Now she was uncerta⟨...⟩ Although he was still smiling, she had a feeling he was in earnest. Was it possible? *Oh, certainly not,* she chided herself. *What a nonsensical notion!* She could honestly say that the thought of marrying Rupert had not entered her mind for a good many years, and she had no intention of giving it any consideration now. She no longer loved him and could not believe that he loved her. The very idea was preposterous. They both had rejected marriage to one another years ago, and one did not simply change one's mind about such a thing just because it became convenient, did one? Not after all this time. And surely they both had changed—it did not occur to Charlotte that such a development might have been a good thing—so there was no reason to expect that the feelings they had once shared could be revived.

"Good heavens, Rupert, stop funning me. We thankfully avoided such a mistake a long time ago." She shook her head and gave a little laugh. "No, it is better, I think, that we leave all that in the past. Let us just be friends."

Despite her smile, Charlotte's words did not welcome dispute, nor did Rupert find he was prepared to accept out-and-out rejection by pressing the matter at this juncture. He looked at her fondly.

"As you wish, my dear."

So she wanted to be friends, did she? Very well. Friends they would be, but he intended to win her all over again in the process.

BOOK YOUR PLACE ON OUR WEBSITE AND MAKE THE READING CONNECTION!

We've created a customized website just for our very special readers, where you can get the inside scoop on everything that's going on with Zebra, Pinnacle and Kensington books.

When you come online, you'll have the exciting opportunity to:

- View covers of upcoming books

- Read sample chapters

- Learn about our future publishing schedule (listed by publication month *and author*)

- Find out when your favorite authors will be visiting a city near you

- Search for and order backlist books from our online catalog

- Check out author bios and background information

- Send e-mail to your favorite authors

- Meet the Kensington staff online

- Join us in weekly chats with authors, readers and other guests

- Get writing guidelines

- AND MUCH MORE!

**Visit our website at
http://www.zebrabooks.com**

CHANGING SEASONS

Jessie Watson

Zebra Books
Kensington Publishing Corp.

http://www.zebrabooks.com

For Lucky, my special bear.

ZEBRA BOOKS are published by

Kensington Publishing Corp.
850 Third Avenue
New York, NY 10022

Zebra and the Z logo Reg. U.S. Pat. & TM Off.

First Printing: August, 1999
10 9 8 7 6 5 4 3 2 1

Printed in the United States of America

Prologue

"Never! I shall never marry you now. You are a—a deceiver. I cannot think whatever made me believe I loved you!"

"But you don't understand. . . ."

"Understand! How dare you? I *understand* only too well. I *understand* that you have been consorting with a—a— Oh! How could you?" She began to sob.

"I love you," he said simply. "It was just a lark." She glared at him. "I never meant to hurt you."

"A lark might have lasted a night. God knows that would have been bad enough. But you have kept that woman in London these past three months, Rupert. Oh, what a fool I have been." Charlotte did not add that the humiliation hurt her almost as much as his actions, for half the town must have heard the tale, nor could she say how let down she had felt by the young man she had known for so many years that she had called him friend long before she ever wanted to call him lover.

He could have throttled Denys Parker for letting the story out. He might have known it would reach Charlotte's ears, even here in Marlowe. How could he explain? He could hardly tell her that a rich young man with too much time on his hands had had second thoughts about their impending wedding and let his friends convince him that Jane Cummings, whose bed was at that time to let, could put all to rights. He had barely thought of Charlotte these past months, as he found one excuse after another to travel to the Metropolis and lose himself in the arms of an experienced ladybird. It was only when another friend, Allen Merrill, found him and Jane dining at Grillon's one night and told him of Denys's blunder that he had come to his senses and reminded himself that he did indeed love Charlotte Middleton.

But that was doing him precious little good now, confronted as he was with a weeping, furious fiancée. He very nearly pointed out to Charlotte that Jane Cummings had not been best pleased with the turn of events, which of necessity involved his permanent leave-taking. She, however, had the common sense to realize when and how to minimize her losses and had grudgingly taken solace in a ruby necklace that would keep her quite nicely until the next man came along. Well, he could hardly tell Charlotte that either, could he? But what the devil was he supposed to say? Why could she not just understand? They both knew perfectly well that many a husband kept his light-o'-love. Of course, he and Charlotte were not even married yet, but it seemed a pretty fine distinction to him. After all, it was not as if he planned to keep Jane after the wedding! His guilt began to make him angry and then defensive. Then he said just what he shouldn't have.

"Blast it, Charlotte. You're doing it up much too brown!" She tossed a pillow at his head. "It was nothing, nothing to me at all."

She knew what he was trying to say, felt that she should try to be more forgiving, but her pain betrayed her. "Yes, Rupert, but it was a great deal to me."

"Damn it, Charlotte. Be reasonable. It is over, and we can overcome this—peccadillo—and wed just as we had planned."

She was devastated by his apparent inability to see his wrong, and he was baffled by her failure to see the triviality of the problem. Neither could conceive how to make the other understand.

"No," she said quite simply and quietly. Then she removed the betrothal ring from her finger and handed it to him.

He was stung, never having believed, never having *expected,* that she would react so drastically. There was a great deal of hurt in her eyes, but he could not see it, nor could she see his. "I would have made you a good husband, you know."

"Hah!"

"And what will you do now? Marry someone else?" he asked sarcastically, his anger returned.

"Yes, I shall!"

"Hah!" he said back at her.

"Yes! I shall marry Digby Fayerweather! There!"

He laughed. "That clunch? Whatever for?"

"Because *he* loves me."

Unhappily, Rupert did not take this perfect opportunity to point out that *he* loved her. "Good God, Charlotte, he has the manners of a farm animal. He doesn't love you, and he knows no more about how to treat a wife than . . . "

"Than you do?"

He gave her a black look.

"And what will you do, Rupert? Go back to your lightskirt?"

"No." A thought suddenly popped into his head.

"I shall sign up. I shall buy my colors, and if you care to find me, I daresay you will be able to locate mc somewhere on the Continent fighting Bonaparte."

It was her turn to laugh. "You? Please, Rupert. You have no more interest in fighting Napoleon than I in . . ."

"In marrying Fayerweather?"

"But I shall marry him."

"And I shall join the army. You might consider that this is the last time you may see me alive. I could be killed, you know."

She stiffened. "While I, so you would have me believe, will make a horrible marriage. I shall marry Digby."

"Fine," he ground out. "And I shall buy my colors."

And each kept his promise.

One

Nine years later

He sat back in his chair to read the letter.

I cannot say how your letters over these past fourteen months have eased my mind. It was, I know, most difficult for you to give me the news of Randolph's death, but your kind words and my faith have helped me immeasurably to come to terms with the loss of my beloved nephew. I know that you admired him greatly and I was comforted to know that you were at his side when he died from his wounds.

The letter continued for three more pages, but having read these words, he paused. Why on earth was the old man bringing this up again, for it was ground well covered in the past.

And so, Rupert, you will forgive me for importuning you once again to make me a long visit when you have returned home.

Ah, so that was it. He chuckled and shook his head. Randolph Elmont, his late comrade, had spoken often of his uncle, Lowell Goodspeed, and his blissful visits to the vicar's parish of Edenshade in Essex. He began to read again until, stunned by the words of the last paragraph but one, he sat frozen for a moment. Could it all finally fall into place so simply?

He and the vicar had corresponded for more than a year. Rupert's personal letter telling him of Elmont's death had been followed by a grateful acknowledgment, and they had slipped into an easy intimacy that he could not recall having had with another human being. In the beginning, Rupert's letters had filled the void Goodspeed felt after his nephew's death, for the two had been close since Elmont had been a child, and the latter had written to him as often as the war would allow. Once the horror of his loss had abated to a level that he could bear, Goodspeed found that he had come to care a great deal about his new correspondent, who, after notifying Randolph's parents, had been concerned enough to inform a mere uncle, who had loved the young man as a son.

The arrival of Rupert's letters was always a special event at the rectory. Goodspeed would hole up in his study, his yet half-written Sunday sermon or the household accounts cast aside, and sit in his favorite old chair, a glass of wine in hand, losing himself in the closely written pages and their details of bivouacs and sorties, victories and losses. Not wishing to remind him of the brutality that had taken his nephew, Rupert initially confined his commentary to the more tedious side of making war. After receiving two such letters, Goodspeed had pointed out that he had more and better information about what was happening on the Continent from his local newspaper.

And that, I must tell you, is saying very little, since
The Valley Messenger *generally limits itself to village gossip: births, deaths, marriages, who has come
to our little hamlet, and who has left it. And of course
(and this pleases me greatly, for I am the most avid
of gardeners) our gardens, for they are quite something.
Still, I digress. What I am trying to say, my boy, is
that I expect more of you than I do of* The Messenger. *I wish you to tell me what is* happening. *I do
appreciate and thank you for your circumspection, for
I know you think to spare my feelings, but I assure
you, that is quite unnecessary.*

Rupert had chuckled upon reading that letter. The
vicar sounded quite the character, just as Elmont had
described him. He had obliged this "request," and
thereafter, his stories were as full of detail as the man
could have wished.

For Rupert, those first few letters were written out
of respect for the vicar and for his friend, who, he
felt, would have wanted him to do so. It was not until
some months later that he became aware of the relief
he found in writing home. He came to find himself,
for the first time, awaiting the erratic mail deliveries
to troops constantly on the move. He laughed over
the antics of Goodspeed's beloved ragamuffin dog,
Fortune ("for he is worth that and more to me, my
boy"). He followed the long illness and eventual demise of farmer Gareth Pennyworth, the birth of twins
to Goodspeed's nearest neighbors, and the myriad
events of Edenshade that he assured the vicar he
longed to hear.

And he did long to hear them. When Rupert had
departed England nine years earlier, he had left no
family to speak of, no friends particular enough to

correspond with, not even a lady who might weep at
the death that stalked him almost daily on the Continent. All of that had bothered him a great deal for
a very long time. But there was plenty of time yet to
find a wife and make a family. And a home. He had
been only too glad to quit England, never mind that
the prospect of war had terrified him. But of course,
he had been much younger then. The house he had
lived in in Marlowe had been sold for him after he
had bought his colors and sailed for Europe. Well,
God knew he had sufficient blunt to support a family
in high style. But it was not until he heard Elmont's
stories about Uncle Lowell that he began to experience a sort of emptiness. His friend's death had in-
tensified that hunger, but it was his correspondence
with Goodspeed that had turned it to an ache, a
yearning to return that he had never felt before.

And so he had determined to leave the only home,
if such it could be called, that he had known for many
years, to return to England. But to where exactly and
to what? Charlotte had married after all, just as she
had sworn she would. Rupert was restless now, had
been for weeks. He was at once thrilled at the prospect of leaving and baffled and confused by what he
would find at home. Until today.

Shaking off his wandering thoughts, Rupert reread
the penultimate paragraph of the letter. It told no
more nor less about the meanderings of Edenshade
than did his friend's other letters, now carefully
stowed in the box at his feet, and yet it changed everything because it contained a name that Goodspeed had never before mentioned.

*And Charlotte Fayerweather, a widow of our little
village, has a few of the old fusspots up in arms, al-*

though I hasten to add that she is otherwise greatly liked here. Her heinous crime? She had waltzing at a party she gave the other week. I cannot say that I was not just a bit taken aback myself at first. It is rather an intimate dance, as you doubtless know, my boy! But I must say that I took to it soon enough, as Mrs. Fayerweather was so good as to show me the steps right there and then, and we had enormous fun. I must tell you, with the deadly sin of pride guiding my pen, that I feel I acquitted myself well. Mrs. Fayerweather said so, too, but then, she is a very charming and good-hearted person. Some folk did make mice feet of it (and those are well-chosen words) for a bit, but we all enjoyed ourselves tremendously. I whisper to you my suspicion that those few who complained were those who could not master the steps!

The rest of the letter concerned Fortune, but this he did not feel compelled to reread. Smiling, Rupert fished in the box until he found a letter received nearly four years earlier—this one from a discreet man of inquiry back in Marlowe, who, prior to Goodspeed, had been his only correspondent. But then, he had been paid to be.

And so I must inform you, Major Frost, that I can no longer in good conscience continue my efforts in your behalf or accept further remuneration from you. Once Mrs. Fayerweather had sold up here (as I've explained before), she journeyed to the Lake Country on holiday for a time, then departed. I went to Windermere myself three weeks ago, having learned from my contact there that she had left without providing a forwarding address. I had hoped to obtain more information in person. To my distress, neither the inn-

*keeper nor anyone else in town could assist me. As you
know, she had informed no one here in Marlowe of
her plans—she was not on the best of terms with her
late husband's family, and her parents died some years
ago. Therefore, sir, I must admit defeat and beg forgiveness for my inability to conclude my commission
to your earnest desires. Should I learn anything in the
future, I shall, of course, so inform you.*

Grinning, Rupert took up his pen to answer Goodspeed's letter. At last, he knew where he would go
and what he would do when he went home.

Two

"Who did you say, vicar?" Charlotte asked although she believed she knew very well what he had said.

"Rupert Frost. Major Rupert Frost, that is. But he has told me he doesn't wish to be addressed by his rank now that he is out of the army. Wants to leave all of that behind. Although he certainly worked hard enough for it—his rank, that is. Oh, my, the stories he has told me—well, written me, I should say. Well, I do not mean to imply that he has boasted to me, for he has not—not his way at all. No, no, my nephew, young Elmont, you remember, he often wrote . . . Oh, my, are you ill, Mrs. Fayerweather?"

Charlotte had sunk down on the pew when she had felt the blood draining from her head. But the color was returning to her cheeks now, and she threw back her head and laughed. "My dear sir, do you mean to tell me that Rupert made *major*? Well, blast it, good for him! Oh!" she put a hand to her lips. "I do apologize, vicar." But she could not contain her broad smile.

Goodspeed could not have said which surprised him more: her language or her apparently knowing Rupert Frost. "I, um . . ." He sat down one pew ahead of her and turned to look at her. "Do you mean to say that you know him, my dear?"

She giggled, then sobered. "Yes, vicar, I do."

"But that is fantastic! How?"

She looked down at the prayer book in her hand. Several dozen of them had been delivered just a short while ago, and since they were her gift to the church, and a surprise, she had come to make a little speech to her good friend and present them herself. But now she was uncertain what to say. Charlotte knew that she could tell him anything, and she certainly had no shame about her and Rupert's past relationship, but it was long ago pushed to the back of her mind and it was much too soon to know how she felt about his impending arrival. Moreover, she had no way of knowing how Rupert might feel about her telling the vicar. Best that she say as little as possible for the moment.

"Well, we lived in the same town—you know, in Marlowe—before he bought his colors."

"Did you indeed? My, my. What an incredible coincidence. Have you and he been in correspondence then?" he asked her hopefully.

"Er, no. He never, um, that is I did not . . . No, vicar, we have not had any communication in many years. Not since he left Marlowe, in fact. I am glad to hear that he has fared so well." She smiled in fond memory, then put down the prayer book and rose, shaking out her skirt.

"I see."

"Well, I must be off. Mrs. Ruffle will be wondering where I've got to. When did you say that he will be arriving?"

"It is difficult to be precise, but I should think in a few weeks' time."

Charlotte nodded and began to walk briskly down the aisle.

"Oh, Mrs. Fayerweather, thank you once more for the prayer books. It is most generous of you."

She seemed to him a bit preoccupied. "Not at all, vicar. It is my pleasure." Charlotte opened the heavy door and stepped out into the cold early January sunlight.

Charlotte's thoughts ran in a half-dozen different directions at once, all revolving around the same theme: Rupert. She never noticed the antiwaltzing Mrs. Derwent coming out of the little shop in the High Street and thus did not return the frosty nod that worthy lady, who apparently deemed that Charlotte had served sufficient penance for her transgression, condescended to bestow upon her. This new faux pas would consign Charlotte to at least an additional six weeks on Mrs. Derwent's list of people to cut, but she was not to know that then and would not have cared if she had.

The rising wind tugged at the brim of her hat and Charlotte absentmindedly adjusted it. How long was it exactly? Eight—no, nine years. In truth, she had not given Rupert a great deal of thought in some time. Oh, in the beginning, of course, she had. In fact, she'd thought of little else but her broken heart for quite a while. But she had been as stubborn as he, and when she had learned that he had actually done it—gone off just like that, as if . . . as if he did not care one farthing for her or what they had meant to one another. She had hoped that, by the day following the argument, he would return to once again

declare his love and ask her forgiveness, which she
would then gladly have given.

But he did not come the next day, or the next, and
soon she learned that he was gone. And so Digby
Fayerweather became the sudden, quite amazed, but
entirely welcoming, recipient of her attentions. Once
word got round that she and Rupert would not make
a match of it after all, it had taken little effort to bring
Digby to the point. She had worried for a bit that the
talk inevitably deriving from her broken engagement
might frighten him off, but Fayerweather was too
smitten and too puffed up with his own consequence
to question her change of affections. If, before, the
old Charlotte had been put off by his shallowness and
lack of ready wit, the new Charlotte told herself that
she only found him so in comparison to the none-
such that was Rupert. *Stop comparing them,* she scolded
herself again and again, *and Digby can be seen on his
own merits.* The new Charlotte managed to convince
herself that marriage to Digby was a wonderful prospect, for how could a lady believe that the man who
would be her husband was anything but a paragon?

And her husband Digby was to be, for, not being
a complete flat, he waited an entire two weeks to be
sure of her sincerity before he proposed. While Digby
spent the time of their short engagement counting
his blessings, when he was sufficiently able to see
through the stars in his eyes to do so, Charlotte spent
many a sleepless night berating herself for agreeing
to marry a man she did not, could not, love. More
than once, she was on the point of crying off, as much
for his sake as for hers, but always she drew back.

It was not until she found herself wishing that she
had not called Rupert to account, that she had not
been so unwilling to forgive his unfaithfulness, that

finally she accepted her predicament. *Do not be an idiot,* she told herself. *You had every right to be furious with him.* Still, she considered further, she might have been less implacable. If she had not taken the great step of breaking their betrothal, they might have been able to make things right. But she had and there was an end to it. Rupert has gone. *He left you without much of a fight and evidently with as little thought. Maybe he did not love you, just as you suspected when you heard about his ladybird. And you, my girl, got yourself and Digby into this situation* (as she was wont to call it), *so you had better make the best of it.*

And make the best of it she had. In the end, Charlotte was not a blissful bride, but she forced herself to be a reasonably contented one. Although their marriage was not an especially good one, it was not quite the disaster that Rupert had predicted. Digby, for all his shortcomings, and they were rather numerous, was not a bad man, nor even a bad husband. He was neither indulgent nor parsimonious, passionate nor cold. He was, once the novelty of his good luck in a bride had worn off, indifferent, but she kept her loneliness at bay with her household duties and a newfound interest in gardening. What Charlotte found she missed the most was the depth of understanding that had existed between her and Rupert. Their close friendship would only have deepened, she knew, through marriage, and she felt terribly cheated by that loss.

Completely unprepared for the circumstances following Digby's sudden demise, precipitated by a fall on the ice outside a baker's shop, Charlotte surprised even herself by realizing that she had no desire to remain in Marlowe, although she had no idea where to remove to. After selling the house and bidding good-bye to her husband's parents and siblings, who did not care a bit what she did, Charlotte decided to visit the Lake Country for a time, an old acquaintance having always spoken of it so fondly. She had hired a new housekeeper, Mrs. Irene Ruffle, a widow who had waxed poetic of Edenshade, where she had lived until moving with her former employer, now deceased, to Windermere.

During all the years of her marriage, Charlotte never heard a word of Rupert. She had assumed him to be alive, thank God, for even though no one in Marlowe corresponded with him—Denys Parker had moved away and Allen Merrill had enlisted and been killed in battle—she had been convinced that word of his death would somehow reach her, and there were always the constant and horrific casualty lists to scan. Once the hostilities had been concluded, however, and the Corsican Devil routed for good and all and sent to his final exile, the casualty lists became but a bad memory, and she had lost hope of ever knowing what had become of Rupert once she departed the town. Perhaps, she had acknowledged to herself later, it was for the best. Perhaps she had needed to finally put Rupert in the past, where he belonged.

But now he was back in her life, or would be soon enough. Charlotte misjudged her footing and stepped into a slush puddle. Grumbling as the dirty, ice-cold water soaked through her boot, she picked up her pace and quickly covered the last yards to her house, calling to Mrs. Ruffle as she let herself in. A short time later, she was warming herself by the fire in the small library, a mug of steaming chocolate cupped in her hands.

What is he like now? she wondered. *Perhaps he has*

married. Perhaps he even has children, for soldiers do get leave, so it is quite possible that he met someone to his liking at such a time. But, no. Although the vicar had not said much on the subject of Rupert, he had not implied that Rupert would be accompanied by anyone, and certainly not a wife. Charlotte expected that he had changed a great deal. After all, she considered, one did not rise to the rank of major in His Majesty's service by being cloth headed. *No, that is unfair, for Rupert was never stupid, only rather immature and short-sighted, at least in his treatment of me,* she thought wryly. *Doubtless he is now a sober and serious fellow, quite unlike the man I knew. Perhaps I shall not even recognize the person he has become.* She did not know quite why this possibility should bother her, but it did.

Charlotte sipped the last drops of her chocolate and set the cup and saucer on the fender in front of the fireplace. Then she sat back in the comfortable old chair and closed her eyes. *And just what will he think of you, old girl?* Suddenly, her eyes popped open. Throwing back the shawl spread across her lap, she jumped from the chair and ran to the mirror hanging on the far wall. This was hardly the first time that Charlotte had ever gazed at her reflection, but judging by the close inspection that she now made, it might as well have been.

The woman on the other side of the glass looked back at her first in surprise, then with some consternation. Good God, did she always look like this? Not that there was anything especially wrong with her appearance. There was the proper number of every-thing on her face and the spots that had plagued her for a brief time in her youth had long since departed, but she had remembered herself as having been, well, less boring. Her lips twisted in a grimace of self-mockery. *Not necessarily boring, Charlotte. Perhaps just no longer young,* she whispered to herself. A plain oval face—without high, finely planed cheekbones to give it the least bit of distinction or assurance that, in its old age, it would soften into lines of graceful maturity—was blessed with a perfect complexion normally highlighted by a lovely rose tint, but now gone almost a sickly white. Charlotte pinched her cheeks hard, but the resulting red spots succeeded only in making her appear the victim of a particularly ghastly kind of fever. Brown eyes trimmed with full lashes—her best feature, she had long ago realized—were round with something that she decided could not possibly be panic. Charlotte's gaze traveled up, and in disgust, she tore off the cap that covered most of her head. Her dark brown hair was wound around her head in the same plain fashion in which she had worn it since she had first put it up after leaving girlhood. Well, there had never been any reason to have it styled when the fashion changed since she and Digby had never gone anywhere or seen anyone who would ever care what she looked like. Certainly, Digby never had, not after the first weeks of their marriage.

But what will Rupert think? Good heavens, you have not cared what Rupert thinks these many years, she berated herself. *You cannot suppose for a moment that, once he meets you again*—here Charlotte allowed herself a chuckle, for wouldn't he be as surprised as she?—*that he will take the smallest notice of how you look? Certainly, he is bound to be curious after all this time, for clearly, you are curious about him, but no more than that, surely. After that, you may go about with a garter on your head like Lady Castlereagh, and he would neither notice nor care.*

She pulled the pins from her hair and it fell past

her shoulders in heavy waves picked out here and there with lighter threads of brown. Still, her hair was dreadfully out of style—a rather odd circumstance in one who took such pains to always dress herself in the first kick of fashion. Charlotte gathered up the hairpins scattered on the table and headed for her bedroom. Mrs. Ruffle, met halfway down the hall, barely paused when she caught sight of her lady's appearance. Always impeccably turned out and up to the minute—a condition reached Charlotte had never understood how, given a housekeeper's wage, no matter how generous—Mrs. Ruffle had long ago despaired of convincing her to cut her hair to conform with the latest fashion.

"That will never do, you know," she announced airily, nodding in the direction of all that hair. Squeezing past Charlotte with arms full of the linen just removed from her employer's bed, she peered closely at her. "You look a bit pale. It's all those *hairpins*, haven't I been telling you?" Charlotte glared. "Someday, it's all going to fall out, you'll see. Then you won't have to be complaining, like you always do, about drying it for hours before the fire every time you wash it."

"Yes, well, as a matter of fact—"

"And where's that terrible cap?" Mrs. Ruffle had refused to wear one from the beginning of her service with Charlotte. "But, if you decide to take me on, Mrs. Fayerweather, I tell you fair here and now, I shall *not* wear one of those ridiculous caps. Oh, er, begging your pardon, ma'am," she had amended in acknowledgment of the frills atop her would-be employer's head. But it had been the last time that she had been so accommodating in her estimation of what Charlotte had deemed to be a matron's lot, although she had told Mrs. Ruffle that she did not care two figs if her housekeeper wore one.

"Oh, dear," she continued now, "could you just pick up that pillowcase I've dropped? There's a good girl. That child," she went on, referring to Nell, their maid of all work, who should have been changing the linen, "burned her hand at the stove this morning and she's still moaning about it, so I thought I had better see to this. Well, I'm that certain you are never going out with your hair all anyhow like that."

"Of course not, I wondered if . . ."

"Good, thought you would not. Now what were you saying, ma'am?"

Charlotte smiled. *"Trying* to say, is more like, Mrs. Ruffle . . ."

"Yes, dear, do go ahead. I've got to see to the washing of this, you know." She held the sheets aloft.

No one who heard this exchange would have thought the familiarity between mistress and housekeeper the least bit wonderful, not if they knew the participants. For it had also been clear from their first meeting that Mrs. Ruffle, although in her own way always respectful, was not the sort to toadeat, and Charlotte was not the sort to want her to. Their relationship, always proper, had been an easy one.

Charlotte gave a little laugh. "What is the name of that hairdresser you have mentioned to me once or twice, I . . ."

"Once or twice? A hundred times, if it's been once, Mrs. Fayerweather," she clucked, but looked more hopefully at her employer. "And what would you be wanting with his name then?"

"Just find him, Mrs. Ruffle, before I change my mind," Charlotte replied archly.

Mrs. Ruffle beamed. "So you're going to cut it

then. Good for you. I shall send Nigel off to fetch him right away."

"Oh and, Mrs. Ruffle, to answer your other question: I left my cap in the library."

"That's fine then, ma'am. I'll just toss it in the fire."

"In the fire?" Charlotte was aghast.

"Or maybe I'll use it instead to dress that chicken I've got roasting for your supper."

"Good grief!"

"Now, Mrs. Fayerweather, you won't be needing it anymore, not if you're going to be having your hair fixed properly, will you?"

"Well, ladies do still wear caps, even if their hair is *fashionable,* Mrs. Ruffle," Charlotte pointed out a little desperately.

"Now why would you be wanting to do that? If you are going to all the trouble of having it cut, you want to show it off, you know. Caps are for old women and those who might as well be." She grinned at her mistress with fondness and added softly, "You'll not really be wanting the thing anymore, will you?"

Charlotte gave way with a laugh. "I suppose not. Unless this fellow makes me look a fright!"

"Oh, he won't, ma'am," she called gaily as she bustled off "You'll see. You're going to look fine as sixpence!"

Three

Meanwhile, the vicarage was in a turmoil not seen since the bishop had come to visit a dozen or more years ago. Goodspeed's housekeeper, Mrs. Barclay, had reminded her employer that his houseguest was not expected for some weeks and, anyway, didn't she see to it that his house was always clean and presentable?

"Certainly, Mrs. Barclay, always. Still, this is a very special guest, and I want everything to be just so. Major—that is, Mr. Frost has been in the army for a long time, and I wish the house to be all that he could want after years of living in tents and such."

"Well, if he's been away that long, vicar, I should think he'll be glad of the sight of anything with a roof and a proper cup of English tea," she said with a practical sniff "But if you're that concerned about the place being so perfect, you might let me do a proper cleaning in your study. Now, *that's* a sight, sir!"

He threw back his head and laughed as she glared at him, her hands on her hips. "Touché, Mrs. Barclay. You've caught me out fair and square! All right, you may do your worst, for I know you have been itching to turn out my study for years." The housekeeper nodded with satisfaction. "Only do not throw anything away, and please, I implore you, do not feel compelled to be *too* neat."

Mrs. Barclay smiled and, shaking her head, hurried off to get started before he changed his mind. Goodspeed, deprived of the sanctuary of his study, decided he might as well make some visits in his small parish.

Wrapping two mufflers around his neck, for the day was bitterly cold, and calling to Fortune, he left the vicarage to walk down the small hill toward the cottages in the village proper. Despite the cold, he paused a moment at the top of the little humpbacked bridge that crossed the narrow river running past the shops in the High Street and the homes of the good souls residing in Edenshade. It was a small, old town, hardly more than a village in size, located in the Colne valley of Essex. The river that rushed and tumbled over itself down nearby hills, as if in a panic to get wherever it was going, was only barely worthy of the name by the time it meandered through Edenshade. It was so narrow and shallow in spots that residents could cross it easily via a series of large, flat stepping-stones that had long ago been laid across its middle.

Goodspeed looked about him and smiled. He had lived in the village for nearly thirty years, having come here when he was in his late twenties, and he dearly hoped he would never have to leave. Life here was good. His parishioners were as happy as folk had a right to expect to be. They were sufficiently prosperous to lead relatively peaceful and law-abiding lives that did not place onerous demands on their vicar, a circumstance of which was he heartily glad.

For if Goodspeed was a competent and caring clergyman, he had never felt a particular calling to the church, nor believed that he was so much closer to

God than the next person that he had a right to censure their lives. Rather he had taken orders as so many did, because he was the younger son with a good education in his pocket, but not much else. Fortunately, the living was one that permitted him to live most comfortably. His flock genuinely liked Goodspeed, recognizing that, in him, they got the clergyman they needed, without the arrogance and interference they did not. The sermons that he composed, frequently as an afterthought, often were peppered with biblical allusions to gardens and flowers. Fortunately, those in attendance at services found this quite appropriate.

There was still some snow on the ground here and there, although the last snowfall had been more than a week earlier. A large portion of the duck pond had frozen and a few venturesome folk were ice-skating, although Goodspeed could not imagine how they managed to move, so bundled up were they against the cold. He pictured the landscape as it would appear in just a few months. The low-slung branches of the chestnut trees testing the cool water of the tiny river, the green grass rolling off into the distance of the hills enclosing the little valley in which the village lay. The dewdrops that would speckle the village green. And the gardens.

"Good morning to you, vicar. Were you planning to claim this bridge for your own, or can a body get to the other side of this stream without putting on a pair of those skates?"

The good-natured voice woke Goodspeed from his thoughts and the warm Spring breeze of his reverie became, once again, the biting January wind. He clapped his hands to encourage his circulation and completed the passage across the water.

"Mr. Trent," he laughed, "I was just thinking about the Spring."

Silas Trent gave him a dour look and shook his head. "Might be farther off than usual, you know. Mrs. Trent's old cousin says we're in for a good long Winter, according to her rheumatism or some such."

"Oh, dear, that isn't good, for Celia Lathrop's joints are seldom wrong." His companion nodded dispiritedly. "Still"—Goodspeed slapped him on the arm with more optimism than he felt—"we must trust in the good Lord to bring us Spring as soon as may be."

Trent's lips twisted, but he chose not to respond to this bit of wisdom, remarking instead that the long weeks would give them plenty of time to plan their gardens. "For what else is a body to do if he can't put a spade to the soil?"

Goodspeed readily agreed. "I've rearranged my flower beds on paper three times already this Winter."

Gardening was the standard form of conversational currency in Edenshade, only its tenor varying with the seasons. Winters could be cruel in Edenshade, but its Springs and Summers more than made up for the lapse. Even its Falls were special, when leaves were stained with flashing colors. But it must be said that most of its residents lived for the warm weather, for it was then that they broke out their trowels and pruning shears and the small pots of fragile green shoots lovingly and painstakingly nurtured indoors during the last days of Winter and took to their gardens where, so it was said, the good citizens of Edenshade were at their best and their happiest.

Edenshade was as much a village of gardens as it was of cottages and people. It was at its finest in high

Summer when the ducks paddled in the pond and swam in the river. And the gardens—for there seemed to be one attached to every building, even the shopkeepers priding themselves on the window boxes or tubs of flowers congregated around their old wooden doorways—were magnificent. Some were naught but tiny patches nestled under a window or bordering the front walk, some old herb gardens, but many were stunning accomplishments of the gardener's art and hard work. There were gardens, like the vicar's and the Trents', dominated by roses, others by herbaceous flowers. The Norwell cottage, sitting beside the river, boasted a much coveted water garden, and the big old house up on the hill had formal walks of neatly trimmed ornamental shrubbery and trees. But the toplofty owners of Sherbourne Place had never cared to mix with the villagers down the hill, had never shared their enthusiasm for matters horticultural, and were only waiting for a buyer to come along and set them free of Edenshade and the fervid customs of its inhabitants.

The good residents took enormous pride in their efforts, frequently working well into the evening on the long Summer days. Their gardens were not just for enjoyment. Most of their keepers were contenders in the annual Valley Garden Show, virtually the only time of the year when tempers could flare and the normally placid life of the village almost became a cautionary tale of pride and covetousness.

"And have you given any thought to those tea roses I was telling you about, vicar?" Mr. and Mrs. Trent intended to throw village convention to the wind and turn out their musks and damasks in favor of the imported hybrids, and he had been trying to convince his old friend to do the same.

The vicar chuckled. "I'm afraid that I am not so radical as you, Mr. Trent. No, my old cabbage and damask roses are good enough for me."

"Can't say that I blame you. They've won you so many prizes that I wonder the judges don't just retire the ribbon in your name."

Goodspeed puffed up a bit with pride. "They have done me proud, bless 'em. But I wish you joy with the new ones. I'll be most interested to see how they do."

"Well, I hope to give you a run for your money this Summer, vicar."

"Good, good. Always like a challenge, my friend." Fortune, who had been barking playfully at the skaters on the pond, now bounded ahead, and with a wave and a laugh, Goodspeed followed after him.

Mrs. Ruffle set her shopping basket on the scrubbed wooden table. "Prepare Mrs. Fayerweather's tea tray. Then put away that meat I've brought home for supper," she directed Nell. "It should take me at least that long to take off all these clothes," she said, referring to her numerous outer garments.

By the time she had returned to the kitchen, Nell had completed her assigned tasks and poured a cup of tea for the housekeeper. Mrs. Ruffle held the hot cup between her two hands to warm them and sipped carefully. "Oh, there's a good child, Nell. Thank you."

"Yes'm. Shall I take the tray to Mrs. Fayerweather now?"

"I'll see to it. Has that bread finished its second rise yet?"

"Yes, Mrs. Ruffle."

"Good. You see to that and I shall go to Mrs. Fayerweather." She headed for the morning room.

"Thank you, Mrs. Ruffle. I was just thinking how nice a cup of tea would taste." Charlotte eyed the extra cup on the tray knowingly. "Evidently, so were you. Do join me, Mrs. Ruffle, if you can spare the time," she invited with a twinkle in her eye.

"Good of you to ask me, Mrs. Fayerweather. I'm that chilled. I'll pour."

The housekeeper enacted this ritual whenever she had village news to report. If Charlotte had cared to, she might have boasted that she usually had all the news sooner than almost anyone in the small town, with the possible exception of the vicar. She had once teased that the housekeeper probably knew Mrs. Parsons had been delivered of twins before the midwife told Mr. Parsons. Charlotte would never have admitted, even to herself, that her willingness to always play this game said almost as much about her curiosity, since the plain fact was that everyday life in Edenshade could be less than captivating.

"You have been to the village, I collect." She smiled.

Mrs. Ruffle nodded. "Went to visit my sister and to get those chops for your supper. And who should I meet at Mr. Mendon's?"

"Do tell."

"Mrs. Barclay. You know," she prompted, "the vicar's housekeeper. And do you know what she told me?"

"Speaking to you again, is she?"

"Oh, bless you. She never really stopped. We've known one another longer than the cat's had whiskers." Both Mrs. Ruffle and Mrs. Barclay had been born in Edenshade, and while the former had re-moved to Windermere for several years, the latter had never left. "No, no, Louise—Mrs. Barclay—wasn't that upset."

"I seem to recall that you said she was in quite a taking after you told her she dressed like a dowd," Charlotte reminded her with a little smile.

Mrs. Ruffle waved a plump hand. "And so she does. 'You'd think a clergyman's housekeeper could stand to hear the truth,' I told her. And do you know what she said?" Charlotte did, since Mrs. Ruffle had related the whole story when it had taken place the week before, but she let her go on.

"She said, 'A vicar's housekeeper has no business tricking herself out in all those colors and fancy fabrics as you do.' Imagine that, Mrs. Fayerweather." She straightened the tucker at her neck and put down her cup. "Well, I promised not to say another word about those dreadful dresses and caps."

"A wise decision, I should think." Long-standing friendship aside, Louise Barclay's employment by the vicar put her in the way of a goodly amount of village gossip gleaned from the unsuspecting Goodspeed, which she willingly shared with her old friend, who would be loath to jeopardize the getting of such in-formation.

"Well, Mrs. Barclay told me that the vicar has a houseguest. Arrived yesterday. Rupert Frost, his name is. A handsome young gentleman, she said. That is, not exactly young, but not old either. Perhaps a few years older than you, Mrs. Fayerweather." Mrs. Ruffle had been encouraging her employer to find a new husband and had made a couple of unsuccessful at-tempts at matchmaking for at least as long as she had been after her to cut her hair and throw away her caps. She eyed Charlotte now hopefully.

"Yes, I know. We are acquainted, Mr. Frost and I. That is, we were acquainted." Mrs. Ruffle caught her breath. "We were friends back in Marlowe a number of years ago."

"Good heavens! You knew he was here then?"

"Not exactly. Mr. Frost and I had not maintained contact. It was the vicar who happened to mention to me that he was coming."

"Well, you must be looking forward to seeing him again."

Charlotte put down her cup. "I—oh, certainly."

Mrs. Ruffle glanced at her employer over her teacup. "Humph. You don't look too pleased with the prospect if you don't mind me saying so."

The truth was, Charlotte was not at all certain how she felt about seeing Rupert again. One moment she looked forward to it; the next, she dreaded it.

"Mrs. Ruffle, weren't you going to look over the linen this afternoon?" she asked pointedly.

The housekeeper sighed and rose. "Yes, ma'am. Oh, did I mention," she tossed back as she reached the door, "that I saw the new issue of *The Ladies' Cabinet* at Mrs. Robards's shop? It had some lovely patterns. You might want to spruce up your wardrobe."

Charlotte raised a brow. "And what is wrong with my current wardrobe, may I inquire?" They both knew that her clothes were up to the minute.

"Oh, not a thing, I'm sure. But you've an excuse now to replace all of that." She dismissed her mistress's gowns as if they were so many old rags.

"What are you talking about?"

"Well, surely now that Mr. Frost is come—"

"Mrs. Ruffle!"

"I'll see to that linen now, ma'am." She had a little smile on her face as she closed the door behind her.

"Fortune! Here boy!"

The dog—a medium-size beast with a dark yellow coat, one slightly ragged ear, and an alert, expressive face—was tramping happily through the damp grass of the hillside. Spotting Charlotte, he loped enthusiastically in her direction, ignoring Rupert's calls.

"Fortune!"

Both dog and woman turned and cast a look in the direction of the voice. The dog continued his pace while the woman stood still as a post. Never mind that she had not heard the voice in years, she would know it anywhere. She extended her arm to pat the head of Fortune, who now sat at her side, looking questioningly from her expectant face to Rupert's as the latter approached alternately whistling and calling to him in a carefree voice.

She had the advantage over him, and just before he came close enough to recognize her, she spoke.

"Hello, Rupert."

Fortune hesitated a moment, then punctuated her greeting with a small bark. Rupert had narrowed the distance between them now and stopped in his tracks. He could not have said for certain whether her voice, like his, had triggered memory or if he had recognized her face or figure. With a broad smile, he crossed the remaining few feet and took her hands in his.

"Charlotte."

He held her at arm's length, his eyes glancing from bonnet to half boots, and shook his head. "You look just the same."

He was not surprised to see her and she thought Lowell Goodspeed must have mentioned her name over supper at the vicarage. Her misgivings about this meeting flew away and she found herself almost at her ease in her old friend's company. She laughed.

"Rupert. I had heard of your coming. It is good to see you."

The wind picked up then and began to deposit a light layer of snow flurries on them. They shrugged deeper into their cloaks. "The weather here can be capricious. This morning, it looked as if the day would be fine, but the temperature seems to have fallen dramatically. Why don't you and Fortune come back to my cottage? It's nearly teatime anyway and I can fortify you with a hot drink before you walk back to the vicarage."

As they removed their outer garments in the hallway, Charlotte sent Nell ahead to the drawing room to build up the fire there. She took off her tartan cape and silk plush hat. Mrs. Ruffle appeared fortuitously with a towel to dry off Fortune's coat.

"I just happened to be looking out the window and saw you coming down the lane." She leaned down, rubbing Fortune's only slightly damp fur, and smiled up at Rupert. Then she looked expectantly at Charlotte.

Charlotte's lips twitched in a wry smile. "How kind of you, Mrs. Ruffle. I am certain Fortune would have caught his death if not for your consideration. But, ahem, so long as you are here, please meet Mr. Rupert Frost." She turned to him. "Rupert, this is Mrs. Ruffle, who keeps house for me."

"How do you do, Mrs. Ruffle?"

She straightened only to dip in a tiny curtsy. "How do you do, sir? And welcome to Edenshade." Her smile broadened. "I am sure that we all are most happy to have you here."

Charlotte groaned inwardly. If Mrs. Ruffle tried her hand at matchmaking, she would throttle her. She decided to ignore the comment. "Come, Rupert. Shall we go into the drawing room? The fire should be going strongly now." He nodded and followed in her wake. "Mrs. Ruffle, please have Nell bring in the tea tray. Mr. Frost and I are chilled to the bone."

Fortune pushed his way into the drawing room ahead of them and immediately headed for the fire, where he lay as close to the blaze as the heat permitted.

Rupert chuckled. "Do you suppose that His Highness will allow us to share the fire, Charlotte?"

"If he knows what is good for him," she rejoined with a laugh.

They sat on either end of the fender and for a few minutes occupied themselves with the dog, who wriggled playfully on his back, four paws in the air, as Rupert rubbed his ears. When Fortune stilled and stretched out again, Charlotte tucked her icy-cold feet under his belly. She had been watching Rupert as he crooned to the dog. He had changed a little, which was hardly surprising after so many years. There was some gray in his dark hair now. His long frame was leaner, harder than it had needed to be when he was a callow young man with no responsibilities. And his green eyes, which now returned her gaze with an old familiarity, seemed somehow more aware, more perceptive than she remembered. Then he smiled at her and he suddenly became again the Rupert from those long ago days.

Nell arrived with the tea tray, which Charlotte directed her to place on the low table next to the fireplace. Charlotte filled a cup and returned his smile. "Two sugars, is it not?" She dipped the silver tongs into the sugar bowl.

"Just one actually."

She raised her brows in a question.

"Your memory is correct, but when we were in the field, we often had little or no sugar—or milk come to that. I learned to do without either. Since I've returned, I enjoy both again, but find that one lump of sugar instead of two does me quite well."

"I see."

He laughed lightly at his protracted telling of what must seem to her trivial detail. "Forgive me. You hardly wanted the entire tale, but I did want to explain."

"On the contrary, Rupert, I should like to hear about your adventures. The vicar says you were a hero, you know."

She indicated with a nod that they might move to the nearby chairs, for the fire was almost too warm, even if Fortune did not seem to mind it. Rupert sipped his tea and leaned back in the chair.

"I imagine that quite surprised you, Charlotte. After all, you seemed so certain that I was not, um, hero material."

As soon as the words were out he regretted them. He could not even have said what had possessed him to make such a foolish remark, since his purpose in coming to Edenshade was to win her back, not alienate her. Stung by his words, Charlotte blinked. His easy manner in their short time together had led her to drop her guard and his referral to their late hostilities caught her unprepared. Well, if this was how he wanted their relationship to be, it certainly was all right with her. She sat up straighter, taking pains to stir her tea, so she did not see the regret cross his features, and perhaps she had long ago lost the knack for reading the thoughts behind his eyes, which now would have disclosed his uncertainty as to how to undo his misstep.

"Yes, now that you mention it," she replied stiffly, "I do of course recall that we did not part on the best of terms. Thank you for reminding me, Rupert." Her tone was nearly as cold as the late Winter day.

"Charlotte, forgive me. I had not meant to rake up the past. It's all so long ago, we ought to leave it there and . . ."

"No, Rupert, we ought not to do that," she interrupted thoughtfully.

The look he returned was a mixture of dismay and surprise. "Listen . . ."

Charlotte held up a hand, her features softened. "I only mean that I do not think it a good idea to behave as if our acquaintance began today. We have known one another too long, shared too much . . ." She bit her lip, uncertain how to continue or even if she should. "Don't you think that it would be—healthier—to say what we must to one another and *then* to put it all to rest for good?"

Rupert thought a moment, hating to bring all of that back to life with words, but there was a good deal of sense in what she suggested. He nodded, albeit with little enthusiasm. "Yes," he agreed, "I must concede you are right. I suppose I had hoped to avoid any—conflict or hurt—but not speaking of it cannot make it go away and could cause it to fester."

She nodded and refilled his teacup. But now that the decision had been reached, each was loath to begin the process. Charlotte gave her close attention to tracing the pattern on her cup and finally ventured, "The vicar *did* tell me how brave you were. He said you were a hero. I am so pleased to know how well your army career turned out."

She might have thought he flushed, but his face, like hers, was somewhat reddened by the fire. He waved a hand dismissively. "Lowell embellished my record considerably, I am sure. There is a great deal to be said for the courage and ability of the men who fight under one, you know."

She smiled. "I make no doubt that is true. Still, you provided the leadership, the example, Rupert. You ought not to be so modest." Charlotte hesitated. "You acquitted yourself well. I was wrong to mock you when you said you would enlist."

Rupert threw back his head and laughed. "You were not!" He retorted heartily. "The truth was, I was terrified and about as ill fit for the job as a man ever was. I must tell you that in the early days my commanding officers would have been in complete agreement with you. It took quite a long time to make me a real soldier."

"Yes, but you did become one, and a gallant one at that."

He bowed his head in mock surrender. "Very well, Charlotte. I shall not come to cuffs with you. If hero you would have me be, hero I am!"

They spoke for several minutes of his years of service. He soon realized that there was little point or need to minimize his accomplishments on the field, for she did not begrudge him his success. Indeed she seemed quite happy for him. After a while, he turned the conversation.

"And while I was off soldiering, you married Digby. I should not have spoken so harshly of him. I hope

he made a better husband than I foretold. Did he?"
He watched her carefully.

"Digby was not a bad husband, Rupert. I cannot
say we were deeply happy, but neither were we mis-
erable. In any case, the poor man died in a fall several
years ago, and eventually, I moved here." She
grinned. "Mrs. Ruffle, who had come to keep house
for me in Windermere, recommended Edenshade as
a good place to settle, and I have been very happy
here." Her contentment was evident in her voice.

Neither of them wished to mention the circumstances that had precipitated these developments,
but at length, Rupert spoke. "I was an arrogant fool,
Charlotte, too caught up in myself to realize what I
was tossing away. I could say that I never meant to
hurt you. I am certain that I must have said it then—
only I know now how callous and self-serving that
sounds. For if I had honestly considered the matter,
I would have known that my actions could do nothing
but hurt you . . ."

"Rupert, please stop. We both were young. I suppose I should not have reacted so strongly—should
have forgiven you, but I could think only of myself.
It seems we both were more than a little caught up
in ourselves." He opened his mouth to respond, but
she forestalled him with a smile and a little toss of
her head. "We both have grown and changed. Perhaps we *should* talk of something else. Tell me, how
did you come to choose Edenshade as your new
home? The vicar says you plan to settle here."

He decided it would not be fruitful to persist in a
conversation she did not want to continue. Rupert
was unable to judge her feelings about him as well.
Apparently, she was willing to welcome him back into
her life but she seemed to be ready to consider him

a friend and nothing more. No matter, Rupert would be damned before he would give up. Their betrothal had grown from an initial strong friendship. He was more than willing to woo her back—only this time he did not intend to lose her.

He told her how he had come to know Lowell Goodspeed, about their correspondence and how he had looked forward to reading about the little town of Edenshade and its occupants. "His letters became my link to England. It's strange, but I came to care about this place and its inhabitants. It all sounded so blissful. When I'd decided to leave the army, I needed someplace to go and it seemed natural to come here. After all, I certainly felt as if I knew Lowell and I felt almost the same about the town." He hesitated for just a moment, then said, "And to be honest, he had mentioned you in one of his last letters. I cannot deny that your being here helped me to decide." *There, let her make of that what she will.*

Charlotte gave him a startled look.

"You did not remarry." It was a statement rather than a question.

She gave a little shake of her head. "No. After Digby died, I decided not to. I am happy with my life as it is." She gave him no time to press for details. "And what of you?"

"I? Oh," he prevaricated, "I could not have asked a woman to marry me when I was a soldier. We would have seen one another so little and she would have worried for my safety. Such a life could not be a happy one for a woman." He chuckled. "But I am not getting any younger, as they say, so it is time I think that I sought a wife—before I am so old and decrepit that no lady will look at me!"

"Ah, I am certain you have not a moment to lose,

Rupert." Charlotte tilted her head and smiled at him. "There are some young misses here in Edenshade who might suit."

He could not tell if she was serious.

"And suppose I do not care for young misses? Suppose I prefer a somewhat—more mature—woman?" His tone and expression were playful. "What would you say to me then, Charlotte?"

She returned his grin and matched his tone. "So long as you are not looking at *this* mature woman, Rupert."

"So you will not give us another chance, Charlotte."

Now she was uncertain how to interpret his words. Although he was still smiling, she had a feeling he was in earnest. Was it possible? *Oh, certainly not,* she chided herself. *What a nonsensical notion!* She could honestly say that the thought of marrying Rupert had not entered her mind for a good many years, and she had no intention of giving it any consideration now. She no longer loved him and could not believe that he loved her. The very idea was preposterous. They both had rejected marriage to one another years ago, and one did not simply change one's mind about such a thing just because it became convenient, did one? Not after all this time. And surely they both had changed—it did not occur to Charlotte that such a development might have been a good thing—so there was no reason to expect that the feelings they had once shared could be revived.

"Good heavens, Rupert, stop funning me. We thankfully avoided such a mistake a long time ago." She shook her head and gave a little laugh. "No, it is better, I think, that we leave all that in the past. Let us just be friends."

Despite her smile, Charlotte's words did not welcome dispute, nor did Rupert find he was prepared to accept out-and-out rejection by pressing the matter at this juncture. He looked at her fondly.

"As you wish, my dear."

So she wanted to be friends, did she? Very well. Friends they would be, but he intended to win her all over again in the process.

Four

Before the Winter at last released its tenacious grasp on Edenshade and its environs, a highly productive snowstorm descended on the valley for the better part of two days. Once the inhabitants burrowed out of their homes on the third day, they found themselves in a world encased in snow and ice. The braver, or perhaps more bored, residents exchanged visits with their closer neighbors, even those whose company they might have eschewed under less confining circumstances. Not surprisingly, Rupert's arrival was included in most conversations.

One hardy soul who had his fill of enforced solitude told his wife that they should put what he dearly hoped was the last of the Winter to good use and organize a skating party, an activity not unusual during Edenshade Winters. Given the present weaknesses in the town's communication system, Lowell Goodspeed announced the planned event from the pulpit on Sunday and the outing was arranged in no time. A group of village boys cleared the frozen duck pond of snow and shoveled paths from the narrow road. Here and there around the pond were benches, where, in warmer months, folk sat to feed the ducks or to pass the time of day with a neighbor. Late in the morning of the agreed-upon day, people from all over the village stepped carefully down the shallow embankment and began to converge on the pond, many having to wait their turn while others before them sat on the benches to don their skates.

It had been several years since Charlotte had skated, but she was looking forward to the chance to breathe the fresh air and exercise her muscles. She exchanged waves and greetings with acquaintances and soon was part of a happy group chattering loudly, each relating how they had passed the snowbound days. People jostled good-naturedly for space on the benches, eager to test the ice. Several fires were being tended on the banks of the pond and people already were gathered around them for warmth, for the day despite the bright sun remained very cold. Hot cider was being sold at one fire, roasted chestnuts at another, and both vendors were doing brisk business.

"Oh ho! Brandon, if you eat any more of those chestnuts, you'll be too stuffed for ice-skating!"

The man so addressed grinned, tossing a steaming chestnut from one hand to another before popping it into his mouth.

"That's right, old man," joked another of his friends. "Leave some for the rest of us, will you?"

"Not to worry, sir," called Mr. Crawford, the grocer selling the treats. "I've plenty for all!"

Not far off, a young man began to play a concertina, accompanied by another on a fiddle, and the gay music floated through the crisp air. The ice was already becoming crowded and many of the skaters began moving in time to the music. From their vantage point atop the embankment, Rupert, Goodspeed, and Fortune observed the festive scene below.

"Ah, Rupert, this should be great fun! Why, it looks as if half the village is here!"

Fortune gave an impatient bark and bounded ahead. Goodspeed laughed and, with great agility, followed the dog, calling to Rupert, "Come along, my boy. Come along!"

When Charlotte first ventured onto the ice, she hugged the perimeter for security. A neighborly young gentleman of some twenty-six years was rather enamored of her and gladly took the opportunity to give her his arm in support.

"Oh, thank you, Mr. Pike. I shall appreciate it if you can see to it I do not fall on my head or crash into the others or otherwise make a complete cake of myself. I have only done this once or twice before, you see, and that was a thousand years ago when I was not much more than a girl. It was my house-keeper who talked me into this." She gave him a quick smile, then looked immediately back to her feet.

"Hardly that long ago, surely, Mrs. Fayerweather," he dared, smiling back, his cheeks colored from more than just the cold. Jeremy Pike had been out of mourning for his deceased wife, Elizabeth, for better than two years. A kind and likable man, he had always been awkward with women and had married his Beth, whom he had come to love, largely because she was a willing and convenient choice.

"Er, if you can lengthen your stride, as it were, you will find that you will go along much more smoothly."

"Like this, you mean?" Charlotte tried to suit movement to his direction.

"Um, yes, yes, that's perfect. You see how much more easily you can glide?"

Charlotte grinned and nodded. "I do. Oh, this is

much better, isn't it? And it is a good deal less work, too!"

Soon, they had become part of the larger crowd moving round the pond, and she felt less conspicuous. The setting was rather like that of a country dance set on ice. People swayed and swung happily to the frolicsome tunes played by the "orchestra," who wove in and out of the small groups of gaily dressed townfolk still scattered on the shore clapping their hands in time to the music. Those who, by inclination, age, or ability, chose not to participate in the ice dancing kept a more sedate, but no less cheerful, pace on the fringes of the pond. The sounds of laughter and voices mingled with the notes drifting unimpeded through the cold, still air.

Fortune, like many of the other good citizens of Edenshade, was undeterred by his lack of skates and slid happily around the ice on his feet. He loved people, and just as they did, he welcomed the opportunity to meet and mingle after days of confinement. The fact that many people seemed unable, perhaps even unwilling, to keep up their end of the conversation with him did not diminish his enthusiasm, for Fortune was always quite willing to overlook the shortcomings of these large, two-legged dogs.

Goodspeed soon was covering the pond in the long strides that were characteristic of his walk on dry land, his hands tucked confidently behind his back, a long, brilliant red muffler flying out almost straight behind him so fast did he fly, vivid against the white landscape and his black clerical garb. He nodded and grinned at parishioners as he glided past them. For the most part, Fortune trotted beside the vicar, only now and then losing his footing and sliding two or three yards on his belly, but to him, it was part of the fun.

"Jeremy!" A shrill, peremptory cry pierced the air, rising above the general level of noise. He looked quickly in the direction of The Voice, as he called it—although only to himself of course, for despite her tendency to be overprotective, his widowed mother was very dear to him. When Beth had died, Henrietta Pike had left her own house in Edenshade and moved into his to save him from loneliness, she had said, during those first hard months. She had not yet left. He spied her now bearing down on them, her cloak billowing, and Good God, whatever had possessed her to wear such a hat? The bonnet was, indeed, ill suited to the occasion, being overlarge, its broad brim and its long feather now were laid flat by her propulsion. Those around her were giving Mrs. Pike a wide berth, for her athletic skills and grace were negligible, resulting in a kind of staggering but rapid step that made her appear like a parody of a clumsy and arthritic ballerina.

"Oh, dear." Jeremy sighed, reluctant to abandon Charlotte, but cognizant of his familial responsibilities.

She rescued him. "Mr. Pike, please do not concern yourself for me, for I think I can manage now. Do go to your mother."

He gave her a look of gratitude. "You are all kindness, Mrs. Fayerweather."

As he spoke these words, he heard his mother shriek, and he turned to see both of her skates begin to leave the ice.

"Mother!"

Jeremy never could have reached her in time, but Rupert came up behind Mrs. Pike just in time to catch her before she could fall. Calamity thus averted, the crowd only barely hesitated before resuming its circumnavigation of the pond.

"Mother! Good heavens, are you hurt?"

Both he and Rupert helped her to right herself, and Charlotte, skating more slowly, appeared a few moments later. Mrs. Pike assured them all that she was undamaged, but agreed to be escorted to a nearby bench, where she set her bonnet to rights and pulled her woolen dress in tight against the cold. Rupert left them and soon returned carrying a cup of hot cider for each of the ladies.

"Sir," Jeremy asked, rising from his seat, "whom do I have the honor of thanking for coming to my mother's aid?" That lady seconded the question.

Before Rupert could respond, Charlotte spoke.

"Mrs. Pike, Mr. Pike, may I introduce Mr. Rupert Frost? Rupert, please meet Mrs. Henrietta Pike and her son, Jeremy."

The niceties were observed and the older lady asked Rupert, "You are new to our little town then, Mr. Frost?" She sipped her hot drink.

He inclined his head. "I am, madam. I am late of His Majesty's service and plan to settle here. Until I can find a house of my own, the vicar has been good enough to let me stay with him."

"So you are a bachelor then?"

"Mother—"

"Calm yourself, Jeremy. I was not going to put him—or you—to the blush. I was merely inquiring. How is a body ever to learn anything without asking?" She chuckled and patted her son's arm. "All right, my dear, I shan't tease you anymore."

"Thank you, Mother. Now tell me what you are doing here. I offered to escort you, but you told me you did not care to come. You really should not have ventured onto the ice alone," he scolded affectionately.

"Nor did I, Jeremy. Your brother accompanied me here, but almost as soon as we began to skate, he met up with some of his friends. He did promise to come right back, but you know Jaspar, I am afraid I have not seen him since."

"The little cub abandoned you!" Jeremy growled in reference to the thirteen-year-old also resident in his house, who often tried the maturity of his brother beyond endurance. Jeremy turned to look back at the pond in an attempt to pick out the miscreant from amongst the crowd of skaters. "When I get him, I swear I'll box his ears!"

"You will do nothing of the kind, Jeremy. Do you hear me?" his mother ordered in The Voice. "However, dear, it would be nice if you could just see where he is. I want to be certain that he is all right. There's a good boy."

Jeremy managed a chuckle and shook his head. "As you wish, Mother. But never calling him to book is largely why he has become such an imp, you know." He cocked a brow at Rupert and grinning conspiratorially whispered, "And when I do find the little heathen, I shall have more than a word or two to say to him!"

Mrs. Pike half turned to Charlotte, who sat beside her on the bench, and also spoke in an undertone. "Honestly, Mrs. Fayerweather, Jeremy has been so protective of me. Of course, it is most gratifying that he takes his responsibilities so to heart, what with Mr. Pike having passed on and all, but sometimes he can get, well, carried away."

"Yes," Charlotte agreed. "You are fortunate to

have him to care about you. But I expect you know that already." She gave her companion a teasing grin and cradled the hot cup in her mittened hands, letting the steam warm her frigid nose.

Mrs. Pike chuckled. "Indeed I do, Mrs. Fayerweather."

Rupert had accompanied Jeremy on his errand and they had reached the pond, where the latter was able to pick out his brother skating merrily with some companions and oblivious to his abandoned responsibility. Jeremy opened his mouth to call out to Jaspar, then thought better of it.

"Oh, there's no point in tweaking his nose here, not in front of his friends, although I daresay he does not deserve better." He glanced at Rupert. "I can recall only too well the time that Father berated me in front of some schoolmates about a chore I'd neglected. I was mortified. But you may be sure he'll get the sharp edge of my tongue when we get home."

The man spoke as if he had left his youth behind many years before and Rupert smiled and nodded. "Shall we see if Mrs. Fayerweather and your mother would like to skate again?"

The four returned to the ice and Jeremy led his mother in a slow and careful promenade away from the more energetic skaters. Mrs. Pike's repeated turning to call or wave to acquaintances nearly caused her to lose her balance more than once, and Jeremy was hard-pressed to keep his patience. Rupert and Charlotte skated easily side by side. They made a handsome couple, each above average in height, one fair and slender, the other dark and muscular. She introduced Rupert to neighbor after neighbor, each willing to accept the newcomer who had the good opinion of both Charlotte Fayerweather and Lowell Goodspeed.

"We seem to be doing passably well, Charlotte," Rupert remarked after a while in reference to their skating.

"Yes, we do, thank heaven." She grinned up at him. "I have not had such fun in ages."

"Needless to say, nor have I," he replied dryly. "And you are quite charming with your red nose and cheeks, my dear."

"Oh ho! I can only imagine, Rupert! Have you seen the vicar?" It seemed sensible to change the subject.

"No, actually, I have . . . Good God, the man is a source of constant surprise. Look, Charlotte!" He pointed toward the center of the pond and laughed. She joined in when she saw what he meant. Toward the middle of the pond, a few people had joined hands to form a line that turned like the hand of a clock from a base formed by Lowell Goodspeed.

"Oh, look a whip!" someone cried.

"A whip! A whip!"

Adults and youngsters quickly attached themselves to the line, each grabbing hold of the last person's hand. The swing of the whip at first slowed, but soon picked up momentum. The musicians drew closer to the line, bringing the music of the concertina and fiddle to a mad tempo. The line grew and grew, its components squealing with delight as the velocity increased. It was impossible to tell if the music was causing the hectic speed of the whip or vice versa.

Just as Charlotte and Rupert exchanged questioning glances and decided to join the fun, the long line snapped apart. People slid—some on their skates, others in a less dignified manner—to all areas of the ice, and all those who were not part of the line had to dash aside or else risk being virtually swept away. Miraculously, no one was hurt; in fact, all appeared to enjoy the dismemberment of the whip as much as they had its spin. Joyous laughter and squeals came from every direction and Charlotte and Rupert could see Goodspeed, still on his feet, clapping his hands and laughing harder than he had in years.

"Oh, too bad we missed out," she sighed.

At that moment, one last person who had been part of the whip and who had hitherto maintained remarkable control over her skates made a full ninety-degree turn and steered herself straight into Rupert's arms.

"Wha—" he croaked in surprise, since only a second before he had seen no one in danger of careening into him.

The young lady threw her arms around his neck ostensibly to keep from falling. She looked into his green eyes and managed a breathless, "Thank you, sir, for so kindly rescuing me. Please do forgive my clumsiness."

Charlotte could only barely contain a snicker at how neatly the chit managed the business, and she turned to catch Rupert's eye to share the joke, but instead blinked in disbelief.

He looked down, for the creature was much smaller than he, into enormous blue eyes. A fur-trimmed bonnet framed a plump, round face, and her lips formed a captivating smile as she maintained a deathlike grip on Rupert, despite her having come to a complete and, Charlotte had noticed, gracefully athletic stop in his arms. He dropped said arms immediately only because convention demanded it. His urge to hold her even closer was promptly squelched by his realization of her age, for surely she could not be more than sixteen. For the life of him, Rupert could not remove his eyes from her.

And for a moment, Charlotte could not take her eyes from him. Rupert looked like a man besotted. It had not been so long ago that he had intimated a desire to rekindle their love and here he was behaving like a halfling. Charlotte suddenly was most pleased that she had laughed off his suggestion. Thank heaven, she thought, that *her* heart had not been engaged—again—for clearly her instinct that his feelings were not sincere had been correct. Oh, she was ready to believe that Rupert did wish to marry, but she was unconvinced that he was very particular about *who* he met at the altar. Well, it was certainly no skin off her nose if he chose to become smitten by such transparent behavior, and from a mere child at that.

"Oh, my," the young thing breathed. "I do believe you have saved my life, sir."

"I am privileged to be at your service."

Good grief, this could turn out to be quite amusing after all, Charlotte thought.

"Rupert, I should like to introduce Miss Penelope Logan." He beamed and bowed. "Pen—" for Charlotte was acquainted with Miss Logan and her family—"this is Mr. Rupert Frost. He is recently come to Edenshade and is staying for the present with the vicar." She feared any mention of Rupert's war record might send the chit completely around the twist.

"Miss Logan, perhaps you would like to sit down on that bench." He waved his arm vaguely in that general direction and gave a little frown of concern. "Please allow me to give you my arm, for I fear you could be a bit wobbly after such an adventure."

"You are so kind to be concerned, Mr. Frost. I do

feel a bit unsteady and I think your advice is correct. Perhaps I should sit down. Just for a while, you understand, until I might catch my breath."

Rupert gave Charlotte an absentminded smile. "Oh, you will excuse us, Charlotte?"

"Of course, Rupert." She smiled back. "You must look after Pen."

As he led her away, Penelope looked back over her shoulder at Charlotte and gave her an ecstatic smile and a little wink. The minx!

The vicar joined Charlotte and inclined his head in the direction of the departing couple.

"I must confess, Mrs. Fayerweather, that until now I have never known Penelope Logan to be anything other than the heartiest of young women."

"Oh, yes, vicar, but if her body has weakened, I do believe that her *mind* still is working quite well. Don't you agree?" She looked at him from the corner of her eye and both burst into laughter.

"Would you care to take a turn, Mrs. Fayerweather?"

Five

Spring

The ice on the duck pond melted eventually, and Spring crept in furtively, first leaving shy offerings of snowdrops and aconite in the shady parts of the hills; then, more daring, smudging the hollows with blue gentian and depositing narcissus and early iris in the sunny spots, where none could miss their triumphant splashes of color and all could be assured that the last frost was but a memory and that Winter had, at last, been made so unwelcome as to depart the area entirely, doubtless in a miff. The good residents of Edenshade were quite prepared for the changing seasons. Winter months had meant an end to actual work in their gardens—no more weeding or pruning, no more worrying about this infestation or that blight, no more good-natured rivalry to see who had the better showing of pinks or primroses or poppies. But people's enthusiasm was transferred indoors in the harsh weather.

Many happy hours were spent planning and replanning gardens. Husbands and wives, heads together before the Winter fire, talked of where to lay out herbaceous beds and how much room a fruit tree would require, should they plant one, and whether it might give too much shade. Seeds—carefully harvested and saved from the previous year or received from relatives or neighbors, for most would gladly share the fruits of an especially admired plant with a friend—were started indoors in the final dark days of Winter. It was true, however, that some neighbors were too proud by half and jealously guarded their gardens; some were even known to patrol their plots at all hours to ensure that no particularly admiring or envious neighbor crept in during the night to steal seeds or cuttings.

Some eighteen years earlier, a desperate inhabitant, one Herbert Chauncy, outraged by the success of his neighbor's irises, sneaked into her yard one night and dug up all the coveted bulbs. Mrs. Flavia Asquith, on discovering her unlatched garden gate and the conspicuous absence of her beautiful irises together with the prompt realization that she would not be blessed with their sight in the Springs to come, knew exactly where to look and whom to blame for this horticultural mayhem. She wasted no time—no matter that she was an early riser and the cock had not yet crowed in Hartwell Dickey's little barn down the lane—in marching two cottages down to that of Mr. Chauncy. There, she beat on his door loud enough to wake the dead, not to mention Mrs. Chauncy, who happened to be entirely innocent in the crime. Then she rang a peal over his head that he would not forget for many a day. Finally, she cursed his garden, willing it never to grow the lovely disputed flowers. As it happened, Chauncy had thrown his booty into the river, too late realizing he could never plant them in his own garden, so the bulbs were lost. Mrs. Asquith, now gone to her rest

these past six Summers—although she outlived her
enemy by two years, which pleased her to no end—
never lost an opportunity to point out her loss and
Mr. Chauncy's part in it to all and sundry. If Augustus
Panghurst bragged of his beautiful deep blue veron-
ica, Mrs. Asquith, she could be heard to remark that
the color was, indeed, lovely and she would dearly
have loved to compare it to that of her beloved irises,
but Mr. Herbert Chauncy had deprived her of that
pleasure. She *always* referred to him by his full name,
as it seemed to her to make the accusation that much
more official, since the local constabulary had done
nothing at the time, the alleged perpetrator having
admitted no wrongdoing and his accuser having no
evidence to bring to the proceedings.

The story of the Midnight Raid on Asquith Cottage
for a time took on epic proportions; then it dwindled
to not much more than a dimly remembered local
legend whose details were disputed. The older inhabitants related it almost as a cautionary tale of what
could happen "to a perfectly God-fearing, law-abiding
person like Herbert Chauncy, when he let pride and
covetousness get the better of him." The younger or
more recent residents in Edenshade swore the story
must be apocryphal, but the family who bought the
Chauncy's cottage after Jane Chauncy went to live with
her daughter in London, where she greatly hoped
never to hear of or see a flower again, never could
grow irises there, try as they might.

Fireside discussions in Edenshade could range
from the innocuous: *Should we lift the peonies, dear, and
put them against the far wall? They might give a better
display there. No, no, they hate being moved once they're
established, Deborah. They will do quite well where they are.*
To the profane: *I'll not have those damned petunias in*

*the garden any longer. Do you hear me? The mere sight of
those jolly little trumpets makes me sick.*

Mostly, the conversations were pleasant and productive, but even within households they could become heated—who wanted to dig up all their hated rhododendrons and replace them with lilacs, for example, could and did, in one memorable instance, pit brother against brother.

The vicar often talked to himself when he was preparing his sermon and Fortune usually lazed at his feet, every now and then looking up as if to render his opinion on the aptness of a phrase or the length of the homily. He did so now, lifting his head, then lowering it once again to Goodspeed's slippered foot and sighing mightily.

"Yes, I am happy that you agree with me." He smiled as he massaged one of Fortune's ears, and the dog groaned with pleasure. "Well, what shall it be then, eh? How about . . ." He riffled through the Old Testament. "Ah! I have it, Fortune, Psalms, chapter 73 . . ."

"Ahem."

The sound came from the doorway across the room. Goodspeed peered shortsightedly, pen poised above paper, and looked into Rupert's laughing eyes.

"Ah, Rupert, back already?"

"And not a moment too soon, it seems," he teased. "What would your flock think if they knew that Fortune helped you write your sermons?"

"Ha, ha. Have fits, I make no doubt," the vicar rejoined, neither he nor the dog bothering to deny the charge. "Some of 'em can be very testy, you know. And few of 'em recognize the true intelligence of our canine friends." His eyes twinkled.

"I shouldn't be surprised." Honestly, at times the man seemed totally unsuited for the priestly life, but then Rupert would see him comfort the sick or bereaved and know how fortunate Edenshade was to have such a one to help save all their souls.

"I shall not interrupt you," he said, turning to leave.

"No, no, do stay. Just let me jot down this verse number." Goodspeed muttered and scratched with his pen; then he looked up with a grin. "There, you see that was all it needed to finish it." Fortune rolled over and sighed gustily again, grateful to see the end of so much work. "Now tell me, what did you think of the place?"

Rupert sat across from Goodspeed and stretched out long legs covered in kerseymere.

"I liked it very much indeed, Lowell. I bought it." He related this news quite matter-of-factly, but the sparkle in his eyes betrayed his pleasure.

"You bou— Why, that is splendid, my boy! Congratulations!"

The purchase of which they spoke was Sherbourne Place—the large house on the hill whose owners were, even at such an early hour, celebrating their impending deliverance from the nightmarish idyll that was Edenshade.

The sparkle remained in Rupert's eye. "Thank you. You will not be surprised to learn that the Redmunds have told me I may move in within the month."

"Ha! To be sure." Goodspeed reverted almost immediately to the subject dearest to the hearts of Edenshaders. "You know, old Thomas Redmund, that was Donald's father, took an *interest* in his garden. Donald never has, nor has his wife. Not that Thomas lifted a spade himself of course, not him; he had servants aplenty for that. Still, they grew some very fine things at Sherbourne Place," he conceded. "Although the whole setup was much too formal for my taste. Still. Of course, they haven't had a really decent showing in years. Donald and his family have never cared about that, and ever since the place finally became his to do with as he pleased, his main concern has been to sell it, especially since he has gambled his way through so much of his income. But now you will change all that."

Rupert felt obliged to remind his friend that growing flowers was something of which he had no experience, nor was he altogether certain that he cared to learn, although he wisely kept this last bit to himself, especially since he had the feeling that such an admission could put him beyond the pale with the natives.

"Well, I cannot promise you that my abilities in the gardening line will be very impressive," he offered gamely, "but I shall see to it that the place is properly kept up."

The vicar blinked. "Kept up? Ke— My dear boy, you will have to do better than that, you know. People will expect it of you. Why, the Peppers *keep up* that pathetic patch *they* choose to call a garden, but I promise you that Sherbourne Place needs, indeed *deserves* a great deal more than *upkeep*. Why, it is the finest manor in town, probably one of the finest in the valley. Certainly it is one of the oldest and largest. And while I daresay that the house and outbuildings and so on are in tip-top condition, it is time that the garden resumes its rightful place . . ." Seeing the blind terror on his listener's face, he modified his approach. "Now, don't worry, Rupert. It is not as bad as all that. I like to think that I know more than a little about roses, and I shall be happy to advise you on that head at any time."

"Er, thank you, Lowell. Oh my, I suppose I need time to let it all sink in. It seems I have bought not just a property, but a horticultural responsibility."

"Good. You see, you're beginning to get into the spirit already. Will you be in to luncheon? We could talk more about it then."

"No! That is, I thank you for your offer of help, but I find I am not very hungry. Perhaps I might take Fortune with me for a walk?"

The dog, hearing the magic word, rose. He stretched his legs and ambled over to Rupert to lick his hand, then gave a beseeching look to Goodspeed. You couldn't be too careful about these things. After all, the vicar could say no, although he seldom did, or Rupert might change his mind, although Fortune didn't think this likely as the man seemed to be a bit pale and a romp would do him good. Dancing with anticipation, he glanced from Rupert to the vicar, who smiled down at him.

"Very well, my friend. You may go with Rupert. But do not overtire him, mind. He looks rather peaked to me."

Fortune gave a sharp answering bark and swung quickly toward the door, his tail wagging rapidly. He and Rupert had become great friends and often went walking together. But it must be told that Rupert's charms, abundant though they might be in the dog's eyes, had not been, after all, sufficient to long sustain the interest of Miss Penelope Logan. To be fair, the maturity that Pen had at first found so compelling in him soon became a liability when compared to the youthful exuberance of young gentlemen of her own age. Thus, following a brief, but merry, period of flirting with Rupert at teas, card parties, and the like, she had turned up her pretty nose and, in the politest way possible, bestowed her affections elsewhere.

Rupert had been flattered by Pen's attention—indeed he had enjoyed her company—but had felt nothing more. He had, however, hoped that the sight of him and Penelope would stir Charlotte to action. Unhappily, this had not occurred. Their chance meetings in the village provoked from Charlotte no more than a cheerful "Good morning, Pen. Good morning, Rupert, lovely day!" before she continued on her way. At Mrs. Black's tea, she had even been heard to remark how charming the two looked together. Clearly, she took the pair in her stride, and Rupert had all he could do to keep from grinding his teeth so loudly that she might hear. And so, although he had experienced just a prickle of surprise at Miss Logan's desertion, he could not feel real distress. During a chance meeting at a hop, Charlotte had teased him with the young lady's defection.

"Fickle, I call it," he had responded dryly, and the two old friends had enjoyed a chuckle at the turn of events.

Pen had lately been keeping company with Frederick Barnstead, and the couple had begun to evidence signs of quite a serious attachment.

"My dear," she had recently confided to her oldest friend, Violet Beardsley, "I cannot imagine my life without Frederick. I am even able to overlook—well, I must be completely honest and say *largely* overlook his annoying habit of making that dreadful *ahem* noise every two or three sentences."

Like more than one child in this garden-mad town, Penelope's dear friend had been named after a parent's favorite flower. And like most of her peers, she detested her name, comforting herself only with the fact that it was infinitely better than Petunia or Aster or Myrtle. Her friend's traditional name as well as her usually good judgment were two of the many reasons that Violet so admired Penelope. Still, Violet, who privately thought she surely would lose her sanity whenever she had to spend above five minutes listening to Mr. Barnstead punctuate his words with his throat clearing, deemed it wise to keep her opinion on this head to herself; however she was befuddled by anyone's summary disposal of Rupert Frost.

"But, Pen, are you quite sure about choosing Mr. Barnstead over Mr. Frost? After all, you said yourself that he—that is, Mr. Frost—is an exemplary gentleman, a very handsome man who . . ."

"Yes, yes, I know what I said, Vi, but that was *ages* ago. Anyway, Mr. Frost is, well, *old,* isn't he? My Frederick is at least as handsome as Mr. Frost and ever so much *younger* besides."

"Well, if you do not want him, there are those of us who think that Mr. Frost is quite perfect just as he is," her friend said rather defensively.

Penelope patted her hand. "And you are welcome to him, Vi, for he is a sweet man. But I do not want him now, for I love Frederick." She tapped her lips pensively. "Oh, but if I could just think of a way to stop all that awful *aheming.*"

Henrietta Pike's regard for Rupert had not abated with time. She had told him on the second occasion of their meeting that she intended to "take you under my wing, my dear," and she had kept to her word. Translated, this apparently meant that she would see to it that he met everyone in town (his former rather more sheltered, and preferred, life with the vicar came to an abrupt end), especially particular young ladies of marriageable age, and that she would put him in the way of a permanent residence, besides giving him all the advice and more that he might need to make it habitable.

Mrs. Pike made a great show of her support, and more than one inhabitant of Edenshade wondered why she did not try to attach him herself. After all, she was kind, attractive, well off, and not so very many years older than he; the age difference would have been large enough to be gossiped about without being scandalous, and small enough to bridge without endangering the esteem of either party or the village. Still, when a close friend broached the subject, Mrs. Pike would say only that, while others might not exclaim over the years she had in *her* dish compared to those so far accumulated by Rupert, *she* found such matches ridiculous in the extreme. She refused to acknowledge, even to herself, a loneliness that had crept into her life and remained firmly lodged there after the demise of Mr. Pike, no matter how busy she kept herself.

And with her boys to see to, when did she have time to think of herself? Of course, Jeremy did not take a great deal of looking after, but she did want to see him resettled again, so matchmaking for Rupert would not add greatly to her burden. So far, her efforts in this regard for both gentlemen had been unsuccessful. The last attempt she had made on Rupert's behalf had been a luncheon she had given, on which occasion she had hoped to introduce to him her prime candidate. However, the chit had been taken with a stomach ailment that had prevented her attendance, and Mrs. Pike had to make do with her second choice, Joan Allerdyce, who turned out to be too featherheaded to attract his interest. She soldiered on in her efforts on Rupert's behalf, while her oldest son flatly refused to countenance any such machinations for him.

Edenshade's old church of St. Michael and All Angels was built of flint in a hodgepodge of architectural styles, most noticeably Norman. The flock assembled for Sunday service listened to the vicar's voice swing through the repeated cadences of the Benedicite.

" 'O ye Winter and Summer, bless ye the Lord . . .' "

Henrietta Pike sat flanked in the family pew by her two sons and looked at the large containers of flowers near the altar. The ladies of the parish took turns supplying St. Michael's with flowers, and this week, it was Dora Hooper's turn. Henrietta sniffed with both disapproval and satisfaction. Once again, Dora had provided nothing more interesting than a few pots of wallflowers, and those arranged with little taste or imagination, in Henrietta's opinion, but then she and Dora Hooper had been at daggers drawn these twenty years past.

As happened whenever he came to church, Jaspar Pike's eyes moved slowly over the lovely vaulted ceiling of the chancel. *Perhaps he will grow up to be an architect, like Sir Christopher Wren,* thought his mother, not for the first time. A noble calling, especially if one designed churches. But this was neither the place nor the time for either of them to indulge in daydreaming, she decided, and gave her youngest a smart jab in the ribs with her elbow.

"Oof." He glanced resentfully at his mother, but her eyes were fastened innocently on the vicar.

" 'Glory be to the Father, and to the Son . . .' " Goodspeed was concluding.

Something else caught Henrietta's attention. Sev-

eral pews to the left sat a young girl with a dashing
bonnet tied in coquelicot ribbons beneath a dimpled
little chin. Ellen Waring's sparkling brown eyes
peeped across at Jeremy, and a quick look in his direction showed him returning the girl's gaze. Although Henrietta wanted Jeremy to remarry, she was
not eager to lose him, especially if the young woman
in question did not meet her standards. If Charlotte
Fayerweather had been rather too old for him, at
least she had been a safe crush (Mrs. Pike was quite
up to snuff and did not miss much that went on
around her, particularly when it concerned her
sons), for she had a good head on her shoulders and
no more notion of tying herself to a mere cub than
the vicar's dog had to marry the Dickeys' rooster.

Evidently, that infatuation had fled, or at least
cooled sufficiently to allow her son to notice another
pretty face. And this one certainly had that. Golden
curls framed by that ridiculous bonnet, a tiny rose
bow of a mouth, and a complexion that Henrietta
was prepared to wager her best kid gloves on owed
more to the rouge pot than it did to nature. Unhappily, looks were all Ellen Waring had. Those she got
from her mother, while her wit came to her from her
father, the greatest idiot in town, and Henrietta Pike
was not the only one who thought so. Neither Ellen
nor her parents were bad people, quite the contrary.
Harford and Leta Waring had two beautiful daugh-
ters, Ellen and the younger, Pearl—now there was a
complete chucklehead, and even prettier than her
sister, heaven help us. Henrietta made a mental note
to keep Jaspar as far from her as possible. The entire
family simply smiled at everyone as the world went
by and never ventured an opinion because they
hadn't sense or energy enough among all of 'em to

form one. Oh, no. If the wind was blowing in *that* direction, Jeremy had better come about, and the sooner the better. Her other elbow found her older son's ribs while, simultaneously, she shot a baleful glare in Ellen Waring's direction that flustered the poor girl for the remainder of morning service.

"Mother!" Jeremy whispered.

"Sssh!" She gazed angelically at the altar.

Jeremy, who actually had no interest in Ellen Waring beyond the desire to steal a kiss from those beautiful lips, gave a little smile and joined the congregation as it whispered, "Amen."

The vicar concluded the second lesson and, in a glad voice, read the marriage banns, the first of this Spring season, of Petrie Norbert and Hester Wilmot.

The congregation filed out into the Spring sunshine and assembled in informal groups on the grass. Some ladies of the parish had taken the trouble to set out a few tables with tea and some modest cakes and buns, and most folk were doing grateful justice to their efforts. Fortune, unbeknownst to the assembly inside the church, had occupied his usual place within the confines of the simply carved but commodious wooden pulpit. Now he strolled amongst the faithful meeting and greeting, having his head patted and the odd morsel smuggled from a hand momentarily dropped to someone's side with a too casual air.

Two middle-aged women, each thin to the point of gauntness, were dissecting the service.

"Well, we have had our annual homily on pride, Mrs. Tibbetts. It is to be hoped that *some* in the parish will listen this time. I mention no names, of course."

"Yes, well, at least this year the vicar didn't revert to Proverbs as he always does." Fortune decided that the vicar apparently was as predictable to Mrs. Tibbetts as she was to him. "Off with you, Fortune. Go on now." Mrs. Tibbetts spoke brusquely but not unkindly, and the dog wandered off to mingle.

"These seedcakes are awfully good," the greengrocer's wife remarked. "I do wish that Mariah would give up her recipe. There, Fortune, they are delicious, don't you agree?"

"Well, that is what I explained to him, don't you know. 'Isaac,' I said, 'you cannot plant them in that sort of soil and expect them to do anything but rot.' Oh, hello, Fortune. 'It's too damp.' But, would he listen? No, he . . ."

"Excellent sermon, vicar. Interesting choice using Psalms for pride. Me, I've always liked Proverbs. Gets right to the point. 'Pride goeth before destruction and . . .' "

"I must say, Pen, ahem, you look awfully pretty in that bonnet."

"I got the seeds from my cousin, Ambrose, in Trimble-Over-Water. He grows the most incredible snapdragons you've ever seen. If I can get half as good a showing, I'll be a happy man."

"Now, Julius, we both know that you won't truly be happy unless your snapdragons can win you a prize in the contest."

The man laughed. "That's true, Robert. Here, Fortune. There's a good boy. Ambrose has been promising me those seeds for years, and now that I have them, I intend to win that prize."

Rupert handed Charlotte a cup of tea and nodded over his shoulder at the two men.

"What contest are they talking about?"

"Thank you," Charlotte said accepting the cup. "Oh, you mean you have not heard yet of our little contest?" She smiled understandingly at his blank stare and explained. "The Valley Garden Show is held every Summer, usually around late July. Well, the name is something of a misnomer, actually, since only two towns in the valley actually participate, and it is known familiarly as the *contest*, rather than the *show*, because prizes are given—just ribbons, but I promise you they are worth their weight in gold here—and competition can be very, um, heated."

He guided her to a bench by an old tree and they sat down. "Really? And who enters this contest?"

"Well, anyone who wants to and whose garden or particular flowers are fine enough. You see, there are all sorts of categories. Best Overall Garden, Best Roses—that's one of those with the keenest competition; the vicar has won seven years running—Best Herb Garden, Best Water Garden . . ."

"Best snapdragons?"

She sat back and laughed, nodding her head, and he joined in her amusement. "Folks here take their gardens quite seriously. I am sure you have realized that by now."

"Indeed, how could I miss it? It's so early in the season, and already gardening seems to be all most people do or talk about."

Charlotte shook her head. "Rupert, what you do not understand is that it never really stopped. All that gardening—energy—was simply moved indoors for the Winter. For the past few months, people have been planning flower beds, reading gardening treatises, and cultivating seeds."

"Good God! And what of you, Charlotte? Are you part of this collective madness?"

"When I came here, I did not know a great deal about the subject. It is difficult not to want to participate, to try to grow something and to have a pretty garden that you and your neighbors can appreciate, however. In fact, there is a great deal of expectation in that regard. Heaven forbid that anyone should let their plot of land, large or small, be less than it could be. My efforts satisfy me and, so far, have not shamed me before my neighbors, so last year, I let Mrs. Ruffle convince me into entering some flowers." She chuckled at the memory. "I was sadly trounced! Ha! I have learned my lesson, I promise you. This year, I shall watch from the sidelines." She eyed him with arched brows and asked teasingly, "Well, now that you are a landowner, and of such an important property at that, shall I be cheering for you? I make certain that the village will expect nothing less of you."

"Charlotte, please! I have hardly settled in at Sherbourne Place yet. I haven't had time to examine the gardens."

She pretended shock. "You have not looked at the gardens? What kind of Edenshader are you? Why, don't you know that a proper resident of this town looks first at his or her prospective garden, *then* at the drains and walls and so on? This will never do, you know, Rupert."

The poor man put his head in his hands and pleaded for mercy. "I swear to you, Charlotte, if one more person,"—he gave her a menacing look—"mentions my responsibility to the gardens at Sherbourne Place, I shall—"

"Ah, there you are, Mr. Frost. I was just saying to my husband that, now you are resident on the hill, we shall doubtless be seeing great things in the gardens there. It has been too long, dear sir."

Charlotte managed to turn her guffaw into a fairly credible cough. Rupert quelled her with a look. "I,

ah, have only just moved in, Mrs. Bartlett, Mr. Bartlett.
I must confess that I have not yet had time to" —they
blinked at him in utter confusion—"that is to say,
there has been so much else to do that I have not been
able to see to the gardens, and . . ."

"Not been . . . Well, you must remedy that just as
soon as may be, you know. There are any number of
us who are only too willing to give you advice and—"

"Yes, well, I have been thinking that I should look
for a few gardeners to see to it all . . ."

"Gardeners! Oh, I see," declared Mr. Bartlett, who
did not see at all. "You mean for scything the grass
and to help with the heavy planting and pruning and
weeding. Well, that is understandable, for the
grounds are extensive, but surely you mean to be
your own man, as it were, to oversee the entire op-
eration—what goes in, what comes out—you know
the sort of thing."

By this time, Rupert had risen and was running his
index finger inside his neckcloth to ease his suddenly
labored breathing. "Well, you know, it is just that I
know so little of . . ."

"Tut, tut." God, would they ever let him finish a
sentence? "We are all here to help, dear Mr. Frost,"
explained Mrs. Bartlett. "You may depend upon us."

In fact, this was part of Rupert's fear—that he
would have no waking moment at Sherbourne Place,
no solitude to plan his campaign for Charlotte, no
peace, without some Edenshader or other eagerly
turning up on his doorstep to lend a hand with the
damned garden! No, he simply would have to take a
firm stand and do so immediately.

"Awfully kind of you all, I am sure, Mrs. Bartlett,
Mr. Bartlett. But, you see, I shall advertise for a team
of gardeners not only to do the lion's share of the

work"—even he had to admit that all this horticultural industriousness had roused his curiosity and
made his own hands itchy to dig into the soil, even
if only for a bit—"but to advise me on what to
plant and how and so on." He raised a hand in a
self-sacrificing manner. "No, no, I am afraid my
mind is made up. The place is too big. There is too
much to be done for me to take advantage of my
neighbors' generosity. And I do not say that I shall
not come begging at your doors for advice and assistance now and again. Who could not, after all,
with the beautiful gardens I see all around me, even
this early in the Spring?"

"But, Mr. Fr—"

"No, Mr. Bartlett, you are too good, but I *must* insist. Why, think of it. The extent of the work to be
done would have me calling on you constantly and
then what would become of your own garden?" It
was a brilliant stroke and Rupert knew it even before
he heard Charlotte stifle another laugh.

"Oh! Er, that is . . . Well, I suppose we must not
browbeat our new neighbor, my dear." Mr. Bartlett
waggled his eyebrows meaningfully at his wife, who
did not need the hint.

"Heavens no! Mr. Frost, far be it from us to interfere. You must, of course, do as you think is right. I
seem to recall my brother in the next village men-
tioning an excellent fellow who should be just the
sort you need. I shall send someone to you with his
name. Oh, Mr. Bartlett, we must be off!" The couple
fled in evident relief.

Rupert turned to Charlotte and smiled trium-
phantly. "There, I believe that I have taken care of
that matter."

Before she could reply, the Bartletts suddenly

turned back. "Oh, Mr. Frost!" Mr. Bartlett called. "I wondered if anyone had mentioned it to you. Surely the Redmunds never did—about the contest, I mean."

He inclined his head in Charlotte's direction. "Yes, Mrs. Fayerweather had just been explaining it to me when you first arrived."

"Ah, good. Then you understand about the honor of the town and so forth . . ."

"Pardon me? The 'honor of the town?' What are you talking about, sir?"

Mrs. Bartlett chimed in. "Well, you see, the Redmunds haven't participated in the garden show for donkeys' years and that is our largest and finest property. And all this time, the honor of Best Manor House Garden has gone to Clayton Park in Great Tipton, the next village over, you know. So ever since the Redmunds withdrew Sherbourne Place from the competition, we have had to put up with all manner of jibes and insults from them. It has been *too* awful. But this year will be different. We are all depending on you. And the Great Tipton entry really only ever won by default anyway. I cannot say it has had anything *that* wonderful to recommend it."

"Now, dear, there are some very fine topiary and the knot gardens . . ."

She gave him a pitiful look. *"Honestly,* Lucius. Nobody does topiary anymore, and a child can put together a knot garden." Charlotte bristled a bit at this, since she had tried unsuccessfully in previous years to create one. "I mean that a garden must make a statement, one that is as grand as the house it surrounds. Oh, you know the kind of thing, Mr. Frost." She peered closely at his pale face. "Or perhaps you do not. Hmm. Well, I shall be sure to send that name round to you just as soon as we get home. Just remember, you and Sherbourne Place are upholding the honor of Edenshade."

"Good God, Charlotte, lead me home. I need a drink."

Six

Summer

By the time Spring had ripened into early Summer, Edenshade had seen two weddings and Goodspeed had just the previous Sunday read the banns for three more. Rupert had hired the gardener recommended by Mrs. Bartlett, and the man had already proved to be an expert in his profession. He and his supporting staff were making good progress in putting the "damned gardens," as their new owner called them, to rights. Rupert had finally settled in to his new home and was feeling so comfortable with his surroundings, inside and out, that he thought it time to return the hospitality that had been shown him by various neighbors over the preceding months and to allow everyone to see what he had done so far at Sherbourne Place.

An all-day outdoor party was to be held in the parkland surrounding the huge house. Fortunately, the weather was perfect and the gaily striped marquees erected in the event of rain now could serve to give shade to those who preferred it. There would be games and a puppet show for the children. For the adults, there would be archery, bowls, races of

both carriages and horses, and dancing to a brass
band. Food, with plenty of sweets for the children,
would be available throughout the day on tables scattered under the trees. The menu was eclectic and
casual, as Rupert hoped the entire entertainment
would be more reminiscent of a fairground than a
party at a grand house. While jugglers wandered
through the crowd miraculously keeping crockery
and balls dancing in midair, people feasted on plat-
ters of joint, sausage rolls, various kinds of fruit, gin-
gerbread, and sweetmeats, and they slaked their
thirst with ale, spruce beer, mead, and lemonade.
Children searched under the shrubbery and in the
cool, shallow pool of the fountain for hidden prizes
of trinkets, while adults wagered on their favorites
playing at bowls or madly dashing their carriages or
horses through the woods.

Charlotte enjoyed herself immensely and stood up
for more than one dance with Rupert, and she was
quite surprised to find herself rather flustered by his
nearness. She was careful not to communicate her
reaction to him, rather joking with him as old friends
might. Rupert was unaware of her feelings in part
because he was at great pains to conceal his own,
which were considerably more than friendly. Both his
duties as host and his plan to try to make Charlotte
jealous meant that he had to dance with other ladies,
and more than one had her heart set to fluttering at
his attention. Violet Beardsley only managed to get
through the country dance with Rupert without trip-
ping because she knew her mother would murder
her otherwise. Fortunately, it was not until after this
exertion had been concluded that he chanced to
mention how charming he thought her name, else
Violet surely would have disgraced herself. As it was,

she, like Charlotte, had all she could do to disguise her feelings for him. Since Violet had not yet acquired Charlotte's refinement or social dexterity, her feelings were less a mystery than she might have preferred them to be.

Celia Lathrop, who claimed to see the future even without the assistance of her arthritic joints, had volunteered to dress up as a fortune-teller. Rupert had wanted to put up a small tent for her use, but she preferred to do her prognostications, as she called them, out on the lawn where everyone could hear. She sat at a table under a large chestnut tree and a long line of Edenshaders waited their turn to learn their futures. Celia claimed that her knowledge came from simply holding the hand of her visitor. She then shut her eyes tight, rocking slightly from side to side as her petitioner begged enlightenment.

One farmer was glad to learn how well his crops would do that year, but another fellow was more than a little disgruntled to find out he would soon be visiting London.

"Never been there. Never want to go. Told you this was all nonsense, Gertrude," he remarked to his wife, who was quite pleased at the prospect. "London indeed!"

Not surprisingly, a large number of her predictions concerned the upcoming garden show—whose entries would fare well (most everyone's), and one or two that would not (these individuals not being among Mrs. Lathrop's favorite people). But again and again, Celia Lathrop foretold a marriage. This was, to a certain extent, not unusual, given that many citizens of Edenshade were of the customary marrying age. Thus, there were many blushes from maidens and sidelong glances from hopeful suitors, and more than one knowing nod from an approving parent. Among the maidens fated to become matrons in the near future were Penelope Logan, who giggled and held tightly to Frederick Barnstead's hand, and Violet Beardsley, who, much to her delight, was to be courted by an "older gentleman."

But the number of marriages that were to be expected in Edenshade rose and rose and began to include some who, for varying reasons, might not have been expected to enter the lists. Rupert, being such an eligible bachelor, was naturally counted among those to go to the altar, as was Charlotte, no matter that she had no particular desires in that direction. Even the vicar and Henrietta Pike were included. Eventually, the fortune-telling ended with much good-natured laughter, some teasing Mrs. Lathrop for not being more varied in her performance, others swearing they would have nought to do with parson's mousetrap.

"Just between you and me, Edward, I like my life just fine the way it is. I'm not saying that I'm happy Eloise was finally carried off by that fever, mind, but I can do what I like in my own house now. I can even blow a cloud at my own supper table without her waving her hands at me and carping about the smell. No, sir, you won't see me with another wife."

"Never mind, Geneva, just because Mrs. Lathrop told you that you'll marry this year—and I cannot see why you believe such moonshine anyway; it's just a bit of fun—does *not* mean that you'll wed James Rider, not while I'm alive, and certainly not while your father still breathes. That young man is worth ten pounds less than nothing and we will not even begin to discuss his family. You are not to even *think* of him as a potential husband, do you hear? Geneva, I am *speaking* to you!"

The area was well lit with torches and lanterns strung through the trees, and those who did not have children to put to bed stayed on into the late evening enjoying "one more dance" or telling "just this last story, dear." The party was the talk of Edenshade for all the next day and the day after that, Rupert being declared a "great fellow" by one and all, not only for his generous hospitality, but for not being too high in the instep to join in the fun and get to know his neighbors.

"Oh, Pen, what wonderful news! I do wish you happy!" Charlotte leaned forward and lightly bussed both of Penelope Logan's cheeks.

"Do sit down, Mrs. Fayerweather. It is so good of you to call. I am sorry that Mama is laid low with one of her sick headaches today and cannot join us. You are acquainted with my very dear friend, Miss Violet Beardsley, I think?"

Charlotte smiled and nodded at Violet, a plump, sweet-faced girl with soft brown eyes. "I do hope that Mrs. Logan will be better soon, dear. I can stay only a moment, but I wanted to call and offer my felicitations. Mr. Barnstead is such an admirable young man. I am certain he will make you a good husband."

Penelope flushed with happiness. "Thank you. We both are so happy. I cannot believe that our wedding is just a little more than a month away! Vi is to stand up for me." She gazed fondly at her friend and a thought began to form in her mind, but she waited until Charlotte had left to speak of it.

Whenever the two young women were together of

late they seemed to talk of only two things: Frederick
Barnstead and Rupert Frost. But while the former
had pledged his heart, the latter had yet to do more
than bestow an idle compliment, a circumstance of
which Violet was only too painfully aware. Since
Penelope was a young lady of both goodness and sen-
sibility, she refrained from rhapsodizing *too* much
about her beloved and their imminent nuptials, in
order to spare her friend's feelings. But such restraint
was neither pleasant for its benefactor, nor productive for its recipient. Mr. Frost was everything that was
polite whenever he and Violet chanced to meet—and
the two friends had arranged for *that* occasion more
times than he would ever have guessed—but no more
than that, and it did not help that Violet remembered
quite well how easily he had once taken to Penelope.

Clearly, Vi was besotted with Mr. Frost and her friend
saw no earthly reason why he should not, in his turn,
fall head over ears in love with her. She was convinced
that the situation needed only the right spark to set it
alight, but Pen had been very nearly at her wit's end
as to how to accomplish such a thing. Until Charlotte
Fayerweather had paid her call this morning.

Violet sat by the open window, chin in hand, trying
to pretend an interest in the wedding breakfast plans
they had been discussing when Charlotte had arrived.

"Will you really be serving champagne, Pen? What
a treat that will be."

"Yes, yes. But I think that I may have a way to deal
with your problem, Vi." She smiled fondly at her old
friend.

"You do? Oh, Pen, honestly?"

Her shining curls bobbed as she nodded her head.
"I believe so. You know, it was not until Mrs. Fayerweather was here that I recalled she and Mr. Frost

are old friends. I heard that they knew one another many years ago back in, oh, wherever they used to live, and they are friends again now."

"So?"

"Oh, Vi, you goose, don't you see? Mrs. Fayerweather *knows* him. She will know what he likes and does not like, and probably what you might do to catch his eye."

"Do you really think so?"

Penelope, rather taken with her own scheme, nodded again, even more vigorously. "Why not? As his oldest and dearest friend," she decided, "surely she must want to see him happy and settled. We need only help her to see that *you* are the woman he needs."

"But she hardly knows me, Pen. How can I expect her to help me?"

Penelope took her hand and patted it. "Vi, that part should be easy. We shall just see to it that the two of you meet frequently, just as we have done with Mr. Frost—oh, but with much more success, I am convinced! Once she knows you better, she is certain to see how perfect you are for him, and the rest should be easy!"

Violet was reluctant to be too hopeful. "Well . . ."

"You will see."

And the two set to planning their strategy for securing the endorsement of the unsuspecting Mrs. Fayerweather.

Charlotte turned in front of her glass, trying to get a better look at the back of her hair. Unsuccessful in her effort, she patted it ineffectually and told herself that Mrs. Ruffle would hardly let her leave the house with untidy hair. If the housekeeper had said her coiffure was properly arranged, then surely it was. She was much more sanguine about her gown. The fabric, an airy lawn, had a tiny check pattern of soft blue and green, with sheer sleeves of the same material extending to the elbow. It was a perfect costume for the wedding—yet another one!—that she was to attend with Rupert.

Setting a floppy straw hat on her head, she surveyed herself one last time in the mirror and smiled. *Not too bad for a woman of my age,* she decided. *I wonder what Ru—* Then stopped herself. This was not the first time of late that she had found herself wondering what Rupert would think about this or say about that. Honestly, as if she cared for his opinions after all this time! They did seem to spend quite a bit of time together, but she felt that was purely happenstance. Still, it was nice to hear him laugh again in that comical way he had, and when he asked, she was pleased to give her advice on improvements and changes he was making at Sherbourne Place. She felt comfortable with him and she was enjoying herself very much, but that was all, she assured herself.

Two thoughts suddenly emerged and struck her with such force that she stopped halfway down the steps. Was that truly all she really wanted? Did she wish to live the rest of her life without the companionship of a mate, without the assurance of a hand to hold, a love to sustain her? Charlotte very nearly sat down on the stairs at the sudden realization that, indeed, she did not! But when had this change of heart occurred and what had caused it? She made her way into the morning room and sat down. She had a few minutes before Rupert arrived to escort her to the church, and she was grateful that Mrs.

Ruffle was out doing the shopping and that Nell was attending to her chores in the kitchen, so she could be alone to consider.

Charlotte had been perfectly content with her life as it had been. She was a respected and liked member of the Edenshade community and wanted for nothing. Until five minutes ago. Now she wanted only to marry and live a long and happy life with the man that she loved. Perhaps it was all the weddings that had been, and were to be, celebrated in Edenshade this Summer. The whole town was headed for the altar at St. Michael's. Marriages, plans for marriages, proposals of marriage, marriage breakfasts, marriage clothes, marriage banns, and premarriage tiffs had taken on a life of their own and vied for preeminence only with Edenshade's gardens. The local cynic might have said that marriage fever had infected the village like an infestation in a rose garden. Actually, it was more like a sudden fog that seeped into unsuspecting corners of the townspeople's lives involving them in the happy event whether they wanted to be or not. Some people had even begun to keep time by weddings, so common had they become.

"Let's see. You wrote to your brother, oh, must have been three weddings ago. I should think you'd have an answer by now."

"But, Mother, I *cannot* wait that long! Why that is two whole weddings from now!"

Mrs. Derwent and several other ladies found that the town's two dressmakers had no time to make their new Summer frocks, because they had all they could do to sew new bride clothes. Farmer Bradley had to wait a whole day to have his wagon wheel repaired—"And me with real work to do, mind!"—because the smith had promised Mr. and Mrs. Stevens that their carriage would be in good enough repair to carry their Eleanor to her wedding on Saturday.

Well, of course, all of this certainly could put one in a mind to marry, Charlotte decided with cheerful relief. And what more logical person to wish to wed than the one who attended so many of those weddings with you? *Just a minute, my girl,* she brought herself up short. *You saw the vicar at those weddings, too,* and *danced with him besides, and you don't wish to marry him! But then he does not dance half so well as Rupert, and . . .* Oh, dear, this was not leading anywhere that she wished to go. Still, she did know Rupert so very well, it made sense then that . . . The voice interrupted again. *You thought you knew him all those years ago, too, but you did not. Oh, all right! I did not know him then, but I was also much younger and much less experienced, and so was he. Well, he was younger, at any rate. In any event, he has changed since then. He is responsible and mature now. So was the vicar, and remember Celia Lathrop predicted he would marry, too,* she reminded herself with a chuckle. Charlotte thought the world and all of Lowell Goodspeed, but could not envision him as a husband—not hers, at any rate.

Oh, well, it hardly matters, I suppose. Rupert is nowhere near to being in love with me. At least, I do not think he is. She twisted the net gloves in her hands, staring blankly out the window into the garden, recalling what he had said to her when they first met again after all those years. "You will not give us another chance, Charlotte?" he had asked. And she had laughed off the question because he had only been teasing her, after all. Hadn't he? *Of course, he was, stupid,* she reminded herself, *and just recall how he practically turned himself inside out whenever Penelope Logan was near.* That was over and done with, but he certainly had taken her dismissal of him in his stride, and Charlotte had seen him look at other women and preen himself at their attention. It was then that the second thought struck her with much force. Suppose he married—everyone else was, after all—what then?

Charlotte sighed. She would not—she would absolutely *not*—let herself fall in love with Rupert Frost all over again. Probably he would prove to be as faithless a lover now as he had been before. Perhaps a younger women would be more tolerant in that regard, perhaps just more naive. Her abstraction was broken by three sharp raps and she opened the door to smile at the man of her thoughts and walk with him up the street to the church.

"For as much as David and Catherine have consented together in holy wedlock, and have witnessed the same before God and this company . . ."

Soon the newly wedded couple were dashing merrily through the carved wooden doorway of St. Michael's and into the sunshine, where the crowd of invited guests shouted its good wishes. The group presently reassembled in the garden of the bride's parents, where toasts were made again and again to the couple's happiness. Like most of the houses in the area, the Albrights' was constructed of brick, whose surface had mellowed over the years to a soft reddish hue. Their garden, divided by gravel paths, was one of the smallest but finest in Edenshade.

As Charlotte enjoyed a few quiet moments admiring some lilies, she noticed Violet Beardsley, accompanied by Pen Logan, strike up a conversation with Rupert beneath the rose arbor. He smiled charmingly at Violet, then threw back his head and laughed at something she said. It seemed to Charlotte that Pen deliberately stood on the periphery saying little, so that her friend could command all of the gentleman's attention. Well, he certainly did not seem to mind. She shrugged and turned back to the lilies.

"Mrs. Fayerweather, are you having a pleasant afternoon?"

It was Penelope. She smiled. "Why, yes, Pen, I am." She was not accompanied by Violet and a quick glance showed the other girl to be still at Rupert's side.

Penelope followed her eyes. "She is with Mr. Frost." Then she added with all the experience in the world in her voice, "They do make a perfect couple, do they not?"

Charlotte was about to chuckle at this observation, but another look in their direction made her stop. They did look good together. Before she could do more than register this condition, Penelope went on in a lowered voice, although the only other guests nearby all were too involved in their own conversations to overhear.

"Er, Mrs. Fayerweather, if I might have a word?"

Charlotte nodded.

"I know that I may speak with you in confidence."

Penelope's listener's brows rose the fraction that politeness prescribed.

"It is Violet. Miss Beardsley. You may not be terribly surprised to learn that she is quite fond of Mr. Frost. I want very much for my friend to be happy—as happy as I am with Mr. Barnstead. Will you help us?"

"I beg your pardon?"

"Oh, dear. I am not saying this properly at all. Mrs. Fayerweather, you and Mr. Frost are very old friends, are you not?"

Charlotte gave a little nod.

"Well, as you can see, Mr. Frost is not at all averse to Miss Beardsley's company, but he does not have a special regard for her. Not yet, at any rate. But I believe that all Mr. Frost needs is some, um, inspiration."

"Inspiration?"

"Well, what I mean to say is, could you speak to Mr. Frost on her behalf? Oh, not in an obvious way, as I need not tell you, of course. Rather, if you could just mention her good points—she is a splendid horsewoman, you know, and her watercolors are so lovely—you have seen them yourself . . ."

"Pen, are you asking me to play matchmaker for Miss Beardsley?"

"Oh, my, no! Oh, I never would suggest such a thing, Mrs. Fayerweather!" Penelope became quite flustered at her poor handling of the matter—and after all her fine promises to Vi! Especially since she now realized that she must have sounded exactly as if she wanted Mrs. Fayerweather to be a matchmaker.

Charlotte took pity on her young friend. "Come, Pen. Let us sit over there, so that you might catch your breath."

She took Penelope's arm and led her past some shining red poppies and to a seat under an old beech tree.

"Mrs. Fayerweather, I do apologize. Whatever must you think of me?"

Charlotte smiled, but squinted a bit in puzzlement. "Now, Pen, I promise I do not think ill of you. But surely you cannot honestly expect that I should attempt to intercede between Mr. Frost and Miss Beardsley?"

Penelope toyed with the wide satin ribbons of her bonnet and started to speak. "Well, but Mrs.—"

"Not another word, Pen. Come," she said gently. "You must know it would be the height of bad manners in me to speak of her to Mr. Frost. And I might also remind you that Miss Beardsley's parents may have entirely other plans for her and may not thank me for interfering. I could never enter into such a havey-cavey business."

"But, Mrs. Fayerweather, they would not mind, I promise you." The look Charlotte returned was less than encouraging. "Truly, all I want is for you to speak well of her when the opportunity arises." In actuality, Penelope had originally wanted a great deal more from Charlotte, but the situation being what it was, she would happily settle for whatever aid she could beg. "Vi's parents do not yet have anyone in mind for her to wed, but you may be sure that they would be more than pleased if she were courted by Mr. Frost! He is very eligible, you see."

Charlotte was silent. He certainly was. She stole another look toward Rupert and Violet. They had been joined by several other people, but he appeared to be enjoying both her presence and her part in the conversation. He had made it rather clear to Charlotte that he wanted a wife, after all. And Violet Beardsley was as suitable a candidate as any. She was well bred and pretty, she probably would have a good income, and she was as accomplished as any young lady of her station—indeed, her watercolors were just as fine as her friend had claimed they were. Pen's request had sounded outré at first, but she saw now that the girl was not asking anything so terrible. It would be the easiest thing in the world for her to speak well of Violet Beardsley when the circumstances were right; such things were done in polite society all the time. Why then had she been so quick to recoil from helping to advance Violet's cause? If jealousy had caused her re-action, why had she not felt the same when Rupert and Pen had flirted with one another? Charlotte could not have explained her feelings then, but she was rather certain now that if she declined Pen's request, she would be doing so for very selfish reasons. She glanced once more over toward the arbor and saw again how happy they looked together.

"Very well, Pen."

Penelope blinked. Charlotte had seemed to be in a brown study for so long with a peculiar crease between her brows that Penelope had despaired of her changing her mind.

"Mrs. Fayerweather, you will help?"

She smiled. "Yes. But only when the right situation presents itself. And if Mr. Frost shows no inclination toward Miss Beardsley, I shall drop the entire matter. Is that understood?"

"Oh, yes. Thank you, Mrs. Fayerweather."

That had been hours and hours ago. Now Charlotte opened her bedroom windows as wide as she could to tempt whatever air she might from the heavy Summer night. Back in bed and still unable to sleep, she punched her pillow much more fiercely than was called for and turned over again. When she finally drifted off, Charlotte dreamt she was at St. Michael's as Rupert and Violet exchanged marriage vows. Suddenly, all those in attendance were holding gigantic golden goblets and toasting her in loud, raucous voices.

"To Charlotte Fayerweather! Matchmaker *par excellence!*"

Rupert and Violet declared their gratitude for her intervention in their romance, promising to name their firstborn after her.

"It can be Charlotte or Charles, so it matters not if it is a boy or a girl!" Violet giggled.

"We might have twins. That would be even better!" declared Rupert.

Violet hugged her so tightly that Charlotte thought she might suffocate. She struggled and struggled to free herself and finally broke loose, only to wake in her own bed, the sheet that had wound around her now kicked onto the floor. She sat up and pulled her nightdress close around her legs, for the rain that was sweeping down from the hills was heralded by a brisk, damp wind that whooshed the curtains far into the bedchamber. Charlotte sat for a few moments, enjoying the cool air and berating herself for being such a ninny. *I have no claims on Rupert,* she thought, *nor do I wish for any. Violet Beardsley is a perfectly nice young woman, who, for all I know, could make him an ideal wife.* Thunder roared briefly in the near distance just before torrents of rain began to blow into her room. She rose quickly, closing the windows to the storm and, before she fell asleep again, determined that, if things progressed as Pen hoped they would, she would simply be glad that her old friend was happy.

Seven

As the time of the flower show drew nearer, those folks who would participate in one way or another began to exhibit behavioral traits that might be considered unusual during any other time of the year. In the days approaching Flower Week, as it was commonly called—despite its duration of just four-and-a-half days—the gardeners of Edenshade showed increasing anxiety, fretting over every little problem, real or imagined, amongst their blooms. Domestic tranquility, sleep, and chores became disposable commodities as long hours spent weeding, pruning, eliminating pests, and otherwise cosseting precious plants took precedence over almost everything else. Arguments between and amongst families and neighbors took on fabled proportions, leading one wag to remark, "The Capulets and the Montagues couldn't hold a candle to some of the folk hereabouts." Of course, this gentleman had won ribbons three years running and had little to be concerned about—"Or so he thinks," one of the "Capulets" predicted ominously.

As in years past, Goodspeed had used his homily in an attempt to deter such feelings. But this year, his words (or Peter's actually) appeared to have little effect on his flock, for when he entreated them to "greet ye one another with a kiss of charity," he would have sworn that he heard at least one harumph from amongst the pews, a suspicion confirmed after the service when he was admonished by no fewer than three parishioners that the garden contest was a serious business and *not* for the faint-hearted. True, almost the entire village could be seen to take part in the wedding celebrations that continued to occur with a bizarre frequency, but by a day or two after the nuptials, otherwise friendly folk were all too often heard sniping at one another or cursing the weather—which, in truth, had been quite fine all Summer—for failing to provide the necessary sun, rain, heat, or cool necessary for their precious whatevers to flower in the requisite profusion.

Goodspeed's vicarage garden was surrounded by a low stone wall and neat boxwood hedges that provided a perfect frame for his collection of old roses that took up almost the entire space. His damask roses included the beautiful and very old Celsiana, whose petals, almost like crumpled silk, would fade from pale pink to near white and whose scent wafted well beyond the garden walls when the air was humid and warm. His alba roses included the ancient and tall Maiden's Blush, whose large, fragrant blossoms grew in clusters on stems well protected by thorns. To walk along the paths that wound through his rose collection was an almost hedonistic experience, the beauty of the blooms exceeded only by their magnificent fragrances. It was also bound to be a lengthy visit, as the owner liked nothing more than to wax poetic on the blights as well as the beauties of his collection.

The vicar and Fortune were taking a leisurely walk through the lane just down the hill from the vicarage and St. Michael's—that is, the dog scouted out a path that his upright friend could safely follow. Coming upon some particularly interesting smells, Fortune joyously wiggled his way into a yard in meticulous condition.

"Papa! Papa! Look what Fortune is doing!" a small child cried, pointing to the dog, whose leg was at that moment raised to a tree in the far corner of the yard. The man came running, brandishing a hoe.

"Fortune! That damn dog! I'll . . . Oh, vicar. Good day to you." The fellow, Amos White by name, changed his tone. The dog, having accomplished his mission, came and sat by Goodspeed's side, bestowing on Mr. White what, in dog language, passed for a smile.

"Good day, Mr. White."

"Er, I was just saying what a nice dog your Fortune is . . ."

"No, you were not, Papa. You were very angry at Fortune because he was—"

"Quiet, Timothy! You'll speak when you are spoken to."

"Yes, Papa." He sat down next to Fortune and hugged him with delight.

"Fine dog, that, fine dog," Mr. White managed.

The vicar nodded and smiled. He was as oblivious to his friend's most recent transgression as he was to the holes dug in various spots in the village. For despite the pressure of the contest, no one had the heart to complain to their clergyman, and anyway, Fortune was, otherwise, generally well liked in Edenshade.

The two rambled on through the evening light passing Loring Cottage, whose tubs of flowers and window boxes were thought to have a good chance of success in the contest this year. They wandered out back to where Mr. Loring and his two sons were decorating their carriage with ribbons and nosegays and tinkling bells, for the oldest boy, Lawrence, was to be wed in the morning. The groom was rather nervous and his father and brother were teasing him and slapping his back, so he was more than relieved to see someone who might inject a note of normalcy into the proceedings, no matter that Goodspeed was a living reminder of the source of his unrest. By the time that the vicar departed, things seemed to be somewhat calmer.

As they headed back toward the vicarage, Goodspeed and Fortune passed other Edenshaders taking the evening air, and they stopped to exchange words and news. Walking up the lane by the river, they happened upon Charlotte and Rupert chattering with Cordelia and Arthur Parsons and their twins, Artemisia, the girl, and Achillea, the boy, now more than two years old. The four adults were discussing the previous week's wedding of Martha Foxton and Alford Trask.

"And her that we all supposed would spend her days seeing to her parents instead of a husband!" Mrs. Parsons was exclaiming with pleasure.

The celebration had been a small one, in keeping with the income of Martha's family, but nevertheless quite charming and a good deal of fun. Martha had worn a simple lawn gown with a new bonnet decorated with great care by her and her mother, and she carried a posy of lilies and myrtle from the family's garden. Martha and Alford had left St. Michael's in a shower of flower petals and shouts of good luck. Together with their entourage and guests, they had walked the short distance to her parents' cottage, where simple refreshments were provided under the shade of the chestnut trees and Martha's brothers, those of the skating-party fame, entertained everyone with tunes from their fiddle and concertina. The festivities had lasted well into the evening and had been greatly enjoyed by all.

"Yes, it just goes to show you," Goodspeed joined the conversation, "that great expenditures of money are not necessary either to send a young couple on the road to matrimony or to entertain those extending their good wishes to them. It was a fine day indeed."

"The dancing was a great deal of fun, wasn't it? Charlotte said. "I was just about to say how well you and Miss Beardsley looked, Rupert, when you were dancing that reel. She is quite an accomplished dancer, I think."

"Oh. Yes, she is very graceful," he agreed casually, there being no polite way he could have disagreed had this not been so.

The Parsons soon moved on, as it was time and past to put the young ones in their beds for the night.

"Well," Goodspeed asked, "are you both ready for *this* week's wedding? I just came from Lawrence Loring's house, and his father and younger brother are dividing their time between decorating the carriage and torturing the poor groom. I shall be more than a little surprised if he is able to stand up alone tomorrow, he is so nervous. But I suppose that is why we have groomsmen. And then, of course, Penelope Logan and Frederick Barnstead are soon to exchange their vows. I declare, it seems all I am doing lately is reading banns and marrying people. Praise the good Lord. It is a far sight better than burying folk, but I

hardly have any time left these days for my garden."
He chuckled.

"Oh, vicar, I was just about to tell Charlotte that I
am expecting guests at Sherbourne Place. Friends
from the army you know. One of them, Major Benjamin Nashe, brings with him his wife, Sally, and their
son, Winston, and they will be here for an extended
stay. The other, Captain Alexander Beddoes, will be
accompanied by his cousin, Georgina Hastings. I
have not yet had the pleasure of meeting her, and to
say the truth, I do not know Beddoes nearly as well
as I do Nashe. But both my former comrades are
brave, good fellows. I trust that both of you will join
us at Sherbourne Place for some of the entertain-
ments I have planned. Charlotte, your advice in that
area will not be turned aside, I must confess." He
smiled at her a little sheepishly.

Both assured him of their eagerness to meet his
friends and Charlotte said that she would be pleased
to lend her assistance wherever it might be needed.
She feigned a sudden thought.

"Well, as to guest lists, Rupert, I do hope that you
plan to invite Miss Beardsley?"

He blinked. Charlotte seemed uncommonly interested, of late, in Miss Beardsley's social life and accomplishments. In the recent past, Rupert had found
himself helping Miss Beardsley to notch her arrow at
the Fiskes' archery party, partnering her at whist and
sharing his umbrella during a Summer shower. And
each of those circumstances, he had noticed wryly at
the time, had been engineered—quite deftly, he had
to admit—by Charlotte. Not that Miss Beardsley was
not all that she should be, but she was practically a
child, for heaven's sake. Of course, he was acquainted
with a good many men of his years who would have

jumped at the opportunity to spend time with, indeed probably to wed, such a one as Violet Beardsley, but he was not among them. As he had told Charlotte all those months ago, he was attracted to more mature women. Violet Beardsley would not fit into *that* category for some years yet.

Well, if Charlotte thought to tease him with young misses just because he had said he felt it was time that he wed, let her continue to promote the chit's cause, if that was what she was up to. He had no intention of leg shackling himself to Violet Beardsley or any other of her ilk, but if he were careful, and he *was*, he could enjoy their company without hurting their tender feelings or landing himself in parson's mousetrap with the wrong woman. Rupert gave her his most winning smile.

"Certainly, Charlotte. I had every intention of doing so." He was pleased to notice that she seemed to wilt just a bit at his response, but he put it down to no more than her apparent failure to get a rise from him. "I must be off." He doffed his straw hat. "Charlotte, vicar, Fortune. Good evening to you." He strolled off whistling and Charlotte squinted after him with the uncomfortable sensation that he had been baiting her.

She and Goodspeed strolled on, Fortune first running up ahead, then gamboling back to alert them to some discovery of great moment. Charlotte drew her shawl a little closer and bid the vicar and Fortune a pensive good night at her door.

The uneven stone path that led to Charlotte's house, Hawthorn Cottage, was interspersed with low growing herbs that released their fragrance when trod upon or brushed by ladies' skirts. Daisies edged the path on either side and ended in a wide herba-

ceous border that wrapped like a wide multicolored
ribbon around the front and sides of the neat, two-
story brick house. Deep green ivy slowly crept its way
up the chimney, despite her efforts to halt its progress. Charlotte had once heard an aunt tell of a snake
that found its way into someone's hearth via the convenient means of chimney ivy. Charlotte was terrified
of snakes. In front of the cottage and slightly to one
side was a tall, gnarled old hawthorn tree, which gave
its name to her cottage and whose long branches offered just enough shade to keep the house from becoming too hot in Summer. She had had a wooden
bench built to encircle the tree's wide trunk and Nell
sat there sometimes on warm Summer days to shell
peas or mend the linen. Lattice casement windows
in the rear looked out to a simple plot mostly planted
with lilacs, a couple of roses given her by the vicar
(and which, thankfully, she had managed not to murder), and in their season, lilies, hyacinths, and daffo-
dils. A small kitchen garden of herbs and a few
vegetables completed the immediate landscape.

　　Mrs. Ruffle's hopes had been raised earlier when
her mistress had encountered Mr. Frost quite acci-
dentally in the lane, but here she was come home
with only the vicar and Fortune for company. The
housekeeper was beginning to worry. Once she had
observed Charlotte and Rupert together it was more
than clear to her that they loved one another. She
was clever enough to realize that there had been
more to their previous relationship than Charlotte
had cared to divulge, but obviously they got on well
enough now, whatever might have occurred before.
But it seemed that Mrs. Fayerweather had not yet
come to any such realization of her own, for wasn't
she forever putting forward the Beardsley girl, just as

if the sun rose and set on her head? For pity's sake, did she honestly believe that Violet Beardsley could hold Mr. Frost's interest from one week to the next, much less a lifetime? Whenever Mrs. Ruffle met Mr. Frost in the village, he was always politeness itself and always asked particularly after Mrs. Fayerweather. She could see a sparkle in that man's eye, even if the lady in question could not. Still, Mrs. Ruffle could swear that her mistress harbored particular feelings for her old friend—not that she had let on in any noticeable way—but she was not taking any steps to pursue it. *Well, I shall just have to give her a push in the right direction,* Irene Ruffle decided as she went to Charlotte and asked if there was anything she needed before retiring.

Major Benjamin Nashe had fought bravely with Rupert at Montereau. Rupert had kept his promise to visit his friend and his wife, Sally, on his way home from the Continent, and now they and their son, Winston, were visiting, and he was pleased to be returning their hospitality. As their carriage pulled into the central court of Sherbourne Place, he was waiting impatiently when the groom opened the vehicle's door and pulled down the stairs. The two friends clapped one another soundly on the shoulders.

"Nashe!"

"Frost! Good to see you!" Nashe turned back to the carriage and extended his hand to his wife. The lady who emerged from the shadows of the carriage had, like her husband, passed the first blush of youth. She was, as she had been for most of her life, more than a little plump. The plainness of her oval face was enhanced by an ever cheerful countenance and bright blue eyes. A charming chip straw bonnet sat atop brown curls and tied beneath her chin in a large, green satin bow. Rupert grasped both her hands and kissed her cheeks.

"Sally. You are prettier than ever."

She laughed lightly, pleased with the compliment. "Rupert, how good of you to invite us. Oh, the fresh air is delightful after that stifling carriage. The roads were so dusty that we have had to ride with the windows shut for I do not know how many miles." She waved a handkerchief in front of her face to fan it.

Winston, a young man of almost twenty-two years, had followed his mother from the carriage and now shook his host's hand and offered his compliments.

"Winston! I promise not to remark on how much taller you have grown in just a few months, for I recollect how I used to detest such obvious remarks. Welcome to Sherbourne Place. Please come in. I have refreshments ready and you can cool off."

A short time later, Sally stepped through the French doors onto the lawn. The three men were seated under a shady, sweet-smelling arbor of honeysuckle and they waved to her to join them.

"Oh, I feel so much better. This gown is ever so much cooler than the other," she smiled, holding out the skirt of the soft yellow-and-orange-plaid jaconet fabric. She sipped her lemonade and sat back luxuriously in the chair. "Benjamin, it feels so good to *stretch.*"

Her husband laughed. "Sally dislikes being confined in the carriage, even for shorter trips."

"I cannot say that I blame you, Sally. I am sorry that the twins were unable to accompany you right away."

"Don't be, sir," Winston interjected. "If they were with us I can assure they would only break up our peace. They will be here soon enough." Despite his words, the young man was very fond of his twelve-year-old sisters.

"I wish that I could disagree, Rupert, but Winston has the right of it," their mother chuckled. "They can be extremely taxing. And for the present, they are taxing their grandmother and grandfather in Gillingham, but as I wrote, they will join us here soon."

"Well, if it is quiet you seek, you will be glad to learn that for the next couple of evenings, we shall be just us to supper, as I am sure you are tired after the long journey from Kent and want least of all to make yourselves agreeable to strangers. But on Monday, two good friends will sit down with us, our vicar, Lowell Goodspeed—you remember, Ben, Elmont's uncle—and Charlotte Fayerweather, whom I knew back in Marlowe." He did not elaborate on this last relationship and his guests did not press for details. "Oh, and we shall be joined by Alexander Beddoes and his cousin, Georgina Hastings."

Nashe raised a brow of inquiry and Rupert chuckled.

"I know what you're thinking, Ben, and you are correct. Beddoes and I did not know one another all that well, no better than you and he. I do not really know all that much about him; he is a few years older than you and I and he had been wounded slightly and returned to service before we met him. He seemed a right enough sort, wouldn't you say?" His friend shut his eyes and tilted his head in a way to suggest that he supposed Rupert to have the right of it. "In any event, he wrote me that he and this cousin—think he mentioned that she lives with him, probably a spinster a bit long in the tooth—would be passing in this direction on their return from staying with a relative and would like to break their journey here. Of course, I wrote him that they would be more than welcome to stay as long as they like." This last was uttered with as much interest in seeing his former acquaintance as it was with the enthusiasm of a new landowner proud of his manor and eager to extend its hospitality to all who might venture there.

"Well, I am sure that will be very nice," Sally said. "I shall be glad to have another woman to converse with after a few days here with you men," she teased.

"As to that, my dear," Rupert interjected, "you will be meeting Mrs. Fayerweather, and she, I promise you, will fulfill all your requirements of feminine companionship."

"*Mrs.* Fayerweather?" Sally asked.

"Oh, yes, did I not mention? Charlotte is a widow."

Sally did no more than smile in reply to this, but the pillow talk that night between Mr. and Mrs. Nashe was full of speculation of "this Mrs. Fayerweather" and the extent of Rupert's interest in her.

The vicar sipped his wine appreciatively.

"Tell me, Mrs. Nashe, what are the gardens like in Ashford? I regret to tell you that I have not been to Kent in many a year."

Her son and husband glanced at one another and exchanged grins. Winston laughed.

"Vicar, you have asked the wrong person if you want an unbiased assessment about the place. We all love our home, but Mama's enthusiasm is extraordinary, and she was not even born there!"

"Oh, hush, Winston," his mother chuckled in return; then she spent the next ten minutes entertaining the others with stories about her beloved home. "It is true, vicar. I was used to Cornwall—I grew up there, you know—where the climate is so very different than it is in Ashford or here in Essex. Do you know, we even had palm trees there! But I have come to love Kent dearly. We do have some lovely gardens there, including our own, I dare to say."

"So I have heard, Mrs. Nashe. I should like to hear all about them."

"I shall be happy to oblige, Mr. Goodspeed. I have heard wonderful things about *your* garden, and I am most eager to see it and more of the others here in Edenshade. Mr. Nashe and I strolled through the village this afternoon, but you and I both know that, very often, the real treasures of a garden may not be seen from the lane! And Mrs. Fayerweather was just telling me about your annual contest here in the valley. Competition must be very keen indeed, judging from what we saw today."

Although it was not in his nature to dominate any conversation, the vicar had been known to talk for hours on the floriculture of the area with considerably less encouragement than had been given him by the unsuspecting Mrs. Nashe. She was rescued after a minute or two by her son, who did possess a real interest in the subject and took much more active participation in the discussion, to the vicar's delight, than had his mother.

Charlotte invited Sally to take a turn about the room and the two soon were sitting companionably on a bench near the open French doors and enjoying the fragrant evening breeze. Rupert and Benjamin had, a short while earlier, stepped out on the terrace to enjoy their cheroots, and the low rumble of their voices fell pleasantly on the ear. Sally, never one to miss an opportunity, thought this would be the perfect time to learn more about Charlotte and whether there was or could be anything between her and Rupert.

She had teased her husband, during their whispered conversation two nights earlier, that he sounded to her awfully like a matchmaker, so interested was he in whether or not his friend was courting Mrs. Fayerweather. He had responded with considerable dignity that former majors in His Majesty's service did not play at matchmaking. However, Rupert had always struck him as rather lonely and he would be glad to see him settled with a family. During their campaigning, he had never spoken of a love left at home, or of any woman in particular, beyond the whores that a soldier might encounter from time to time, of course.

Having spoken before thinking, Benjamin quickly explained that he *naturally* had *never* availed himself of such services, and she was a goose if, for even one moment, she believed otherwise. He watched the initial horror on his beloved wife's face change first to fury, then to a grudging uncertainty. If he had been as clumsy as Rupert had been nine years earlier, if Sally had been as stiff as Charlotte had been, poor Benjamin might have found himself haunting his host's halls in the wee hours, searching for a new place to sleep. But he was not clumsy and she was not stiff. After receiving numerous declarations of undying love, Sally cuddled in her husband's arms, said that of course she believed him, and added sweetly that, should she ever learn otherwise, she would have his guts for garters. Laughing, Benjamin accepted her terms, and before the cat could lick his whisker, no one who might have spied the couple (should there be such a contemptible creature) would have suspected that anything had been amiss.

As the two women sat together on the bench, Charlotte smiled in Winston's direction. "He is a charming young man, Mrs. Nashe."

"Thank you. He gets that from his father," she replied.

"Oh, I am sure not!"

"No, honestly. Mr. Nashe can charm the birds from the trees, as they say. I always said he should have been in the diplomatic service. You see, Winston knew to step in before I began to yawn in poor Mr. Goodspeed's face. And I would have, too!" She laughed and changed the subject. "Rupert has told us that you are widowed. I am sorry."

Charlotte nodded. "It is several years now."

"Do you have any children?"

"Mr. Fayerweather and I were not blessed in that way."

"Ah. Did you come to live here with your husband?" Fortunately, Sally Nashe, despite her self-admitted lack of charm, was one of the world's most empathetic souls, who could actually pose such questions without seeming too meddlesome.

"No. I came here after he died. Although I almost feel as if I've always lived here." She explained about Mrs. Ruffle's role in her relocation.

"To be sure. But then, how did you and Rupert end up in the same place again? What made him choose Edenshade as his new home? Was it because you were here?"

"I beg your pardon?"

Sally put her hand to her lips. As soon as she had uttered the words, especially those last ones, she knew she had far overstepped the bounds of polite dis-

course, and with a lady whom she barely knew! "Now
you see what I mean about Winston's charm—or tact
at least. My question was intrusive, Mrs. Fayerweather.
Pray forgive me. I meant no offense."

"Not at all. I do not think that my being here was
all that important to Rupert's decision. We had not
been in communication for many years."

The other woman eyed her shrewdly. Charlotte had
suddenly become engrossed with a bit of lint in her
lap, however, and did not look up. Sally opened her
mouth to say something, then decided she had better
not. Was Mrs. Fayerweather's reluctance to discuss
Rupert's decision evidence of his feelings for her or
vice versa? Or both? Or neither? she reproached herself sternly. In any case, it was none of her business.
Very likely that *is what she intends her few words to convey.
Just keep your nose out of it, my girl,* Sally thought, *or you
will end up like Mr. Chesterton back home, minding everyone's business except your own.* Still, she was quite fond
of Rupert and could see that she might come to feel
the same way about Charlotte Fayerweather. Certainly, she liked Charlotte well enough already.

And the poor woman had been alone here for
years, and from the look of things, was likely to remain in that state. She made a little face. The world
was meant to pass two by two—that was simply the
natural way of things. Even Benjamin thought Rupert
should marry. So why should he not marry Mrs. Fayerweather? They already knew and clearly liked one
another, and she was right here in Edenshade under
his nose, for pity's sake. The more Sally considered
the situation, the more exasperated and determined
she became. She knew Rupert had been correspond-
ing with the vicar while he was still on the Continent,
and it was apparent that the old gentleman, whom

she quite liked, was, to say the least of it, voluble. She thought it unlikely that Rupert had decided to settle in Edenshade just because it was a garden spot; Mr. Goodspeed must have mentioned Mrs. Fayerweather's name. Perhaps while she and Benjamin were here . . .

Two days before Penelope's wedding, she and Violet were on the far side of the duck pond perched on stools before canvases and painting in watercolors. The girls spoke only in desultory undertones, so as not to startle the waterfowl gliding about in intricate patterns and providing an idyllic scene for their brushes. The morning air was heavy and still, disturbed only by the lazy hum of some bees, and the soft plash as one of the half-dozen ducks on the pond stood on its head to snack or to show off to his friends.

Winston Nashe urged his mount to a canter as they broke from the cover of the woods. The rider was blinded by the sunlight for a moment as he and his horse emerged from the shadowed paths of the forest that ran parallel to the river and the pond. Once his eyes became accustomed to the brightness, however, he urged Angus to a gallop and quickly covered the distance to the riverbank. He did not immediately see the two ladies, who were partially hidden by some shrubbery. Angus's snort as he came to a halt by the water frightened the ducks, who swarm hurriedly toward the middle of the pond, quacking indignantly all the way. Just as loud were the admonitions of the two young women, who exclaimed at his lack of manners.

He had first seen Miss Beardsley with Penelope Logan on Sunday, when he, his parents, and Rupert had been walking home from church. Spying Rupert, the two girls slowed their pace—already lagging far behind their own parents—to allow him to catch up. Winston's heart was lost to Violet Beardsley before the introductions were completed. She had not even noticed him, being too busy simpering and blushing as Rupert tipped his hat and smiled at her. Their brief conversation had centered around Penelope's wedding, and the bride had graciously extended invitations to Rupert's guests.

Winston had spent much of his time since then anticipating the chance to further his acquaintance with Miss Beardsley. He dismounted now, letting Angus drink, and approached the girls, hat in hand, still uncertain just what sin he had committed. Violet stood glaring at him, her arms akimbo. This was not the way he had imagined their next meeting. She addressed him in lofty tones.

"Mr. Nashe, is it your custom in Kent to go charging about the countryside willy-nilly terrifying helpless ducks and disturbing the sensibilities of those *trying* to enjoy a peaceful morning painting?"

Miss Beardsley's arm, the top of which was sparsely covered in embroidered pale pink cambric, extended gracefully in the direction of their easels and other accoutrements. Poor Winston suddenly realized what he had done and he reddened in response to her tirade. He cast a glance pondward to see the birds skimming the water looking no less robust than they had before his untoward arrival. Really, he could not see that there was all that much to fuss about. Surely, the ducks would return in time and they could resume their artistic endeavors. He did not say any of this to Miss Beardsley, however, nor to Miss Logan, for Winston was just as charming and tactful as his

mother had claimed, and besides, doing so he knew
would put him in the former girl's black books, and
that was the last thing he wanted. He nodded at both
of them and made his most abject apologies.

"I cannot think what made me do such a rude and
clumsy thing, ladies. I can see that I have quite overset
your pursuit, and I am deeply sorry." He thought they
might be softening just a bit. "Er, perhaps I might
remedy my faux pas. Shall I wade out into the duck
pond and try to round up the little fellows and bring
them back? Although, I must say, I think it would make
much more sense for the *ducks* to be painting *you two.*"
He knew this last was gilding the lily, but he was desperate to be back in their good graces.

Penelope relented first. "Dear me, no, Mr. Nashe."
She laughed. "For you could catch cold, you know,
and be unable to attend my wedding, and that would
be too bad."

Winston grinned and gave her a nod. "Very likely
you are right, Miss Logan." He dared a sidelong
glance at Miss Beardsley, who was staring at him with
rather a peculiar, but no longer angry, look in her
pretty eyes.

He smiled at her and bowed to both of them. "Until Saturday, then, ladies."

Penelope's wedding was all that she could have
wished. St. Michael's was filled with flowers, her parents joyfully sacrificing their chances in this year's
contest to their daughter's nuptial celebrations, and
myriad fragrances floated through the late morning
air. Blooms filled the deeply set stone windows and
surrounded the small group congregated at the altar
for the solemn vows. She carried a wedding posy of
roses of a pink so delicate it seemed almost white,
and delicate, lighter-than-air gypsophila.

Penelope's high-waisted bride dress was of white jaconet muslin. Its minuscule tucked sleeves were trimmed with narrow silver ribbon, and the bottom of the skirt was trimmed with several rows of shirring edged with the same ribbon. She wore a headdress of perfect white rosebuds and myrtle, and a simple coral necklace. As her bridesmaid, Violet Beardsley stood nearby in soft peach muslin banded near the hem with large white rosettes.

Mr. Barnstead's costume was claret colored, and he displayed a determination even he had not known that he possessed, managing to keep his *aheming* to a minimum. Penelope's parents, sitting in the front pew, had finally stopped the bickering brought on by prewedding nerves that their daughter had completely escaped. Mrs. Logan sniffed into her handkerchief, and Mr. Logan was suddenly afflicted with many of Mr. Barnstead's *ahems*.

Because so many had been invited to the wedding breakfast, it had been decided to hold it on the village green, which ran alongside the river. A large number of tables, placed here and there on the grass, were covered with cloths and decorated with swags of greenery, flowers, and ribbon. The tabletops were practically invisible, filled as they were with all manner of food, and champagne toasts were drunk again and again to the giddy, newly married couple.

Charlotte was in a new round dress of pale lavender with a soft yellow stripe. It was trimmed under the bust with a twisted band of the same shade of yellow, which also formed a deep ruffle at the hem. A diaphanous kerchief was knotted loosely around her neck. She wore a cottage bonnet with lavender and green ribbons that set off her coiffure, with which she remained shamefully pleased, to perfection.

Music had started to play and a few people were already dancing. Charlotte had extended her felicitations to the bride and groom and complimented Mr. and Mrs. Logan on the loveliness and success of the entire enterprise. She was doing her subtle best to get Rupert and Violet to join the country dance that had just formed, but her efforts were being foiled, much to her surprise and confusion, by the young lady. Violet's flimsy excuse for not dancing was easily accepted by Rupert, who looked over his shoulder to see Winston Nashe approaching, then back to the girl to see a look of poorly disguised pleasure on her face. He merely smiled at Charlotte's frustration.

In fact, he had seen and *heard* which way the wind was blowing with his young guest, Winston, who had made no attempt to hide his budding interest in Miss Beardsley. Rupert had patiently answered Winston's questions until his mother pointed out to him that he should have a care to his manners, since she had seen Mr. Frost and Miss Beardsley together on more than one occasion.

"Perhaps," she suggested, "Mr. Frost would prefer not to tell you anything that might advance your cause with Miss Beardsley." It was not the done thing, after all, she explained to her abashed son, to cut out one's host. Her poor husband had nearly choked on his coffee. Under other circumstances, he might have chided his wife, but the truth was that he wanted to know if Rupert really was in the way of courting the chit. He dabbed his lips with his serviette and waited, watching his friend. Winston turned scarlet, apologizing for his rag manners, silently wishing he could be dead if he could not have the girl he had, in the intervening days, decided he must marry.

"Not a bit of it, Winston. Miss Beardsley is a fine

Jessie Watson

girl—young woman, I suppose I should say—but I have no, um, personal interest in her. Your field is quite clear so far as I am concerned, my boy."

Winston's pleasure had been boundless and Rupert knew that he would monopolize Miss Beardsley's time at the wedding breakfast. The young man's parents had been relieved, but had been much more circumspect about their feelings. And Rupert was almost smug, having rid himself of the clinging young lady without giving offense, thus freeing him to get back to pursuing Charlotte, who now watched Winston and Violet laughing and running off to join the other dancers. She turned a baffled face to Rupert, who patted her hand, said solemnly, "Never mind, my dear, for I do not," and brought her a glass of lemonade.

"Honestly, Rupert, sometimes I think you are as inconstant now as you were nine years ago." The smile that accompanied her words lessened their sting and he did not take offense.

"Nonsense, Charlotte, that is not true at all. I simply know what I want," he had replied cryptically.

By the time Penelope and Frederick's bride cake had been cut and distributed, the afternoon had faded and the heavy air had cooled. The bride's father, who, like many others in attendance, had taken rather too much champagne, was telling anyone who would listen how he and his wife would miss their beloved and only child. To poor Mr. Barnstead, he declared in as menacing tone as he could muster under the circumstances and in his condition, that failing to make his darling girl happy would put a rapid period to his existence. Mr. Barnstead, suddenly seized with an amazing spate of *ahems*, suggested to his new bride that it might be a good idea to depart

the festivities and leave on their wedding trip to
Brighton. The new Mrs. Barnstead glared at her parent.

"Papa!"

She patted her husband's arm soothingly and
promised him that she was already as happy as she
could ever hope to be and kissed his cheek.

Winston and Violet had just danced yet another
dance together, their fourth if anyone had been
counting, and now stood by the riverbank shyly discovering all those vital things they had in common.

"Oh, I could not agree more. Beets are the most
horrible thing I have ever tasted!"

Fortune and a few of his four-legged friends from
the village had as much fun as anyone, cadging morsels from almost everyone present and paddling
about in the river. True, a couple of guests were not
best pleased to have their clothes splattered by several
dogs shaking the river water from their coats, but
they all dried quickly in the warm Summer sun. The
rabbits the dogs ran after all got away, for none of
them was a hunting dog, but they enjoyed the chase
just the same, and the rabbits remained in their
hutches until quiet descended on the green hours
later. Benjamin and Sally Nashe danced and chatted
as easily with the villagers as if they had been resident
for years.

Charlotte, too, had drunk more champagne than
she should and was a little muzzy. Oddly, though, the
drink seemed to have cleared her head—or at least
cleared her thinking. She had watched Violet and
Winston dancing and chattering and had seen how
suitable they seemed, quite unlike how the girl had
appeared with Rupert. She had thought that a
younger woman would be just the thing for him, but

perhaps she had been wrong. More to the point, she had known how unhappy she had been seeing Rupert with Violet, or Penelope, or with any other woman, for that matter. Like that pretty Mrs. Brent he was chatting with at the moment. She had been trying to deny her feelings for too long, she saw that now. For a moment, she asked herself when she had begun to love him again; then she looked at him and wondered if she had ever really stopped. What had he meant when he said that he knew what he wanted? She had been afraid to ask then, afraid of his answer.

Mrs. Pike appeared, resplendent in royal blue and lace.

"Lovely wedding breakfast, don't you think, Mrs. Fayerweather?"

"Oh, yes. Wasn't Pen a beautiful bride?"

The older woman nodded her head. "Indeed she was. Prettiest yet, I'd say, although I would deny it if you were to breathe that to another soul." She grinned.

Charlotte returned her smile. "I believe I would have to agree with you, Mrs. Pike, so your secret is safe with me."

"The Beardsley gel seems to be getting on *quite* well with that young Nashe. Winston, is it? Handsome fellow. Now that's another good looking couple, if you ask me. Violet Beardsley looks much better with him than she did with Mr. Frost." She gave her companion an arch look. "Not that there is *anything* wrong with Mr. Frost's looks, mind you. But this is much better," she said without explaining how she had arrived at this conclusion. Glancing at Charlotte from the corner of her eye, she remarked in a satisfied tone, "Now, I saw the two of *you* together and you looked very nice, dear."

Charlotte opened her mouth to speak, although she had no idea how to respond to such a comment and the fuzziness in her head did not help her situation, but before she could say a word, Mrs. Pike was off.

"Oh, there's Cordelia Parsons. I want to speak with her about the twins. You will excuse me, won't you? Cordelia!" She hurried off, waving and twittering.

Charlotte considered her situation, one thought skittering madly after another. Should she let on to Rupert that she cherished feelings for him? Would she make a complete fool of herself if she did, or was that just the encouragement he was waiting for to declare his own sentiments? After all, she had been the one to turn him away, she reminded herself, conveniently forgetting for the moment the justification he had given her for doing so. Well, if she did not try to let on her feelings to him, she might grow to regret it for a very long time. Especially if she had to spend the rest of her life in Edenshade watching him and whatever her name might be marrying and raising their own family. She had had this thought before and had pushed it to the back of her mind, but she could not do so now.

He looked in her direction, smiling, then excused himself from the small group that had evolved from the original pair of him and Mrs. Brent and walked toward Charlotte. She gave him a brilliant smile.

"Well, Rupert, I am happy to see that you finally noticed me."

"Charlotte, my dear, how could I not notice you?" Her heart leapt. "But Mrs. Brent did prose on and on, and then the others joined us . . ." He waved his arm behind him in the direction of the group. "And then the talk turned to, can you not guess, the flower contest. Does it ever cease?"

"It is just beginning, Rupert. The contest is not that far off. Everyone is just getting worked up to their usual fever pitch." He groaned. "Are you ready to leave?" Rupert was to walk her home. "I confess that I am a bit tired."

"Mmm. It has been a long day."

The walk from the green to Charlotte's cottage was not far and they moved slowly in the deepening twilight. For the first time since they had met again, she put her arm through his and leaned her head against his shoulder. Neither spoke for a while.

"Look," she said, "the evening star."

They stopped and looked as the first flickerings of light became evident in the sky. Rupert could feel Charlotte's body running along the length of his and pressed rather closer than propriety, or she, would normally permit. He looked down at her, not far, because she was so tall, to see her face upturned, her eyes waiting for his gaze. She was so beautiful. Even more so than she had been nine years ago and willing to be his wife.

"Charlotte . . ."

She touched a hand lightly to the side of his head and smiled sweetly. "My dearest Rupert."

Rupert remembered the kisses they had shared in that other life and knew that he had to taste them again. He bent his head and kissed her as he had never dared kiss before. She did not draw back. Holding him tightly, she pressed her body closer to his and he did the same. At last, he drew back his head and gave a ragged sigh. Did he, at last, have her back?

Charlotte touched his lower lip with her finger and smiled. Then she hiccupped. She gave a little giggle and covered her mouth with both hands. "Oh, my, pardon me."

He felt as if someone had emptied a jug of cold water over his head. She was muzzy, for God's sake! Well, of course she would be, after all that champagne. Ladies were not used to such quantities of spirits. Rupert had no way of knowing whether her behavior resulted from real feelings or merely from the wine. He suspected it was the latter, since she had not given him much hope of her loving him since his arrival in Edenshade. But she had been married, after all, and doubtless missed the physical companionship she had shared with Digby. Relaxed by the champagne, she saw Rupert as a convenience, nothing more. By tomorrow, she would be humiliated— and regretful—over what she had done. He grasped her shoulders gently and put her from him.

"My dear, I am afraid you are just a bit foxed . . ."

"No, Rupert. I admit that my head is slightly fuzzy, but I assure—"

"Now, Charlotte, it is nothing to be ashamed of. Everyone gets a little disguised at some time in his life . . ."

"Rupert, listen to me! You do not understand, I—"

"And I am certain that no one back there was aware of it," he continued as if she had not interrupted. "Why, I do believe that I have had rather too much myself. I beg you to forgive my behavior. For a moment, I thought that you wanted things to be as they had been before, that perhaps you wanted me back, after all. I had no right to think such a thing and less right to take advantage of you in that way." His emotions were beginning to get the better of him now and he spoke more rapidly. "If you can only forgive what I have done, I swear that it will never happen again."

She blinked back a tear of frustration and panic and in a tremulous voice said, "Never?"

Good God! She was going to cry! She did regret what had happened. "Never. You have my word." It struck him that his word—to her—must be of little value, but he had nothing else to give.

Charlotte searched his face for she knew not what. She had seen the way he had looked at her, felt the way he had kissed her, and thought it meant he cared. But he did not; it was only a kiss. And now he was using the champagne as an excuse to fob her off.

She slept surprisingly well that night, but when she awoke late the following morning and recalled the night's events, she was mortified. Had she really thrown herself at his head like that? No wonder he had reacted as he had. She had given him a disgust of her and any gentleman of taste and breeding would have done just the same.

Charlotte pushed away her morning coffee untouched. Since Rupert's return, he had enjoyed the company of other women, been pursued by them, and in the process, whatever interest in her he *might* have possessed had faded away. She pressed her hands to cheeks hot and red with embarrassment. The poor man had not wanted to hurt her feelings, so he pretended that he had been in the wrong. His pointing out that she had drunk too much champagne had been intended to save *her* face, not his. Oh, Lord, could she ever face him again?

A bell tinkled sweetly as Mrs. Ruffle entered the milliner's shop and closed the old wooden door behind her. She had been returning from the green-grocer and had not intended to stop in at Mrs. Robards's establishment, but a shawl of the lightest pink cashmere draped languidly across a settee in the window had caught her eye. She was incapable of resisting at least a look at such a delightful garment.

"Oh, good afternoon, Mrs. Ruffle." Griselda Robards greeted her warmly—Irene Ruffle was a very good customer. "Was it the cashmere shawl that brought you in?"

The flowers on her bonnet shivered with Mrs. Ruffle's anticipation. The dressmaker removed the item from the window and placed it with great care on the display counter, the better to tempt her customer. The housekeeper stroked the shawl and sighed.

"Lovely weave it is, isn't it?" she breathed.

" 'Tis. And that color would be perfect for you."

They discussed the cost, which Mrs. Ruffle found reasonable enough for her budget. As a clerk wrapped the parcel, the dressmaker came bustling out from the rear of the shop, a large bandbox in her arms.

"Mrs. Fayerweather's new bonnet is ready. Betty finished it up just this morning; I was going to send a note around. Do you want to take it with you now, or have you too much to carry as it is?"

"I think I can manage, Mrs. Robards. Thank you. Good day." She gave the woman a jubilant smile.

The smile was returned. "Thank you, Mrs. Ruffle. The shawl will look a treat with that brown striped dress you bought the other week."

As Mrs. Ruffle walked down the road toward Hawthorn Cottage, her vision was obstructed by all of her packages as well as an image of herself in her latest purchase, so she did not see the man coming in her direction.

"Look out there! Careful!"

"Oh! Oh, dear! I . . ."

One of the parcels tumbled to the ground, but a pair of strong arms caught the others and at the same time somehow helped to balance a surprised Mrs. Ruffle.

"Are you all right, ma'am?" He replaced the fallen parcel in her arms.

She liked the way his eyes crinkled when he smiled.

"Yes. So clumsy of me," she fluttered.

"The fault, ma'am, was entirely mine. I am Roswell Dillard." He bowed. "I hope that you will excuse me. I was planting some rhododendrons."

"I beg your pardon?"

"I am a gardener, Mrs.—"

"Irene Ruffle."

"Mrs. Ruffle. I was thinking about whether I should put in some new rhododendrons."

"Do you work up at Sherbourne Place then?"

Dillard nodded. "Guilty as charged, Mrs. Ruffle. Please allow me to help you with these."

"Well, if you insist."

"I do." He took the packages and fell into step by her side.

"How kind. I am just walking home, Mr. Dillard. I keep house for Mrs. Charlotte Fayerweather. It's not far from here."

"No matter."

She peeked up at him from under the large cabbage roses that edged her bonnet. She saw a man of middle height, his face deeply browned by the sun, his hair pulled back in an unfashionable, but practical, queue. The hands that clasped her bundles were calloused from work, but they were clean and the nails neatly trimmed, although she could see that a few of them had broken, probably from digging, she decided.

Mr. Dillard noticed her examination, but contained a smile and said, "Mrs. Fayerweather. I have heard Mr. Frost talk of her." He deliberately kept his pace slow to draw out the time with this lovely new acquaintance.

Mrs. Ruffle, whose step was at all other times brisk and no nonsense, was quite happy to imitate his more leisurely walk. She explained to him that their respective employers had known one another for donkeys' years, and this condition seemed to make more natural the beginnings of their own relationship. It was almost as if Charlotte and Rupert's history encompassed these two, for when conversation might have been halting or unsure, they chatted easily. She even told him all about her new shawl. When they reached the path leading to Hawthorn Cottage, he paused to look at the flowers hemming the walk and gave a small nod of approval.

"Mrs. Ruffle, may I call on you tomorrow?"

"I should be most pleased, sir. Perhaps you would care to come for tea?"

Dillard smiled. "Mrs. Ruffle, you honor me. I shall look forward to it."

Nell had come in answer to her superior's summons. She grinned up at the gardener and accepted the bundles.

"Good day to you, ma'am." He nodded at Nell and went back down the path, whistling.

Mrs. Ruffle hurried up to her bedroom. Nell left her package on the bed and delivered Charlotte's to her bedroom. The housekeeper slowly removed the paper and drew out the soft, light wool. She wrapped it lovingly around her shoulders and looked at her reflection in the glass. Turning, she wondered what Mr. Dillard would think of it. Then she sighed and sat in her chair by the window and dreamed for a while.

"That clue was much too obscure! 'Tisn't fair. You cannot expect me to know such a thing! It happened *years* ago when you two were young!"

Abandoning the game of charades, Benjamin Nashe aimed a green brocade bolster at his son's head, while his mother disowned her "only son," her "former pride and joy," before protesting that, anyway, although the accusation might be true of his father, who was, indeed, ancient, it certainly was not true of his *mother*, who she would like to remind all present was a full six years younger than her husband. Whereupon, Mr. Nashe chased his wife around Rupert's claw-footed sofa, trying to bat the feathers of her turban with the much abused bolster.

Winston collapsed on the floor laughing, as his mother ducked behind a chair, leaving his father to wave the cushion ineffectually in the air. Mrs. Nashe darted for the sofa, where she picked up another bolster and proceeded to engage her husband in a hilarious duel of pillows.

Rupert roared with laughter, but the scene also made him feel rather melancholy, reminding him of what was lacking in his own life. The Nashe family was a close one. Only last week, he had found Sally sniffing over a letter from the twins.

"Look." She had held out the paper proudly. "See how closely Mary's handwriting resembles Daphne's," she said, for the girls had alternated writing the paragraphs.

Rupert had peered at the sheet of paper, but could detect little because so much of the ink had been smeared by Sally's tears. Then, a day or two ago, the three Nashes had engaged in a spirited hour of singing as Sally played on the piano with Ben and Winston sitting on either side of her, each with an arm about her shoulders. He had felt a great happiness well up in him as he watched her pounding gleefully on the keys as the trio swung into one raucous tune after another, then into a ballad that the young man sang in a clear, true voice. He saw the look of deep affection that passed between Ben and Sally and he ached then, as he did now, with the desire for a family of his own to cause mayhem in his drawing room.

He pictured Charlotte with her sewing or at the piano and tried to envision the children they might have. Might. It did not look as if things would ever be as he wanted between them. What had she been about as he walked her home after the wedding breakfast? Was it possible that she had been sincere? Did she harbor real feelings for him? No, she couldn't possibly. She had been very nearly foxed, after all. And what was more, he had seen her the very next day walking with a neighbor, but she had hurried off with little more than a chilly nod in his direction. A day or two later, when he stopped at her cottage hoping for a cup of tea, she had pleaded a headache and refused to see him. That was hardly the way he expected a woman in love to behave. It was possible, surely, that she was simply embarrassed by her condition and the forward way she had acted—not that he would have minded, if only she had been completely sober and he could have been sure of the reason for her actions—but they had known one another too long for her to have such scruples.

But as he continued to observe the Nashe family antics, Rupert knew one thing without question. He did want a wife and a family. And if Charlotte would not marry him—and since she barely acknowledged his existence lately, there was little hope of that— then he would find a woman who would.

Eight

Hosting of the Valley Flower Show alternated each year between Edenshade and its rival town, the somewhat larger Great Tipton. This year, the green in Edenshade would be the one covered with marquees and tables offering seeds, garden treatises, and implements all guaranteed to answer every question, solve every problem, and make the buyer's garden among the finest in next year's contest. Refreshments of all kinds also would be provided, as would amusements for the children. In fact, for four-and-a-half days, the hosting town would be turned into a veritable fairground of merriment.

Judging was conducted by a committee elected via a complicated process developed at the beginning of the show many years ago. Ribbons were awarded in several categories, including Best Herb Garden, Best Herbaceous Borders, Best Roses, Best Manor Garden, and Best Water Garden. Competition between the two villages was, for the most part, amicable, and any bruised feelings were set to rights soon enough. The competition *within* each village, however, could be much more heated, doubtless due to the year-round visual reminders of who had won and who had lost. Winners generally changed from year to year; thus the person or persons who took home one Summer's ribbons for Best Flower Tubs—there were categories for shop tubs and cottage tubs—usually were not the same as the winners the following year.

There were, of course, a few exceptions—those categories that were won by the same people every year and were therefore all the more coveted. Of several such groups, two had persisted the longest: Edenshader Mrs. Trevor Dunstable, whose herbaceous borders had been given the prize for eleven years running; and Lowell Goodspeed, whose roses had been the finest in the two villages (and perhaps beyond) for the past seven Summers. Every year, the best gardeners in Edenshade and Great Tipton did their best to unseat the vicar and Mrs. Dunstable, and since the governing committee had long since learned the advantage of drawing out excitement as much as possible, the final decisions on these two categories were not revealed until the end of the last day. As a result, the suspense, building since the previous year, gripped entrants and townspeople alike, resulting in a huge crowd buzzing with speculation, wagers, predictions, and the occasional argument over favorites.

Lowell Goodspeed flapped his arm in a wide haphazard arc, and the bee that had been droning dizzily around his head for the past ten minutes flew off. He slouched more deeply into his chair, his legs stretched out before him, and he pulled his hat down over his face. The pamphlet he had been reading on rose blight slipped from his lap. The rose garden was at the height of its charm and its heady fragrance acted almost like an opiate. More than anything else he could think of he cherished his moments relaxing here in its peace.

"Vicar, I must speak with you!"

The unnecessarily loud voice was agitated. Goodspeed lifted the brim of his hat just enough to glimpse the identity of this invader of his tranquility. Archibald Stevenson, a contest judge this year, was a large, tall man. His chest as broad as a bull's, his hands and feet enormous, and his voice a veritable trumpet of noise. Goodspeed—and everyone else in church—could hear him whisper to his wife during service, despite her efforts to shush him, and it was said—though with all goodwill, for Archie Stevenson was well liked throughout the village—that everyone else attending St. Michael's knew the state of his bowels as well as his wife did.

"Infidel! Don't you know better than to disturb a man while he is napping, *and* in his own garden, Mr. Stevenson?" Goodspeed asked testily.

"I am sorry, Mr. Goodspeed, but I need your advice. This is very important, I promise you."

Goodspeed groaned. What now? He quickly remembered his calling, however, and said more amiably than he felt, "Very well, man, sit down. Only do moderate your tone. It clashes with the roses." He waved a hand in the direction of the flowers in the event that this intruder did not recognize them.

"It's my borders, vicar."

"Excuse me?"

"My herbaceous borders. *You* know."

So he did. So did everyone. Archibald Stevenson had been trying to wrest the Herbaceous ribbon from Mrs. Dunstable for years. *Perennially*, Goodspeed thought to himself with a snicker, but managed to look interested as well as sympathetic.

"Ah, yes, your borders. Of course. What about them?"

"Well, haven't you *seen*? They are magnificent. They are stunning." His voice went up two or three octaves with each superlative. "They are . . . are . . ."

"Disqualified?"

The man slumped into a chair beside the priest and shook his huge head in despair. "What shall I do? Why this year of all years?"

"Ours is not to question, Archie."

Archie gave him the blackest of looks and did not speak for some moments. Goodspeed had never seen him so quiet and it almost concerned him sufficiently to do something to provoke his visitor to speech once again. The man emitted a long, deep sigh.

"Vicar," he said, "the good Lord grew me this border *this* Summer, and I'll be *damned* if I'll let it go to waste!"

If Stevenson was contrite at his blasphemy or Goodspeed appalled, each managed to conceal it. The vicar did feel it pertinent to point out once more that Stevenson had no choice in the matter.

The man wasn't having any. "Just because I was elected to be a judge this year, I am expected to withhold my garden from the competition. That is an outrage!"

"You did not seem to think so last Summer, as I recall." Goodspeed looked at him waggishly. "You were more than a little pleased and proud to have been named. *And*"—he forestalled an interruption with a raised index finger—"you were apprised then of the rules and did not object. Quite the contrary."

He spoke only the truth. The one thing more desirable than winning a ribbon was being part of the judging panel that awarded it. People lobbied intensely all year long, but especially during Flower Week, to be elected to judgeship for the following

Summer. And Archibald Stevenson had stood a dozen men a pint in the local inn after he had been notified of his election the previous year.

"Suppose not," he admitted very grudgingly. "But that was because I lost again. Figured then I would never win. Might just as well be a judge then. See what I mean?" He looked plaintively at the man beside him.

Goodspeed shut his eyes and raised his brows, his head slightly tilted to one side. "I do, Archie. Unhappily, there is nothing you can do about it now. Perhaps there is a small lesson in faith here. Perhaps you should have believed more strongly in your abilities before asking to be named." *Good God,* he thought, *I should not blame the poor man if he hits me for such a useless remark.*

Stevenson looked as if he wanted to do just that. "Thank you, vicar. I am sure you have the right of it." He cleared his throat loudly. "I, um—that is to say, I would like your advice. . . ."

"So you said."

He nodded. "I want to withdraw from being a judge."

"What? You must be joking!"

"I am not, I assure you."

"Archie. You cannot possibly. It simply isn't done."

Archie's face did not portray a man who was terribly concerned with the niceties of the circumstances.

"Listen to me—you cannot withdraw." Goodspeed spoke firmly.

"Why not? You used to be on the blood . . . er, the dratted committee. Can't you make it all right?" He held up a hand quickly. "No, I do not want a special favor. I just meant, can't you explain to me how to go about it, or could you convince the others to let me out of it?"

Goodspeed shook his head. "No. Archie, you cannot ask to be excused at the last minute and especially not because you have discovered that your borders might *finally* do it this year. Er, sorry. Didn't mean that the way it came out," he amended in response to the hurt look he received, for if they had never won a ribbon, Stevenson's borders were beautiful. "I simply meant that you must not relinquish your responsibilities as a judge—and very important responsibilities they are, I remind you"—he hoped this would help—"so that you can compete for the ribbon."

Archie was crestfallen. "I feared you might say that. You are right, of course, vicar. Only"—he looked, if possible, even more dejected—"I'll probably never have such beautiful borders again, you see."

"Now, now, Archie. If you did it once, you can do it again. Anyway, I've heard that Mrs. Dunstable's borders really are not all that spectacular this season"— this was a blatant lie—"and you would not want to win under such a cloud after all, would you?"

"The missus will be disappointed."

"Perhaps. But she can compensate by reminding one and all that her husband is a *judge* this year!"

"Cold comfort. But what of your chances, vicar?" He looked around him at the roses. "They're beautiful as ever this Summer." There seemed to be just a hint of doubt in his voice and Goodspeed sat up a little straighter.

"Thank you," he said warily.

"Thing is . . . Well, have you heard about the Lady in Great Tipton?"

"What lady are you talking about?"

"Oh, you know." Archie put a finger to his lips. "Dear me, what is her name? You know," he repeated, "the one gave you a run for your money the last couple of Summers. They say this year she may just do it."

Goodspeed blanched. "Serena Woodland?"

His companion nodded in sympathy at his look. "I'll just be off then, vicar. Thanks for the advice. I shall have to let my borders remain under a bushel, as it were, and be a judge." He patted Goodspeed on the shoulder with understanding as he left. "Sorry I disturbed your nap."

Goodspeed sat a few moments, then pushed out of his chair and, eventually, into the house for his tea. He had hardly nibbled through his bread and jam when he wandered back out to the garden to inspect his roses. Serena Woodland. The very name made his head ache. They had been rivals for the past five years, ever since she had arrived in Great Tipton, where she had purchased a house with a neglected, but potentially spectacular, rose garden.

He could see her in his mind's eye, a small mouse of a woman with a sharp nose, a pointed chin, and a great deal of frizzy black hair. He supposed that some men might find her pretty, but he was not attracted to her. She did squint a great deal; still her rosy cheeks and deep blue eyes contrasted against the midnight shade of her hair could be described as not unappealing. No, Miss Woodland was not his cup of tea. Quite the contrary. She had been bold enough in her first Summer in the valley to throw down the gauntlet, telling him outright that she meant to challenge him in future and that she meant to *win*.

Miss Woodland had, along with a crowd of others,

filed into his garden in the traditional fashion for the awarding of his ribbon for Best Rose Garden. She had walked slowly up and down the paths, pausing here and there to sniff a bloom or lean over for a closer look. Her inspection completed, she strode up to him, smiled broadly, then in a most forward manner, introduced herself. She complimented him on the magnificence of his flowers, congratulated him on his winning the award, and informed him that, someday, she would wrest the prize from him. The vicar, far taller than she was, looked down in something of a daze that he would have attributed entirely to her remarkable declaration.

"Indeed?" He had answered her promise with a raised brow. "You are experienced with roses, are you, Miss, ah . . . ?"

"Woodland."

"Woodland. Miss Woodland."

"Yes, vicar, I am."

Lowell Goodspeed had always been a little too busy to pay much attention to females, and he did not pay much attention to this one, at least not for the usual reasons. It was not at all that he disliked women, rather that he simply never thought about them much. It had not even occurred to him that a wife might share the burdens of his parish, because the parish of Edenshade did not present much of a burden for Goodspeed to accept. Miss Woodland stood before him now with all those heavy waves pulled back from her heart-shaped face in a most unfashionable way—at least he had to suppose it was unfashionable, having no experience with a lady's hair, but anyone could see it was dressed, if even *that* were the right word, in a harum-scarum, most unusual way. Did all maiden ladies behave in such a bizarre fashion? The ones in his parish had always seemed quite normal to him.

Her smugness, as he interpreted her confidence, had irked him then and matters had grown worse as one Summer succeeded another. After that first encounter, he had ridden into Great Tipton late one morning to take the competition's measure, although he had known, in general terms, of the condition of her garden from friends in the neighboring town. He stood in the shade of a tree observing, but unobserved. Miss Woodland had only taken possession of the house in the Spring and so had yet had little opportunity to do much to reverse years of virtual neglect. Still, the place had possibilities. He could see that even from the disadvantage of the distance he had kept from the low privet hedge that set off the plot from the lane. There were numerous rose plants interspersed here and there with dense ornamental shrubbery to set them off, and while all appeared to be in a pitiable state, his expertise told him that they could probably be brought round by a proficient gardener. Inadvertently, he moved closer to have a better view of the way the hedge curved on one side to accommodate what must once have been a very tall bush.

"So you've come to see what you are up against, eh?"

He nearly jumped at the sound of her voice. "Oh, Miss Woodland." Goodspeed flushed a bit, for he could hardly lie—he was a man of the cloth after all. "Well, yes, I suppose I have." He gave a sheepish smile.

"Rather pathetic, isn't it?"

"Oh, well, I do not think that—"

"Please, vicar. If you do not agree, I shall begin to

think that someone else is growing your roses, for no one so ignorant could possibly accomplish what you have done. Your roses are remarkable."

He nodded his thanks. "You are too kind."

"Not at all, sir. For if we do not agree now about both your skill and the unfortunate state of my garden, then my victory, when it comes, will not be lauded nearly as much as I hope it will be."

He frowned rather than returning her smile. "You are very sure of yourself, Miss Woodland."

Her grin broadened. "I am. I have been working with roses all my life, sir. The house I previously occupied in Somerset had a rose garden that was admired throughout the county."

"I wonder that you should leave it, ma'am."

Miss Woodland's grin faded and she did not respond to this challenge. "I did bring one or two plants with me. I hope they do well in this soil. Uh, uh, vicar," she teased as he peered over her shoulder for a glimpse, "I shall not give away all my secrets. You cannot see them from here."

"Humph. Well, Miss Woodland, I shall enjoy the contest." The look she gave him said that she doubted the truth of his statement. "But I, too, have given many years to the cultivation of these beautiful flowers," he told her stiffly. "You are correct in one respect, ma'am. You shall not find it easy to outdo my roses."

Miss Woodland wanted very much to return the smile to the vicar's face, for he was more attractive with it than without it, but her deliberate words were instead calculated to provoke, for his warning had vexed her. "I have told you, Mr. Goodspeed, I relish the challenge. And I shall win, you will see. One Summer, you will be standing here surrounded by beautiful roses, as the ribbon is given to me."

"Careful, Miss Woodland, remember that 'pride goeth . . .' "

"Oh, vicar, please, not that old chestnut." She giggled as he reddened, for he never preached when outside his pulpit.

"Will you come in for some refreshment, Mr. Goodspeed?" Her blue eyes sparkled.

He doffed his hat. "Miss Woodland, I must decline your kind offer. I have much to do at home."

Goodspeed had not, thankfully, seen Miss Woodland since last Summer's contest and he had managed to push her and her arrogance to the back of his mind. He snipped off a blossom past its prime. Oh dear. He supposed that, as in years past, she would torment him again about his eventual unseating. It was not so much that he minded losing as he disliked the way she boasted about it, although, to be fair, she never failed to sincerely praise his garden.

Her claims might at some point have been disregarded had she not entered the show in the previous Summer. While it was clear from the Committee's first visit that she would not win the ribbon, it was equally clear that her boasts were not hollow: Miss Woodland's roses, if not as fine as the vicar's or even those grown by Mrs. Leydon or Mr. Humphrey, were beautiful. Goodspeed recalled thinking that she must have labored tirelessly to restore her flowers to health and that she did, indeed, know as much about their care as she had promised him that she did. It had not bothered her to lose. Clearly, she had known that she would, but her attempt was to serve a dual purpose—to show one and all what she was capable of accomplishing, and to find out how it measured up in the judges' eyes.

Well, he supposed that it was time for someone else to win the ribbon. But Miss Woodland? Would this be her year? Goodspeed was so irked by the possibility that he mistakenly lopped off a perfectly good shell pink bud. "Damn," he whispered.

The shower had come on suddenly. Mrs. Ruffle and Mr. Dillard ran laughing up to the back door of Hawthorn Cottage and let themselves in. Charlotte had just come into the kitchen and called to Nell to bring the arrivals something to dry them. She had known that her housekeeper was seeing a man, but had not pressed her for details, and surprisingly, none had been forthcoming.

"Mrs. Fayerweather, this is Mr. Roswell Dillard. Mr. Dillard, this is Mrs. Charlotte Fayerweather, my employer."

"Ma'am."

"Mr. Dillard, I am happy to make your acquaintance."

"Mrs. Fayerweather, Mr. Dillard is the head gardener up at Sherbourne Place. He works for Mr. Frost," Mrs. Ruffle added redundantly. Did she see Charlotte stiffen just a bit?

"Ah. And how are you getting on there, Mr. Dillard?"

"Quite well, thank you, ma'am. There was quite a lot of work to be done. Still is a fair amount, but I like a challenge. You have a nice garden here, if l may say so."

Charlotte beamed. "Do you think so?" He nodded, smiling. "Oh, thank you. I do not know a great deal, except what I like—isn't that what most dilettantes say?" She chuckled.

"Do you plan to enter the show?"

"Ha, ha! Dear me, no. I wouldn't so presume, Mr. Dillard. But it is most kind of you to inquire."

"Have you not seen the Sherbourne Place gardens yet?"

"Er, not since Mr. Frost had his party there some weeks ago."

He darted a glance at Mrs. Ruffle. "You really ought to visit. If I may say so, we have made good progress. Perhaps you might call tomor—"

"I am afraid that I have another commitment tomorrow, Mr. Dillard. Perhaps another time?" She smiled at her housekeeper. "Mrs. Ruffle, I hope that you and Mr. Dillard will have some tea before he goes."

The couple exchanged a glance after Charlotte had left. Mrs. Ruffle passed a plate of sandwiches to Mr. Dillard and shook her head.

"I don't know what it is. She's been, well, a little peculiar ever since Penelope Logan's wedding. And I haven't seen hide nor hair of Mr. Frost. Not here at any rate."

The relationship between Mrs. Ruffle and Mr. Dillard had become a close one over the short time since they had first met. He had already made more than one oblique reference to marriage, and she had made it clear that she would welcome such a proposal. It had become apparent early on that Mr. Dillard was as devoted to Rupert as she was to Charlotte, and before long, they were discussing how they might aid in getting their employers together. The conversation now lingered on that subject while Charlotte let herself out the front door, just missing a puddle left by the now departed rain. As she idly browsed through bolts of fabric for a new gown that she hoped would perk up her spirits, Sally Nashe entered Mrs. Robards's shop.

"Mrs. Fayerweather, how nice to see you!"

Charlotte had not seen Mrs. Nashe to speak with since Pen's wedding breakfast, and although the woman had not witnessed what had occurred between her and Rupert, she found herself a little flustered at meeting her.

"Oh! Mrs. Nashe, good day. You did not get caught in the rain, I hope?"

"No, just missed it. I've come in for a fitting. Mrs. Robards is making me a delicious new gown." The milliner preened in the background. "It is spotted muslin in a good shade of pink and I cannot wait to wear it."

She grinned. "Are you here for anything in particular or are you passing the time? I confess that I should have come here anyway, since Winston is off somewhere with Miss Beardsley and Benjamin and Mr. Frost have gone walking in the hills. I *detest* exercise. Don't you? Actually, I had thought of calling on you to accompany me here, but thought you must be already busy, and here we are!"

Charlotte smiled at Mrs. Nashe's volubility. "I was hoping to find something to lift my spir— I mean, I was in the mood for buying something pretty today. What do you think of this tarlatan?"

Sally Nashe pretended not to notice Charlotte's unfinished sentence. "Very nice, but I think the darker blue would be better on you. Don't you agree, Mrs. Robards?"

After they had both had their fittings, Charlotte having decided on the bishop's blue for her new afternoon dress, the two women strolled along the riverbank, talking companionably and enjoying the air freshened by the rain. Sally was certain that something was troubling Charlotte, but felt she did not know her well enough to inquire about it. Come to that, she had sensed something amiss with Rupert, for all that he remained an excellent host, but she could not put her finger on that source either. She had spoken about it with Benjamin, who had advised her not to worry, for he had seen Rupert in such a pensive mood more than once in the old days.

"Oh, Mrs. Fayerweather, I have news. I had almost forgotten. Captain Beddoes and his cousin—Miss Georgina Hastings, I believe she is called—are expected tomorrow."

Charlotte had forgotten about Rupert's other guests and she nodded her head now as Sally reminded her. "It will be pleasant to see new faces in the village. Oh, do forgive me. That was terribly rude. I only meant . . ."

Sally laughed and waved a hand negligently. "Not at all. I quite agree. It will be good to have someone new to talk with—and about! It is the same in our little village in Ashford. One grows weary—or perhaps *weary* is not precisely the right word—rather shall I say familiar with those we see all the time. Even visitors such as Mr. Nashe and I and Winston must seem so."

"Surely not," Charlotte protested.

"Oh, I promise you we do. Rupert's servants know our tastes as well as ours at home do. They've even learned that Benjamin likes his toast nearly burnt."

Charlotte laughed. "Well, speaking of getting to know people, how are Winston and Violet Beardsley getting along?"

Sally stopped to skip a stone on the river. "Drat," she said, as it sank immediately. "I can never do it. The romance progresses," she replied dryly. "Winston has not lost interest as he has with young ladies before, and Miss Beardsley seems a nice enough girl. Mr. Nashe and I were saying to one another that we would not mind if they should want to marry. We are told that the family is good, and we met her parents after church the other week; they are most agreeable."

Miss Georgina Hastings was definitely not "a bit long in the tooth," as Rupert had predicted. She had, in fact, one of the prettiest faces he had seen in some time. She was slender with fawn-colored eyes and dark blond hair that framed her forehead in soft curls that lent a sweetness to her countenance. But now, her full lips, a natural deep pink, were pursed in impatience.

"Should we not be there by now, Alexander?" She had a low, almost husky voice that more than one man had longed to hear whisper his name.

Her cousin closed his watch with a snap. "Don't get yourself into a pucker, Georgina. The innkeeper said we should reach Edenshade around three o'clock and it lacks nearly a full hour before we can take the poor man out and have him shot for giving out incorrect information."

Captain Alexander Beddoes looked at her with laughing eyes, but she chose not to be mollified by his hyperbole. He decided that he would not come to cuffs with her, for he was too good-natured to argue unless she gave him no choice—an accomplishment she could have proclaimed dozens of times,

their having practically grown up together and she
never having had a disposition that was much more
pleasant than it appeared now. Leaning back in the
carriage seat he stretched out long, muscular legs,
shut his eyes, and tried to enjoy as much serenity as
the rocking, bumping vehicle and his cousin would
permit him. Only a few minutes passed.

"Alexander? The directions cannot have been
right, you know. The coachman probably has been
going to entirely the wrong place for the past one
hundred miles. We shall probably end up God knows
where without any place to sleep and nothing for our
tea. And I am tired and dirty and hungry."

"Georgina." His patience was beginning to wear
just a little thin, for she had been haunting him with
this same complaint framed in various ways. "The
directions are *not* wrong, I assure you. The innkeeper
knew *precisely* where we wanted to go and showed no
hesitation in giving details to our driver. And we are
in Essex, after all. It is hardly as if we were in some
foreign land. So do *please* stop asking why we have
not arrived yet. You are beginning to sound like a
child."

"Well! I think that is a perfectly nasty remark to
make to me, Alexander. I am only *asking*, you know.
We have been penned up in this wretched coach for
hours and. . . ."

"*Wretched?* Did you say wretched? I will have you
know that I paid a ransom—considerably more, I
must tell you, than I would pay to get you back from
anyone silly enough to steal you—to hire this private
coach so that we could travel the last leg of our journey in a reasonable semblance of comfort, and this
is the thanks you give me! You might remember,
coz . . . Look at me, Georgina," he said, for she had

crossed her arms across her bosom and was staring out the window. "I should not have to remind you that we are far from being plump in the pocket, you and I, and private carriages do not come a penny apiece."

"Oh, all right, Alex. I am sorry to pull your ears— only you do know how easily I become bored!"

"I do. God help me, Georgina, I do." Remarkably, there was more affection than sharpness in his voice. "Now please, I beg you once more, *do* give me some peace. We will arrive soon, I promise. Why don't you read that awful romantic novel you insisted on purchasing? Although I cannot imagine how anyone with even an ounce of intelligence can possibly tolerate such drivel."

Alexander actually managed to nap raggedly for the next half hour. Georgina watched him from under hooded eyes. She honestly loved her cousin, but he could be so dull sometimes. When he had first mentioned Rupert Frost to her, she had listened with only one ear, having listened, she felt, to many more war stories and tales of comradeship than any delicately bred female should be expected to tolerate. Besides, while Alexander was talking about the war or his cronies, how could he give proper attention to her and her interests?

But one day, as he related yet another tedious tale of "Life in the Army," her ears pricked. Although she had schooled herself to smile and nod at these times while thinking of something entirely other, part of her must have heard him. How else could she know, when certainly she had not known but twenty minutes before (for that had been the duration of the current chronicle), that Rupert was rich, quite rich, and unmarried. Georgina had tried to sound nonchalant as she suddenly showed an interest in what her neglected cousin had to say.

"Rupert Frost, did you say, dear?" He inclined his head in confirmation. "Hmm. Have you mentioned him before, Alexander? I cannot recall that you have, and I am certain I should remember, for he sounds like a very brave soldier and an altogether charming gentleman. Do tell me more about him." She had poured him another glass of brandy and passed him the plate of macaroons that he was so fond of.

Georgina Hastings was the daughter of Alexander's mother's youngest sister. After being widowed at a very young age, Julia Hastings and her only child had found the need to economize and had purchased a smaller, but lovely, house in the same neighborhood wherein resided Alexander and his family. Georgina had then been but six years old to her cousin's fifteen, but he was even then good-natured, if somewhat gullible—another trait he would not outgrow. He took pity on the fatherless girl, allowing her to traipse after him through the attics of the huge Beddoes house or into the woods to stalk wild animals. If his own playmates were less than enthusiastic about the presence in their midst of a girl, Alexander was big enough to intimidate them into accepting her. Later, when she had grown into a pretty young woman, her giggling and feminine behavior suddenly became alluring, and they vied with one another for her company.

When Alexander went off to war, Georgina, sixteen when he left, missed her best friend desperately. For a time, she had it in mind to marry one of the young men who had remained behind. A few had offered, and despite her lack of any deep feeling for them, she considered their proposals because, if nothing else, marriage would relieve the boredom she had known since Alexander had been sent to the Continent. Georgina had contemplated offers from Herbert Darnell and Wallace Pratt, but neither of them had a sufficiently respectable fortune.

Georgina and her mother had always lived quite well. She had supposed, when she thought about it at all, that this was derived from their own money, but in fact it was due to the generosity of Alexander's father, whose benevolence outside his family was generally known and enjoyed as profligacy. It was, therefore, a considerably unpleasant surprise to Georgina when eventually her mother explained that her father had not left them well provided for.

"But, Mama," she had protested, "never tell me that we are *poor.* I could not bear it!"

"No, my darling, we are not poor, but neither are we rich, nor even close to being so. I am afraid that your dear father made some very, well, unproductive investments and lost the bulk of his fortune."

"Poor Papa," whispered his daughter, who had been terribly fond of him.

Her mother nodded her agreement. "After he died, there was so little income that we had to sell up in Derbyshire and come here to this smaller house." She sighed, looking about her at the breakfast room, which could have fit inside the one they had left behind. The truth was that Julia Hastings had come to love her new residence much more than she had ever cared for their enormous former home. "And so I learned to be careful with our money, the money your father had left us, and with your aunt and uncle Beddoes' assistance, we have been able to have quite a nice life here, have we not, dear? You have not lacked for anything, have you?" she asked softly after a moment had passed and her child had made no reply.

Georgina had put her arms about her mother's neck and squeezed tightly. "Yes, Mama, we have had a good life and there is nothing that I have wanted that you have not given me." She kissed her mother's cheek and smiled, bringing the brightness back to the older woman's eyes. Georgina had declined her suitors' proposals of marriage and learned to paint with watercolors to relieve the tedium of her days. But her mother died following a brief and sudden illness more than a year before Alexander returned from Spain and she felt more alone than she would have thought possible. Worse, she felt more dependent upon her uncle's kindness than she had since learning of it.

Alexander returned home to find a Georgina more worldly than the one he had left. His three sisters had long since married and left home. Within a year of his return, Alexander's father was killed by a stray bullet from a duel in the street outside the Dog and Swan in London, where he had just stood the entire tavern to ale and wine, and his mother took to her bed for what seemed weeks at a time, unwilling to face the financial difficulties with which they all were finally confronted with the demise of Beddoes senior.

It was during one of these prolonged "rest periods," as Mrs. Beddoes chose to call them, that Alexander sat telling Georgina all about Rupert. Certainly, Georgina had thought about the improvement in her fortunes that marriage to a rich man would bring her. But the only truly wealthy, single gentleman in the area was Squire Percival Blaine, more than thirty years her senior, dull as a stick, ruthless, and the widower of two wives already. She knew, therefore, that there was little likelihood of her finding a fortune to marry in the neighborhood and she was conscious that a woman's beauty was hers for only a few years. If a husband did not happen along soon, she might not be capable of attracting him if and when he did.

The day after her conversation with Alexander, Georgina sat thinking in her old swing in the tree beside the house. She could not bear to marry a man without a great deal of money, for she was truly fearful that she might end up just as her dear mother had—only Georgina was too spoiled and extravagant to manage her funds as that lady had and might end up heaven knew where. No, the Herberts and Wallaces of the world might be fine enough young gentlemen, but they could never provide the security Georgina sought. Percival Blaine, although now considered too awful to be an option, might become more appealing as the years passed and her looks faded.

No, her future was not here. But it could just be in Edenshade. It seemed to her that she could as easily marry a rich, handsome, younger gentleman as she could a mean-spirited old one. Not that her cousin had said that Rupert was handsome, not precisely, but she decided that he must be more appealing than Percival Blaine; at least he was younger. As she and Alexander played cribbage the next evening, Georgina carefully broached her plan.

She had decided that she would sell the house her mother had willed to her and move in with Alexander and her aunt. This was altogether a practical idea that she knew they both would second. Indeed, her aunt and cousin had more than once suggested it, but, more importantly, it would give her the capital she would require to finance her campaign to win Rupert Frost. And if she were successful, she would have no need of the little house or the money she got from the sale of it. She could not tell her cousin that she wished to travel to Edenshade for the purpose of catching a rich husband, for even Alexander would not be accommodating enough to permit such a thing. Instead, she must make the journey appeal to him, almost as if it were his own idea.

Georgina realigned her cards and sighed dramatically. Alexander was losing, however, and so preoccupied with his cards that she had to repeat her heavy sigh several times before he lifted his head, by which time she felt near to fainting.

"Georgie, are you ill? You look a bit . . . off."

Perfect, and she had not even planned this part. "Oh, no, Alexander. I am quite up to snuff, thank you," she replied in a lackluster voice.

"Humph. All right then, if you are certain."

He returned his attention to his hand and she wanted to throw her cards at his head. Another sigh and a peek through her eyelashes to see if he noticed how she rubbed her temple with distress. He did.

"Very well, Georgina, out with it. If you are not ill, something has you in the dismals. I'll go bail on it."

"Oh, if you insist, Alexander." He smiled. "Yes, I shall tell you. I am bored to distraction. I shall scream if I do not see a new face or hear a different voice very soon. It is just *too dull*, Alexander."

"I see. Clearly you are blue deviled," he said dryly. "Well, what do you propose to do about your . . . circumstances? I take it you *do* have something in mind, have you not?"

She grinned across at him. "Yes!" she said gaily. "Only listen. I do believe you will like my idea."

"I daresay." He raised a brow in question and returned her smile.

"What do you think about taking a trip?" She laughed. "I make sure that you think I mean Paris or some such, and you know that I should love to go abroad." Georgina raised a perfectly manicured hand to forestall his objection. "I know, Alexander, I know. We cannot afford such an expenditure. However"—she laid down her cards—"if we paid a visit to someone, a holiday need not require a great deal of blunt." He choked back a laugh at her choice of words and she shook a finger at him. "You need not snigger at me in that fashion, for I know that I used the word correctly," she said loftily.

"Yes, you did, Georgie. . . ."

"I wish that you would not call me that, for you know I dislike it."

"Very well, *Georgina*. I was only going to say that I was surprised to hear you use such common language."

She decided it would be better if she did not cut up stiff with him over his patronizing tone if she wanted him to countenance her scheme.

"Yes, well, I was only trying to be au courant, Alexander. Hortense Cavendish—who as you know has traveled to London ever so many times—says that such talk is all the rage among the *ton*. You do wish me to be fashionable, do you not?"

"I lie awake nights worrying that you will not, my dear."

Even Georgina had to laugh at this. "Oh, all right, you frightful man. But you would not want me to shame you among your friends, would you?"

Now he did laugh aloud. "Good heavens, no, Georgie." He had forgotten his promise already, but she chose to overlook his lapse. "Although I cannot say that I would describe Ferdie Mayhew or Arnold Cutter or even Sherwood Polley as fashionable. Ha, ha!"

"I was not referring to them."

"Oh? Well, who did you mean then? Or should I say *whom*?"

Georgina waved her hand impatiently. "Honestly, Alexander, you do have other friends besides tedious people like Ferdie Mayhew." She shuddered for dramatic effect.

"One or two," he replied carefully. "Georgina, what is going on in that bored little brain of yours?"

"You needn't look at me like that! As I said, if we paid someone a visit we would not need an enormous sum of money."

"Mmm. And did you have someone in mind for us to invade?"

"Well of course I do. We could visit Rupert Frost. Your old comrade," she added unnecessarily and held her breath.

Alexander pondered a few moments. "Yes, we could." Georgina nearly leapt with joy. "We might start out by visiting Aunt Anthea. We have not seen her in ages and she is always asking us to stay."

Aunt Anthea had not been a part of Georgina's plan, but she knew her cousin would soon weary of the older lady's stifling house and army of cats and be glad to leave it behind to travel on to Rupert in Essex. She could safely smile and say, "Why, Alexander, what a good idea. You are such a thoughtful nephew. Oh, and Alexander?"

"Hmm?"

"You know how you and Aunt have advised me to

sell the house and come to you?" He nodded. "Well, I have decided that you are right. In fact, an estate agent already thinks he has an interested buyer."

"Georgina, you know that you are always welcome to live with us. I shall be very pleased to have you. Only what finally changed your mind? You used to be against the idea."

"Yes, I did, but I saw the sense of it at last." She smiled.

"Good. Well, I hope that you will find someone with sense to invest the money for you. You might come out of it with a nice little nest egg once the mortgage is repaid."

"I hope so. I shall take your advice. Of course, I shall buy a few things to take on our holiday, too."

"Naturally."

As the coach bowled along a comparatively smooth mile of road, Georgina finally began to doze, the novel open in her lap. Alexander smiled. He could hardly recall a time when Georgina had not been a part of his life. She had grown from an ungainly little girl—who ripped and dirtied her skirts trailing after him as he climbed trees or tore through the woods—into a lovely woman. Alexander realized that she could be self-absorbed and overly concerned about money, but he easily understood the latter worry, not being particularly well fixed himself. As for the other, he supposed that she must be rather lonely with no really eligible men to court her and few friends. He knew that beneath her sometimes selfish manner was a young woman who feared for her future, but who would never harm a soul. So while he would enjoy seeing Rupert, they had not really known one another all that well, and in truth, he had agreed to make this trip more for Georgina's sake than his own.

He knew that she would appreciate such an opportunity to meet new people and visit new places. And
who knew? Perhaps she might even find a husband
there.

Nine

"Oh, ma'am, did you hear about Mr. Nelson?" Before Charlotte had a chance to respond, Mrs. Ruffle continued. "He broke his ankle this morning." She stood back, her hands across the starched white apron covering her midriff and shook her head.

"Good heavens, Mrs. Ruffle, what happened? How did he come to injure himself?"

"Fell off his ladder, didn't he?"

"Oh."

Another shake of her head. "Helping Silas Trent and Mr. Parsons to put up the banners for the flower contest. You know the ones." Charlotte nodded. "He missed a step on his ladder and fell—nearly landed on Mr. Parsons. Louise Barclay told me he screamed fit to wake the dead."

"Poor man." Charlotte swallowed the last bite of her luncheon and Mrs. Ruffle removed the plate.

"Poor Lenore Nelson, more like. That husband of hers is bother enough at the best of times. He'll have that pathetic creature run off her feet in no time at all."

"Mmm, yes, I suppose he will. Well, if I may be so insensitive, did the banners ever get hung in the High Street?" Charlotte's eyes twinkled.

"Bless you. Yes, ma'am, they did. Silas Trent and Mr. Parsons lured in Mr. Dillard as he was coming down the road. He was happy to help."

"Ah, Mr. Dillard. Such a nice man."

Mrs. Ruffle gave a smile that made her face young again.

"I expect that he is rather anxious about the contest. He has been working so hard up at Sherbourne Place, he must be on tenterhooks waiting to see if his work wins the ribbon."

"Well, Mr. Frost did consent to the entry. That is, as Mr. Dillard tells it, Mr. Frost was finally convinced by people like the vicar and Mr. and Mrs. Bartlett to let the gardens be judged this Summer. Mr. Dillard says that *he* advised Mr. Frost to wait, that things are not up to his standards yet—Mr. Dillard's standards, that is. He—Mr. Dillard—thinks it is very unlikely that Sherbourne Place will win."

Mr. Dillard. Mr. Dillard. Charlotte smiled to herself. It was quite apparent that her housekeeper was more than a little enamored of the gardener. Mrs. Ruffle had a great deal to give to a husband and a home of her own, and Charlotte hoped that their relationship would end in marriage. But if it did, she would need to find a new housekeeper, and getting a replacement for the one she had now would be difficult. Her thoughts were interrupted by the chiding tones of that worthy woman.

"But, of course, you have not seen the state of the gardens at Sherbourne Place in some time, have you, Mrs. Fayerweather? Mr. Dillard tells me that he has not seen you there, and you have not mentioned the manor and the gardens or Mr. Frost at all."

"Oh, well, as to—"

"Would it be Mr. Dillard or Mr. Frost that you were avoiding, ma'am? If I might inquire."

"Now, what reason should I have for avoiding Mr. Dillard? Er . . . that is, no, Mrs. Ruffle, you may *not* inquire." She finished tartly.

Mrs. Ruffle was too determined to be daunted by this rejoinder. "Well, then it must be Mr. Frost you don't wish to see, although I cannot imagine why you shouldn't. Why, you have known one another forever and he is a nice gentleman *and* a good catch. All the ladies say so." She sniffed. *"Almost* all."

Charlotte blinked, amazed at her housekeeper's cheek. "Mrs. Ruffle! That will be enough!"

The housekeeper flushed and dipped a tiny curtsy, something she had not done since the day she had been hired. Charlotte could not tell if the woman was being sarcastic or acknowledging her authority.

"Pardon me, Mrs. Fayerweather." That sounded sincere enough. "I am just concerned for your happiness, that is all."

"My happiness, wha—"

"I'll bring these dishes in to Nell, ma'am, before this little bit of leftover sauce sticks to the plate. The girl will never get it off. Excuse me."

Charlotte carried her wineglass into the drawing room and sat in her favorite chair by the window. She looked out at the sundial, which was surrounded by bright flowers. Mrs. Ruffle was right. She had been avoiding Rupert; she just had not realized that anyone else had noticed. Even Mr. Dillard, with whom she had exchanged many a pleasant chat when she used to visit Sherbourne Place, had remarked upon her absence.

She sipped her wine and wondered if Rupert had noticed. Probably not, since he had not made an effort to call on *her* since—well, since they had last spent any length of time together. She preferred not to dwell on her condition and behavior on that occasion. Charlotte had forgotten the time he had called and she had sent him off with the tale that she was unwell. She knew that they would never marry, but she did not want to lose him again as her friend, and she realized now with a start that her actions had brought her dangerously close to just that outcome. *No more of this nonsense,* she berated herself, ashamed of her silly behavior. *Starting tomorrow, you will behave in a more mature fashion and take yourself to Sherbourne Place to look at the flowers and see your old friend.*

"Mr. Frost, I do not think that I have ever seen such beautiful gardens as you have here in Edenshade. I blush to admit that they put our meager efforts at home to shame. Do they not, Alexander?" Her cousin readily agreed. "I am most anxious to see the grounds here at Sherbourne Place. The drive from the main road through your acreage gave me a taste of what we can expect, but one cannot truly appreciate a garden, or even parkland, from a carriage," she said, referring to their arrival in Edenshade just a couple of hours before.

As a servant removed plates containing the last remains of the vegetable pudding, conversation around the dining table continued. Sally Nashe offered to take Georgina on a walk through the village so that she might observe close up the gardens that had so tempted her.

"You are too kind, Mrs. Nashe. I should like that very much." She turned her eyes in Rupert's direction. "And perhaps Mr. Frost will be so kind as to show me the gardens here." Georgina intended to waste no time.

"It will be my privilege, Miss Hastings," that gentleman replied with a smile. She nodded her head slightly in thanks. "I have been very fortunate to find a man who is probably the finest gardener in these parts. He has worked miracles with this place. But I shall say no more about it now. You will see for yourself."

Georgina wanted very much to ask Rupert if he had any plants that bloomed at night, for she understood that some did and it seemed to her a wonderfully romantical thing, but she decided that would be too forward, at least for the present. She contented herself for a while with sitting quietly and looking lovely, speaking sweetly when spoken to, and complimenting her host on his cook's demonstrated abilities.

The gentlemen eschewed their brandies and joined the ladies in the drawing room at the conclusion of the meal. Sally joked that the company had had its fill of her playing and asked if Georgina were skilled on the pianoforte. The young woman colored and replied that, while her abilities were thought to be no more than average, she would be happy to play for their little group. The beautiful old instrument was placed beside large glass doors that looked onto one of the gardens, and as she approached it, her cousin bent to whisper something in her ear. She stiffened a bit, but nodded and sat down on the bench. She had then demonstrated her considerable talent and entertained them for nearly an hour with restful sonatas, and by the time she went to her bed, Georgina was congratulating herself on how smoothly things were progressing.

* * *

The distance between Hawthorn Cottage and Sherbourne Place was not far, but the temperature had
been higher than usual for the past two days and the
heat had settled in the valley. Charlotte found little
noticeable relief even on the portion of the way that
wound through a small glade of trees, and she patted
her damp neck and brushed away the tendrils of hair
clinging to her forehead. Despite the recent weather,
she had not expected it to be quite so hot for her
walk. She shifted the heavy basket she carried from
one hand to the other and wished she had left it at
home; certainly Rupert would welcome her even
without the gift of preserves she had put up the previous season. She decided to take a circuitous route
to the house, detouring through the more secluded
part of the garden to the spot where she remembered
the fountain to be. At length, Charlotte could hear
a soft splashing sound and followed it around tall
shrubbery to find some wrens dipping into the shadowed water. Under other circumstances, Charlotte
might have stopped to watch the birds, letting them
enjoy their bath, but today she did not feel so generous.

"Sorry my little friends. Company has arrived," she
said with a soft laugh. "I do not mind sharing if you
do not, so please do not dash off on my account."
The birds flew off, complaining to one another about
the intruder, their dripping feathers scattering tiny
droplets of water. "Oh, very well, don't stay. It's your
loss, you know."

She set down her basket and sat with a great sigh
on the edge of the fountain. Branches of trees on
the perimeter of the clearing cast delicate patches of

shifting shadows on the water. Charlotte leaned over and dipped her handkerchief into the pool, wrung it out slightly, and applied it to her cheeks, the back of her neck, and the insides of her wrists and elbows. She shut her eyes and sighed with relief, then wet the cloth again and repeated her actions. She could not have said how long she had been listening to the low murmur of voices before realizing they were just a few feet away. Suddenly, she heard a chuckle accompanied by a giggle and Charlotte's eyes shot open to find Rupert watching her and a beautiful young woman clinging to his arm.

"Well, Charlotte, I hope that you find the water refreshing," Rupert laughed. "Tell me, did you come all the way up here just to splash in my fountain as the birds do, or were you planning to pay a call so long as you were in the neighborhood?"

The lady giggled again. Charlotte thought it was quite ridiculous for a grown woman to giggle, and twice in a span of no more than a minute, but she was too polite to point out this defect in the stranger's manners. Before she had the opportunity to redeem her own apparently rag manners to Rupert, however, the lady in question leaned very close to whisper something in his ear whereupon they both laughed at her brilliant wit.

"Oh that is entirely too bad of you, Miss Hastings," Rupert replied, referring to what Charlotte was convinced must have been an unflattering remark on her appearance. Unhappily, his reprimand was made completely ineffectual by the grin that remained on his face.

Charlotte was painfully aware that she must look wilted and damp—even the ribbons of her bonnet were limp—and now red with embarrassment, but

she made an effort at remembering her manners—
something that *other* people seemed to have forgotten. Normally, Charlotte could laugh at herself, but
here she felt at some disadvantage, a circumstance
largely due to her intended mission on this afternoon. She rose to her full height and smiled with as
much grace as she could muster.

"Dear Rupert, ever the cavalier." He gave a tiny
wince, acknowledging the hit. "Do, please, regain
your countenance long enough at least to introduce
Miss . . ." She knew she could not be so lucky as to
learn that this vision was already married.

"Do forgive me, Charlotte." She could not tell
which social lapse he was apologizing for: laughing
at her discomfiture or forgetting to introduce the two
women. "I should like to introduce Miss Georgina
Hastings. Miss Hastings, this is Mrs. Charlotte Fayerweather. She and I are old, um, friends."

Charlotte was surprised to find him stumble over
this description of their relationship, because he had
not done so to her knowledge since arriving in Edenshade.

"Charlotte, you will recall that I told you I was expecting a visit from Captain Alexander Beddoes and
his cousin." He nodded his head in the direction of
The Beauty and nearly skewered his nose on the edge
of her parasol, so close did she stand. Charlotte noticed that Miss Hastings had not released her hold
on his arm and he had not tried to escape her
grasp—she could not have described the lady's hold
on his arm with any other word. Unhappily, Charlotte
also noticed that she looked much cooler and fresher
than anyone had a right to look on such a warm day.
It was too galling.

"Indeed?" breathed Georgina. She lazily twirled

the parasol of cerise trimmed with a delicate white braid and smiled beneficently in the "old friend's" direction. "How nice."

"And what have you there, Charlotte?" The tone of Rupert's voice had lost its teasing bite.

She glanced down at the basket that had caught his attention. "Oh, some jam and candied orange slices that I thought you might enjoy."

"And so I shall. Did you make them yourself?"

"I did." She returned his smile, somewhat mollified at his evident appreciation.

Georgina had worked in the kitchen with her mother making such things as jams and preserves, but had never participated willingly and had not done so since that lady's passing. She had assumed, erroneously, that their engagement in these activities stemmed from their rather straitened circumstances, unaware that they were common pursuits, at least among country women, regardless of their income.

Thus, her dislike for such work as well as a decided feeling of being left out led her to interject in a patronizing tone, "La, ma'am, surely there are other more stimulating ways to pass one's time here in Edenshade?"

Her sweet smile belied the underlying sneer, so Charlotte had to despair of Rupert's perceiving it. The grin she spied from the corner of her eye confirmed this even as his words forestalled the reply she had opened her mouth to utter.

"Oh ho, Miss Hastings, you may be sure that Mrs. Fayerweather is capability personified. Why, she has all sorts of things to keep her busy, and some of them are a good deal of fun, I should think." He cast another teasing glance Charlotte's way. "Her flower arrangements, for example, are among the finest I have

seen. And you know many of the village women, Mrs.
Fayerweather included, take turns dressing our
church with flowers, but she outshines 'em all."

"How . . . gratifying that must be." The Beauty
fluttered long, thick lashes at Rupert.

Charlotte wanted to hit both of them with her basket. He was making her sound like the most boring
creature on earth!

"Honestly, Rupert, if one listened to you, one
would think I spent all of my time doing good works
and putting up preserves!"

"Not at all, Charlotte." He turned to Georgina. "I
cannot say how lively Mrs. Fayerweather's life was before I arrived in Edenshade, but I can say that I have
been most pleased to be her escort on numerous oc-
casions."

Charlotte eyed him dryly. "I would have you know
that before you came here, I did manage to shuffle
out of the house now and again."

"Of course you did, my dear Charlotte."

He was teasing her shamelessly and she willed herself not to lose patience or she would look like a poor
sport as well as a dowd. Charlotte bit her lip in frustration and remarked sarcastically that she was forever in Rupert's debt for his selfless generosity.

"You are so kind, Mr. Frost," The Vision murmured in apparent agreement, entirely missing the
irony. Rupert patted her arm as if to say that modesty
prevented his agreeing with her perspicacity. "I assure you, Miss Hastings, it was my pleasure entirely.
Mrs. Fayerweather is thoroughly enjoyable company.
And I must tell you, she is also a marvelous dance
partner."

Georgina shot Charlotte a narrow-eyed look of assessment that suggested Rupert might not have quite

enough time on his hands in future to squire about an aging, boring widow, no matter how well she danced.

"Well, Charlotte, would you like to join us? I am just showing Miss Hastings about the grounds." He smiled at The Vision, who smiled back radiantly, then dared Charlotte with a look to accept the offer.

"Thank you. Another time. I should like very much to see what Mr. Dillard has accomplished since my last visit. . . ."

"Quite a good deal since *then*, Charlotte. It has been a while since you have visited."

She was taken aback both by the remark and the tone of his voice. Really, one moment he was teasing her unmercifully, and the next he seemed to be complaining of her absence! Still, he did have the right of it and she bowed her head in acknowledgment.

"It has." Her gaze was steady. "But it is a lapse I hope to remedy soon, Rupert."

"Good. Perhaps you will come to dinner tomorrow evening? We can tour the grounds then."

"Oh, I should *love* to see your gardens at *night*, Mr. Frost."

Yes, I am certain that you would, my dear, Charlotte thought.

"And so you shall, Miss Hastings." He smiled again and again patted the hand that remained in a vise-like grip on his arm.

Charlotte wondered if the circulation might be cut off below the elbow. "I shall be very pleased to come, Rupert. But now I must go." She handed him the basket. "I, um, have a dress fitting and I mustn't be late."

An appointment with her milliner was as good an excuse as any to leave and one that Miss Hastings would, doubtless, think worthy of an interesting person's time. Besides, she would die before she told them it was her turn to arrange the flowers for St. Michael's.

At least the church would be cool, but then, unhappily, it was cool in Winter months, thanks to the thick weathered stones laid hundreds of years before. Charlotte and Nell, who loved to help her "do the flowers" especially when it was Charlotte's turn at St. Michael's, passed the churchyard, its uneven surface surrounded by an oaken railing nearly spilling its contents of tilted, ancient stones. Her arms full of flowers, Charlotte pushed open the door set in the elaborately carved chancel arch and held it wide for Nell, who followed carrying more blooms. The dimness of the interior contributed to the blessed coolness and the two women looked at one another and smiled.

"Here, Nell. Let's just sit a moment, shall we? And then we can begin."

Charlotte removed her wide hat and tossed it on the pew beside her. She leaned back in an informal pose and sighed with relief. After a couple of minutes, Nell rose and began the ritual she enjoyed so much. She disposed of the spent blossoms that were the offerings of the previous week and stepped outside to the pump to refill the containers with water. By the time she returned, her mistress had made a good start on sorting through the flowers they had brought and deciding which ones should go where. Now that she had finished her part of the chore, Nell stood at Charlotte's elbow and watched her hands at their graceful work and listened as she explained such arcana as which stems had to be flattened rather than cut to best drink water. But most of all, she wanted to put her own hand to arranging the flowers she had come to love so much for the church that she loved equally well. Charlotte had encouraged Nell to practice what she had taught her on small arrangements for the house. Since her mistress had praised her latest attempt, Nell hoped that she would be permitted to help now, and she was not to be disappointed. After placing a container of mixed flowers near the altar, the bright colors in cheerful relief against the plain white linen cloth that covered the table, she returned to Charlotte for further direction.

"Yes, all right, Nell. You have seen the sort of thing that is appropriate for that spot." She gestured toward one of the windows. "Would you like to give it a try?"

"Oh, ma'am!" The girl beamed.

Charlotte smiled. "Very well. Take this container and some flowers from the two buckets just over there and put them in a simple arrangement, just as you have seen me do—only smaller because it will be for that low space." She nodded her head to the location she meant.

"Yes, ma'am." Nell bobbed, still grinning. She reached into the flower buckets and began to remove half their contents.

"Whoa there, Nell," Charlotte laughed. "You must leave some for the other containers, you know!"

The maid blushed and giggled in her excitement. "Of course, ma'am. Bit carried away I am, I suppose." She replaced a number of flowers and moved off to the other end of the worktable, humming.

When they had nearly finished, Charlotte remarked that she loathed to leave and return to the heat outdoors.

"I am happy to say, ma'am, that the temperature has fallen somewhat in the past hour." The rich baritone voice caught them unaware, for they had not heard anyone enter. The gentleman removed his hat and apologized for his faux pas. "Forgive me, I had not meant to startle you. I came in to have a look at the church and did not expect to see *you* either." He chuckled. "I am sorry."

"Not at all, sir." Charlotte knew who he was. Edenshade was too small and had too few visitors for him to be anyone but the other half of Rupert's most recently arrived company. So this was The Vision's cousin. "I am Mrs. Charlotte Fayerweather and this is Nell, who works in my house. And I think you must be Captain Alexander Beddoes." She could not help but smile at him, for he had the sort of felicitous countenance that allowed nothing else.

Captain Beddoes threw back his head with a hearty laugh. "Well, Mrs. Fayerweather, do you tell fortunes as well?"

"I am afraid not, sir. For that, you must see Celia Lathrop, our local seeress. She can tell you anything. Whether you should believe her is another matter altogether."

She joined in his laughter, while Nell quietly put the finishing touches on her arrangement and peeked at her mistress with great curiosity through lowered lashes.

"You must tell me how you knew me, ma'am, for . . . No wait. Of course! Rupert mentioned you. That is," he amended quickly, realizing how callous he sounded, "he told me about you, Mrs. Fayerweather."

She nodded. "As he told me about you, Captain. And I have also had the pleasure of meeting your cousin, Miss Hastings, just a while ago. She and Rupert were out walking."

"In this heat? Georgina? Humph. Never could have got her to go about in such weather at home. Me, I got used to it on the Continent, doesn't bother me so much, but I did not think Georgina could stand it."

Charlotte contained a smile. "Er, as I understand it, she was most interested in viewing the grounds at Sherbourne Place."

"Was she? Didn't know she was that keen on flowers either. Oh well, just goes to show you how little we really know those we are closest to."

"Yes, that is so true, is it not?" He could not discern the dryness in her words.

Charlotte turned to gather up the scraps of petals and leaves and bits of stems from the table and Captain Beddoes looked appreciatively at the curve of her cheek and the curls that tickled the back of her neck. Rupert had mentioned her in a rather oblique fashion when he told his newest guests about the neighborhood and the people they could expect to meet. Why had he said so little of this fair lady? Was it because he wanted to keep her for himself? Well, if that were the case, Frost was about to learn that he was not alone in his pursuit of the lovely Mrs. Charlotte Fayerweather.

"If you are finished here, perhaps I might have the honor of walking some of the way back with you, ma'am? That way, you could show me a bit of the village, if you would."

"I should be pleased to do so, Captain, although I must warn you that unless you are as enthusiastic about flowers as your cousin seems to be, you may find little of interest here in Edenshade." She put her bonnet in place and tied the ribbons loosely beneath her chin.

"Ma'am, may I say that I have already found a great deal of interest to me in Edenshade." He gave her a serious smile. "Shall we go?"

Captain Beddoes saw Charlotte all the way home as it happened, the two having been so engrossed in their conversation that neither gave a thought to his leaving until they reached the door of Hawthorn Cottage. Nell had walked behind—but not *too* far behind—with a tiny smile of satisfaction that had very little to do with the quite nice arrangement of flowers she had produced, and while they continued their talk at the door, she slipped inside to find Mrs. Ruffle and whisper in her ear.

The housekeeper wasted no time in putting Nell to work. Captain Beddoes was thinking that he should be taking his leave, even though he did not want to do so, and to his surprise, it did not appear that Mrs. Fayerweather wished him to go. The front door opened suddenly, the brief breeze it produced fluttering the clematis that had wound its way around the frame. A smiling face appeared.

"Mrs. Fayerweather, Nell told me you'd brought a guest back with you," Mrs. Ruffle lied. "It's so warm to be standing outside. I've had the girl put out some lemonade and cakes. Will you and the gentleman be coming in now?"

Charlotte blinked. Mrs. Ruffle with her deliberate misconstruction of the circumstances had put her in an awkward position. It would be graceless now to do anything but invite Captain Beddoes in. But she found she wanted him to come inside, no matter that convention said he must not. *Devil take convention,* she decided. *I have not enjoyed anyone's company this much in ages.*

"Captain Beddoes," she smiled graciously. "Do say you will come in."

"Thank you, Captain. I am so pleased that you like it."

Charlotte sipped at a cup of tea and gave a little sigh of satisfaction. She found herself absurdly pleased that her new acquaintance admired her gown, for she had chosen it with great care. That is, she and Mrs. Ruffle had chosen it, for as Charlotte had sat at her dressing table splashing herself with lavender water, the housekeeper had bustled in "just in case I can do anything for you, ma'am," and helped her to decide between an aquamarine sarsenet gown and one of a rich cream muslin shot with tiny primrose love knots. They had finally settled on the blue green gown, which had a low corsage with a ruched edge and narrow banded sleeves. A feather-light shawl with silver spangles, similar to those that wound through her hair, lay across her upper arms.

Before her meeting with Captain Beddoes, Charlotte had not really cared to come to supper at Sherbourne Place and watch The Vision attach herself to Rupert like a limpet. But when Captain Beddoes had heard that she would be dining with them the next evening, he had not attempted to hide his pleasure, and Charlotte had begun to look forward to the occasion with anticipation. She had experienced a twinge upon seeing Georgina Hastings on the arm of her old beau and behaving for all the world as if she belonged *and intended to remain* there, but Charlotte had pushed those feelings aside and determined to enjoy to the full the attentions that Alexander Beddoes paid to her; she had given herself a good talking-to only a day or two before and liked to think she had accepted that Rupert harbored no deep feelings for her.

The senior Nashes entertained the company, which included Lowell Goodspeed, with Sally playing on the pianoforte and singing a duet with Benjamin. While Miss Hastings enjoyed the musical interlude as much as they others did, she soon decided that sitting quietly while attention was focused elsewhere could not be an advancement of her cause, no matter that she had placed herself in close proximity to her host.

"Oh, Mr. Frost, do say that you sing," she begged at the conclusion of a sprightly tune. "I should like above all things for you to join me in a duet at the pianoforte. You know, I feel certain that Mr. and Mrs. Nashe must be hoping that someone will take their place, for they must be a bit fatigued by now." Sally started to rise from the piano bench, aiming to point out to the gel that she and Benjamin were not quite so far into their dotage that a bit of singing should do them in, but that good lady was prevented from imparting this information by her very insightful and more conservative husband, who reminded her sotto voce of their status as guests in his friend's house. She gritted her teeth and relinquished her place on the piano bench.

"Miss Hastings, I must confess that my abilities have never been what I should like them to be. . . ."

"Nonsense, Mr. Frost. I just know that you must be musical. Why, I'll wager that you need only the right, um, accompaniment"—she gave him a small, sweet smile—"to be at your best. You might find that you are a complete hand at singing, you know. Oh, do say you will join me. We shall sing something quite simple, I promise you."

"No, I would not dream of my poor aptitude's distracting in any way from your own musical accomplishments, Miss Hastings." She flushed becomingly. "Please let us all have the pleasure of listening to you alone. We already know how well you play, and I feel sure that you are a gifted singer, as well."

Rupert did not hear the little groan that escaped from Captain Beddoes's lips, nor did he comprehend the arch look Miss Hastings bestowed upon her cousin as she proceeded gracefully to the pianoforte. Charlotte did hear him quite clearly, but good manners required that she pretend not to notice his distress.

Georgina sat down in front of the instrument and smoothed the skirt of her new gown, amber silk trimmed with a gold Grecian key pattern that also edged the tiny puffed sleeves. A breeze blew through an open window and the golden ribbons binding her curls danced tantalizingly. She looked just as lovely as she had hoped to. She gave a delicate little *ahem*— quite unlike anything ever heard from Frederick Barnstead—and began to play the opening notes of the song she knew by heart. For more than a full minute, the room was filled with soft, ethereal music beautifully played, and all the company, even Sally Nashe, was enthralled.

Goodspeed's eyes were closed in rapture as he listened to the sweet notes transporting him beyond the reach of Serena Woodland and all his worries about the contest. *Yes*, he thought, *this year I may actually be happy to see the end of Summer.* The thought was almost sacrilegious, but the clergyman's weariness together with the effects of a full stomach—Rupert's dinner had been a delight—and now this restful music all combined to allow him to relax for the first time in days.

As he leaned back in his chair, Rupert's gaze drifted to a large vase of lilies and his mind began to focus on Miss Hastings. She was such a pretty thing and she played so beautifully. . . .

The quiet was destroyed by a sudden, almost unearthly sound that could only be coming from a creature in great pain. Goodspeed's eyes swept open in expectation of an attack by a horde of vandals, and Rupert was rudely jolted from his reverie. The eyes of the company turned to the spot whence the sound emanated. It was Georgina, and she was singing. Sally Nashe let out a snicker that was, thankfully, masked by the singer's earnest exertions. Charlotte winced. Good God, could such a caterwauling really be coming from The Vision's lips? She nearly chuckled herself when Sally Nashe caught her eye and smirked with glee.

Beside her on the settee, Captain Beddoes murmured, "Oh, dear, I have *told* her not to sing in public." For a moment, he covered his eyes with the fingers of one hand as Georgina gave full throttle to her voice to emphasize the lyric.

Charlotte smiled at him. "Captain Beddoes, please do not be overset." Then she cringed as Georgina crashed through the scale in hot pursuit of an impossibly high note. *Honestly,* she thought, *if I did not know better, I would believe this was some sort of burlesque.* How could Miss Hastings not know that she sounded like a wounded banshee?

Still, Charlotte tried to diminish the awfulness of it all, for Captain Beddoes seemed to feel he was personally responsible for this assault on their ears. "Her voice is not so bad as you would seem to believe it is," she tried to assure him in an undertone.

He raised a brow that questioned her taste, if not her sanity. *Yes,* Charlotte told herself, *the young woman is cursed with a horrible singing voice and pretending anything else would be patronizing as well as ludicrous.* She patted the captain's arm in encouragement. "Oh well, it will soon be over and—"

"No, it will not."

"I beg your pardon?"

"Mrs. Fayerweather, this is one of Georgina's favorite songs and it has at least five verses, perhaps more—blessedly I seem to have been able to forget. Be assured that this could take a while, for I promise you, she will sing each one!"

"Oh."

"Indeed."

And she did sing each and every one. By the time that Georgina Hastings finished torturing the assembled company, each of them would have been hard-pressed to say which had been more difficult: listening to her or keeping the smiles on their faces. When at long last she played the final chord, Rupert rose quickly from his seat.

"Miss Hastings, you have a true gift for playing. And your singing, well . . ."

"Miss Hastings, your performance was most diverting," Charlotte assured her. She could honestly declare that the smile she presented owed its origins entirely to Georgina's performance.

Georgina appeared a trifle flushed, doubtless from her efforts, and she turned to Rupert, obviously waiting for a more fulsome compliment than she had received from Charlotte.

"Well," he said at length. "You certainly do put a great deal of energy into your singing! Er, perhaps we could all step into the garden for some fresh air." He offered her his arm.

She was more than willing to exchange a compliment for something now over and done with for a walk in the moonlight with him and she stepped elegantly onto the stone terrace. "Mr. Frost, how clever of you to know that this would be just the thing after my little entertainment." She paused for a moment, smiling, just in case he had decided to interject the compliment that was owed her, but such was not forthcoming. "It is most pleasant out here, is it not? Now you can take me on a tour of the garden. Do you have any flowers that bloom only at night?"

"Yes, Rupert, do tell." It was Sally, practically dragging Benjamin along beside her.

Rupert did not seem overly perturbed by the appearance of his two friends, or by that of Charlotte and Captain Beddoes walking slowly behind them, but Georgina was more than a little miffed to find that she would not have her host all to herself.

The senior Nashes had, earlier that day, discussed the way "that young woman is throwing herself at Rupert's head" and his evident susceptibility to her charms. Since they had been strongly in favor of a match between him and Charlotte Fayerweather, both were dismayed at this turn up. "Well," Benjamin had ventured over breakfast, their host having ridden out early with Winston, "Mrs. Fayerweather has not shown much interest in Rupert, and you can hardly expect a man to wait forever. Especially not when he has a lovely morsel like Miss Hastings to distract him."

"I cannot say you are wrong, dear, but you must

admit that Rupert has made little effort himself to win Mrs. Fayerweather." He nodded in agreement. "Oh, Benjamin, I just *know* that the two of them should be together! I cannot bear to see him fall prey to Georgina Hastings!"

"Now, Sally, Miss Hastings is not a bad sort, after all. She is a bit forward in that it does seem likely that she intends to have Rupert, but I should say she is rather a fine young woman nevertheless."

"Oh, would you indeed?"

"Sally."

She chuckled and leaned over to kiss his cheek. "Yes, yes, you are right. She is, I suppose, good enough—only she is so obvious, my dear. And I think she must be ruthless, too. I truly believe that, as you say, she means to have him whether he wants her or not!"

"I think he and Mrs. Fayerweather would rub along as happily as we do, Sally, but it does not seem likely to happen. And there is little we can do about that," he said pointedly.

"Of course there is something we can do—only I am not certain yet what that is. You think that we can do nothing only because you are so unromantic, Benjamin."

"Really?" He pulled her onto his lap and kissed her cheeks and her nose and her throat. By the time he reached her lips, Sally was ready to concede her mistake.

Now that Benjamin found himself in the garden chasing after his host and a pretty young woman, he nearly laughed at the farcical situation. What were they supposed to do now? Play gooseberry to the would-be couple? He slowed his pace and held his wife close to his side, letting Rupert and Georgina walk on ahead.

"Sally, for God's sake!"

"Oh, all right!" Sally gave a sigh of disgust and let her husband wind a sprig of myrtle through her hair.

"I remember that you wore this in your hair when we were married." He kissed her nose.

"I do not know about night-blooming flowers, Miss Hastings; however, there is a white garden just over in this direction and this lovely, big moon may light them just for us. Shall we take a look?"

A few moments after the departure of Rupert and Georgina, Benjamin and Sally heard soft voices, and turned to find Charlotte and Alexander coming slowly down the path and talking very companionably. He was looking into her eyes in a way that Sally thought much too bold on such short acquaintance.

Charlotte smiled at them and Captain Beddoes nodded.

"Mr. and Mrs. Nashe, I do apologize for my cousin's, um, singing. She does most things so well, particularly musical things—why, in addition to the pianoforte, she plays the harp beautifully—that she does not realize her voice leaves something to be desired. I have more than once besought her not to sing, at least in public. Generally, she complies, but sometimes she reminds me that I simply do not have a good ear—and I confess I do not, although in this instance I can be glad of it—and so cannot appreciate her talent." He smiled and shrugged.

"Nonsense, Alexander. You can hardly be responsible for what she does. She is of age, after all."

"That is what I have been telling him, Mr. Nashe," Charlotte added, smiling at the captain.

For no reason that she could comprehend, Sally

took Captain Beddoes to task over his treatment of his cousin. "Do you not think you might be rather high-handed, Captain? Miss Hastings was only trying to entertain us, after all." Her tone was not as warm as it might have been.

Benjamin Nashe looked at his wife and blinked. Captain Beddoes nodded. "As you say, Mrs. Nashe. My cousin's motives were kindly meant. As"—he grinned at her—"were mine." He changed the subject. "A beautiful evening for a stroll, is it not?" He led Charlotte off in the direction of a bower of roses.

Before Captain Beddoes had come to Edenshade, he had not intended to look for a wife; in fact, he had never had much interest in marrying. Hardly a week had passed at home when some repair did not present itself demanding immediate attention and his finances were in as poor a state as the roof on his kitchens and getting worse. Even if he did want a wife, how could he offer himself to a woman when he was so behind with the world? Then he had met Charlotte Fayerweather and quickly realized what a singular opportunity thus presented itself. She was attractive enough and intelligent, but best of all, she would bring a very sizable fortune to her husband. Fortunately, he was smitten with her, for Alexander could not have made himself wed a woman he disliked, and he had known almost at once she was a catch too good to leave for another man. He plucked a fragrant lavender rose and handed it to her.

"Mrs. Fayerweather, this lovely flower does not do you justice, rather I hope you will accept the sentiment that it brings."

Charlotte put the half-opened bloom to her nose

and smiled. "Captain, you flatter me. But the night is too perfect for me to tease you with it. Thank you."

Benjamin led his wife to a marble bench in the shape of a Roman sofa. "Do you know, dearest, that I think we are the only ones who wish to see Rupert and Mrs. Fayerweather together?"

"Mmm," she replied, resting her head on his shoulder.

"Not exactly." The soft voice belonged to Lowell Goodspeed, who joined them on the bench.

"Vicar?"

He nodded. "I am pleased to see that someone else feels as I do. Rupert and Charlotte ought to get married. For heaven's sake," he added with a laugh, "everyone else is!"

Rupert had not been blind to the warm looks that his former comrade was bestowing on his former fiancée, nor did he fail to notice the encouraging smiles that she gave him in return. He had tried to engage Charlotte in conversation more than once during the earlier part of the evening, but she did not seem inclined to indulge in anything beyond what would normally pass between a host and his guest. In each instance, however, The Vision had been in close proximity and since he made no effort to dislodge her, Charlotte did not believe his conversational overtures were made from anything but politeness.

Well, if that is the way the wind is blowing, I suppose my presence is de trop, Rupert had decided. *Certainly, she has made no effort to seek* my *company these past weeks. Still, I would not have expected that she would have succumbed to Beddoes's charms; not in her line, I should have thought.* It was not only his pride that was injured. Rupert had honestly believed that, if he had

just made sufficient effort, he could, somehow, have
revived his relationship with Charlotte.

Perhaps, he thought ruefully later that evening in
the quiet of his bedchamber, *I am still as arrogant as
I ever was, still unable, or maybe unwilling, to see the reality
of circumstances. I lost Charlotte in that way once and, it
seems, I have failed to regain her affection due to the same
flaw in my character.* He considered once more what
had happened after Pen Logan's wedding breakfast,
reminding himself that Charlotte had to be foxed to
find him attractive. *Well, I can hardly blame her, can I?*
he asked himself. *Not after what I did to her back in
Marlowe.* Despite the years that had passed, he realized for the second time in his life just what he had
lost, and now, it seemed, he had lost all hope of re-
trieving it.

Rupert had sat by the window in his room and listened to the infinite quiet of the early morning in
the parkland and gardens wrapping the house in a
cocoon of greenery. He enjoyed this peace tremendously, walking in his garden alone in the small
hours, if he could not sleep. Still, it would be good
to share the richness with a wife, to hold her hand
and hear their children come romping through the
French doors and into his arms. He wanted these
things so badly that he now acknowledged a grudging
willingness to leave behind his love for Charlotte and
look for another to build his future with.

Georgina Hastings had made no secret of her interest in him. Rupert was sufficiently experienced in
the world to recognize that her interest, literally on
the heels of their first meeting, might well mean an
interest in his fortune. But she was a lovely thing, full
of fun and bright, and he believed that she liked him
well enough and that she had character enough to

come to care for *him* and not his money. And so, he decided in the dark, silent hours of that morning that, if Georgina Hastings would have him, he would marry her before the year was out.

Ten

A persistent Summer rain eventually dwindled to a fine mist and crept off downriver. It left behind a landscape that was well watered and rinsed clean of dust, and gardeners glad of its nourishment of the flowers and shrubbery, as well as its timely departure just a day before the start of the contest. This left the trees and grass time enough to shake themselves free of rain in the soft breeze and the pathways ample opportunity to sop up the last of their puddles. Contest participants and visitors thus could walk through gardens and green without fear of wetting shoes or hats.

Early on Monday morning, the judging panel and Rupert, now the nearest thing the town had to a squire, who would otherwise have participated in the honors, assembled on the green to bid a formal welcome to the first arrivals. There were seven judges, three from one village and four from the other—the advantage of the extra seat rotating from year-to-year between them. The village that hosted the event always had the smaller number of judges. The judges were elected near the end of Flower Week each Summer for the next contest and each stood a term of only one year, although they could return to office in future years.

This Summer, in addition to Archibald Stevenson, Edenshade had just two other representatives. Pansy Shore, a widow of indeterminate years and boundless cheer, who some folks claimed never actually left her garden except for this single week in the Summer, had served proudly several times in the past. Norton Frobisher, senior judge this year, was a transplanted Londoner and charter member of the Horticultural Society in the Metropolis, who never tired of reminding everyone of this distinction and who was taking his present responsibilities very seriously indeed. Individuals were not required to be past winners to qualify as judges—else poor Archibald Stevenson never would have been elected—but they had to have reached at least the final round of consideration, thereby ensuring that all who had a hand in the decisions were highly accomplished themselves. The Edenshaders' counterparts in Great Tipton were two gentlemen and two ladies: Ann Blaine, a former judge who never liked anything that anyone grew; Tabitha Hatchton, the richest woman in the village; Thornton Ellis, known throughout Essex for his magnificent lilies; and Percy Drysdale, whose family had been among the judges since the contest had begun.

In addition to their primary responsibility of deciding on this Summer's winners, those judges in the host village also formed committees to arrange for and oversee preparation of a program listing all the garden entries, refreshments that would be provided, and the tables and booths that would be set on the green to hold the food and all manner of floricultural information. Refreshments were free to contest participants, while all others paid only a token amount, which proceeds typically were given to the local poor. Since there was much pride at stake in such matters as which town would bring home the most ribbons, folks worked almost as hard planning menus and such as they did in their gardens.

Last Summer had seen the first occasion in many years of musical entertainment. Great Tiptoners had puffed up with pride when two pianofortes and a harp had been placed on rugs on their green. Visitors had been suitably impressed—and dismayed—for the elegant and stately music was sadly out of place in the often boisterous atmosphere of Flower Week. Not a few people—mostly Edenshaders, it must be said—had been delighted when a sudden and unexpected downpour sent visitors running for cover, while the performers and judges scrambled to cover the pianofortes with anything to hand and to drag the harp beneath the thick branches of a maple tree. Gleeful, if drenched, Edenshaders had quickly pointed out the danger of this arrangement and laughed uproariously as Tiptoners had regrouped to hoist the heavy instrument into a nearby cottage. Things might not have gotten worse had the harp not eluded the slippery grasp of its handlers and fallen with an earsplitting crack onto a stone wall.

The ill-starred men had debated in ever rising voices the placement of blame for this accident, nearly coming to blows over the broken pieces of the instrument and soon saw that they were only adding to their rivals' enjoyment. With unspoken agreement, they turned as one and charged at those laughing the loudest, and before the outraged judges could intervene, a fight had erupted that soon escalated to include half a dozen Edenshaders and as many Tiptoners, including those carrying one of the pianos,

who deposited their burden in a puddle and joined
the fray. It had taken several minutes and a number
of strong men from both towns to separate the brawl-
ers and restore order, by which time the sun had re-
appeared and everyone's interest returned to the
contest.

The Edenshade judges realized they would have to
provide something in the way of entertainment, apart
from the time-worn jugglers and predictable fortune
reading courtesy of Celia Lathrop. They settled on
the Foxton brothers, who would wind their way
through the crowd with their fiddle and concertina,
providing a lively background for the proceedings
and, if the gods were in good humor, not give occasion to any other sort of diversion. Phyllida Steele's
cousin, Ambrose, from Trimble-Over-Water visited as
he did every Summer during Flower Week, bringing
with him, in alternate years, his stilts. Shortly after
the contest was officially under way, Ambrose was
abroad in the village, demonstrating his amazing bal-
ancing skill on the uneven surfaces of the lane and
the green. Children shrieked with mirth at his approach, dashing beneath tables and behind skirts to
hide from the great bumblebee, for Ambrose always
sported a costume of black and yellow stripes and
loped after the wee ones, buzzing loudly. A tall, lanky
man whose stature was emphasized by the stilts, Ambrose did not much resemble a bee except for the
stripes, but the children loved him and he took great
joy in his game.

The first task of the judges was to consider the entrants in all of the categories and to winnow each
group down to three finalists, traditionally referred
to as Survivors. This process generally took all of the
first day and sometimes part of the second, since it

meant viewing about a dozen applicants in each category and traveling between the two towns to do so. These results always occasioned a considerable amount of disappointment on the part of those who did not make the final round of judging. For the judges and the finalists, the second day and part of the third were taken up with evaluating the remaining final entries, with the last of the winners being notified and receiving their ribbons on the afternoon of the fourth day.

During these most serious proceedings, everyone else—including, eventually, the losers of the first round and the large numbers of folk who had no direct interest in the contest—played at bowls on the green, partook of the food and beverages, chatted with neighbors from both towns, dispensed and received advice on matters floricultural, and generally had a great deal of fun. Now and then, an argument would break out, sometimes resulting from the contest results, but more often from an overindulgence in drink.

The friendship between Charlotte and Sally Nashe had quickly progressed to the first-name stage, with promises of repeated visits by each woman and regular correspondence once the latter returned to Ashford. As they walked arm in arm down the lane toward the green, Sally, unfamiliar with the code governing the contest, asked Charlotte if she did not have an interest in being a judge. Charlotte explained to her friend that since she had never reached the final round, much less won a ribbon, she did not qualify to be considered as a judge. When Sally made the obligatory protest that all good friends make in such circumstances, Charlotte laughed.

"No, no, do not pity me, Sally, for I do promise you that I am extremely glad not to be a judge."

Sally raised her brows in a question. "But I should think it would be an honor to have the position. And you are involved in village life already, what with your church work and helping out in the school. . . ."

Charlotte shook her head with a smile. "Oh, I grant you it *seems* to be an honor. Certainly those who are elected for the first time feel so—and even some who are repeating the job, I must concede. But the truth, dear Sally, is that it is an awful burden."

Now Sally smiled. "I am beginning to see your point."

"I felt sure you would. You are about to see just how serious the participants are about their gardens and this contest. Competition can be *very* heated and some people who just cannot tolerate losing have been known to hold grudges. If one is not involved directly, it can actually be funny. On the other hand, if one were a *judge,* one could not be quite so cavalier about it all. You will see my meaning, I assure you, Sally."

"I do." They both laughed.

"But I do not mean to imply that Flower Week is not everything it should be. Many people work very hard all year round to see that it is so. And you know, it is not just people from here in Edenshade and Great Tipton who take an interest, although only residents of these two towns are qualified to enter the competition. You will find that folk from other nearby towns come in, too, to join in the fun and to view the gardens. It really is a wonderful event that all of us look forward to, and I am so pleased that you are here to enjoy it with me, Sally."

Sally adjusted the saucerlike brim of her large straw

bonnet to better block the sun. "As am I, Charlotte. You know, I have gotten some ideas already for my garden at home and I hope to learn even more this week."

"No doubt you will have many opportunities to do so. Not just from viewing the gardens in Great Tipton, but from speaking with a whole host of gardeners, each of whom you will find a virtual expert in his or her specialty. And then you will also find lots of books and monographs and other sorts of practical horticultural advice."

Part of the fun of Flower Week lay in the excursions, commonly referred to as Visits, made by hosttown residents to view the gardens entered in the competition in the other village. These Visits usually were planned with great eagerness weeks in advance. Friends, families, and neighbors formed groups, sometimes consisting of a convoy of several carriages, to travel the short distance between villages. More often than not, the Visit was a daylong enterprise, with large, boisterous picnics enjoyed in one of the meadows betwixt the towns. Charlotte was to be one of the Sherbourne Place party, which would consist of three carriages: one for Rupert, the senior Nashes, and Georgina Hastings; another for Captain Beddoes and Charlotte; and the third to carry the extensive provisions for a picnic. Winston had accepted an invitation to join Violet and her parents on their Visit.

As they approached the green, the sounds of voices were nearer and louder, and the few people they had nodded to in the lane seemed to suddenly grow to crowd size. The green was dotted with tables covered with festive cloths and booths gaily decorated in brightly colored fabrics and ribbons. Charlotte and Sally strolled up to the long table set on a low dais from which the judges would announce the contest winners. As the two women approached, the judges had given their opening remarks and Rupert was concluding his welcoming speech.

"And as many of you know, Sherbourne Place is entered in the contest this year after a long absence. . . ." He was interrupted by cheers from the Edenshaders in the crowd. Rupert smiled and waved his arms good-naturedly to forestall the shouts. "Thank you, thank you. And for that reason, in fairness, I shall remove myself from any further participation in these events until all the decisions have been made and the ribbons awarded." Louder cheers now from representatives of both towns. He nodded. "And so, once again, I bid Great Tiptoners welcome to our beautiful Edenshade and to one and all I express my deepest wish that this Flower Week may be the happiest we have known! My very best wishes to all!"

The applause and cheers were long and loud. The Foxton brothers, joined at the last moment by Tommy Miller playing a horn and Paul Holmes beating time on a small drum, paraded onto the green. They played a rollicking tune, then proceeded to the judges' table and escorted those seven individuals to a small booth elegantly draped in navy velvet with its edges trimmed in golden roses. Hidden inside was a large box covered by a sumptuous silk cloth patterned with lilies. The judges stepped to each side of the booth as Tommy played a smart fanfare on his horn, followed by a drumroll by young Paul. With great ceremony the first individual standing on each side—one an Edenshader and the other a Tiptoner—drew back the velvet hangings, then grasped either end of an ornate cord and slowly drew up the silk cloth that covered the box. The crowd cheered once again—this time at the sight of all the prize ribbons displayed on carved wooden boards set inside the box that had been made especially for this purpose many years ago. The ribbons were simple bows of black silk bound at the center with a small enameled trowel engraved with the year and category.

Sally squinted at the boards and shrugged. "With everything I have been hearing since I arrived, I should have thought the prize was at least a bag of guineas!"

Rupert had joined them. "Sally, I told you that the prizes were very simple."

She nodded. "You did, but from all the excitement, I supposed there must be *something* else to it. I know, I know," she laughed. "It is satisfaction and the recognition of one's peers. Still . . ." She waved her arm in an arc that encompassed the ever growing crowd.

"Well, you will find that many people do not care tuppence about gardening prizes. They are here just for fun," Charlotte put in. "It is rather a fairlike atmosphere, as you can see." She glanced at Rupert, who seemed to be searching the crowd for something. Before she could consider what she was doing, she said, "My, my, Rupert, did you lose something? Or someone perhaps? Where *has* Miss Hastings got to? Never say she's left you for the fascinating pamphlets at the fertilizer booth."

Rupert's lips twisted into a wry smile at the jibe. "Perhaps she is with her cousin, Charlotte. When I find them, I shall send Captain Beddoes to you," he said tartly, then nodded to them both and walked smartly off.

Sally Nashe blinked at each of them in turn. "What in heaven's name was that all about?"

"I am sure I do not know what you mean, Sally," said Charlotte stiffly. "Would you like to have a closer look at the ribbons?"

"Oh, it is my fondest wish, Charlotte," she replied dryly. "My dear, why don't you tell me what has happened between you . . . ?"

"Nothing has happened, Sally. *Nothing. Absolutely nothing.* And I tell you that with total honesty. You know, I think you are right; there really is nothing special at all about these ribbons. They are just bits of silk. Oh, I *do* wish they would play those stupid instruments somewhere else!"

The judges began to make their first round decisions by late in the morning. The results were announced from the officials' table by a delegate, since the judges themselves were still visiting and considering the remaining first round entries. There was little surprise when Lowell Goodspeed's name was announced as the first of the Rose category Survivors. Next were read the names of Serena Woodland and James Petersham. Petersham, also of Great Tipton, and Goodspeed were old friends, who had met from time to time as neighborly rivals during Flower Week and they greeted one another happily. Goodspeed's Edenshade gardening cronies, including Silas Trent, clapped him on the shoulder and told him he was a great fellow.

The vicar accepted their good wishes with typical quiet grace and modesty. He turned to shake hands with a neighbor who was not among the Survivors, only to have the man receive him coldly and hurry off. Goodspeed was unused to such treatment and flushed in surprise.

"It is unfortunate, is it not, Mr. Goodspeed, that some people are so lacking in the fundamentals of civilized interchange?"

He turned and looked into a pair of large, dark blue eyes outlined, rather charmingly he thought, by gold-rimmed spectacles. He lifted his hat and offered a smile.

"Miss Woodland. May I offer my congratulations on your success?"

"You may, and I am very grateful for them, Mr. Goodspeed. To be a Survivor puts me in rarified company indeed." She grinned up at him, quite pleased with herself.

The crowd in front of the judges' table had diminished once the first Survivor announcements had been made. Folks began to wander off to celebrate or bemoan their fate. Fortune and some of his friends were frolicking in the cool water of the river while several children waded happily closer to the bank.

"Isn't that your dog?" Miss Woodland asked.

"Why, yes, he is," replied Goodspeed with some surprise. "How did you know?"

"I remembered him. I have seen you together in the past." She smiled.

"Have you?"

She nodded. "Mmm. You bring him everywhere with you, don't you?"

"As a matter of fact, I do, Miss Woodland." He looked at her with particular interest. "And do you think that strange?"

"I cannot imagine why I should think so, sir. He is a good dog—we met when you, um, visited me, or should I say my garden, in Great Tipton some time back. I liked him very much." Miss Woodland tilted her head and the sun glanced off her glasses and straight into his eyes, blinding him for a moment. It hardly mattered, for the poor man could not see much but Miss Woodland anyway.

"He comes to church with me, you know." He had no idea why he felt compelled to make this confession about his beloved companion. "Most of the time he sleeps inside the pulpit—it is very commodious. My parishioners do not know, naturally—well, perhaps one or two." His admission was almost a challenge to her goodwill.

She nodded again and laughed, sparing him the knowledge that it was highly likely that all of his flock knew of Fortune's attendance at Sunday service. "I have a cat of whom I am extremely fond, Mr. Goodspeed. Do you like cats?"

"Very much. Fascinating creatures, cats. Here, do take my arm, Miss Woodland. The ground is becoming a bit uneven. Tell me, what is your cat like?"

"Ah, he is a very special feline, sir. He is a foundling. I came across him near the side of the road beside his dead mother. There was another of her kittens there, as well, but it ran off and I was not able to find it. . . . I have always felt very badly about that, poor little mite. Anyway"—she brightened—"this one's name is Lucky, because he is lucky that I found him. He is not too large and he is so dark a brown that he appears almost black—until you see him in the sunlight, when you can easily detect a beautiful red in his fur." She smiled, not trying in the least to hide her love for him or apologize for running on about a mere animal. Mr. Goodspeed, who understood completely, just as she knew that he would, smiled back. "But I am afraid he is an imp, sir, for he races about my poor cottage as if it were his private meadow, and he tangles my knitting and nips my nose sometimes when I am asleep! Perhaps you might exorcise the little beast for me!"

Goodspeed watched her closely during this animated narration. He could not quite decide why she appeared different to him, and so he simply asked her.

She laughed at him. "Doubtless it is my spectacles, Mr. Goodspeed. I did not have them the last time we met, I think. Also, now that I can see so much better, I do not squint the way I was used to." She removed the spectacles and screwed up her face in a gross imitation of her old mannerism. He agreed that this must have been the change he noticed, but although he did not feel confident enough to add that he liked it very much indeed, he did invite her to take refreshment with him.

"Miss Woodland, perhaps you would like to have some tea and stroll in the shade where it will be much cooler? We might visit one another's gardens afterward?"

"Why, Mr. Goodspeed, what a wonderful idea." She made it sound as if the notion had been entirely his own.

The right carriage wheels dropped heavily in quick succession into and out of a large rut that had been deepened by the recent rain.

"Good heavens!" Georgina Hastings exclaimed, clapping one hand to the crown of her bonnet as she bounced on the seat.

"My dear Miss Hastings, do not fall out. We would not want to lose you!" Rupert said with a smile.

Sally bit back the rejoinder that her host should speak for himself and, instead, smiled at Miss Hastings. Her husband gave her arm a gentle squeeze. They had again discussed the growing relationships between Rupert and Miss Hastings and Charlotte and Captain Beddoes during their walk that morning and decided they must accept that, while Rupert and Charlotte might marry, they apparently would not marry each other.

"In fact, my love, I think there may be a more likely chance they will come to blows than come to the altar," he had remarked, only half in jest.

"Unhappily, I cannot disagree, Benjamin."

"And, since everyone—except us"—he grinned—"seems happy with the way the situations are developing, it would be ludicrous for us to interfere and try to change things to the way *we* would prefer them."

"Oh, I know. And if we honestly care about Rupert and Charlotte, then we ought to be supporting their choices and helping them to realize their happiness."

"So, Miss Hastings," Benjamin began after they had all resettled in their seats, "which gardens do you plan to visit? Sally and I have spent some time working that out. Do you have any particular floricultural interests?"

"I beg pardon? I am afraid that I know little about it, sir." She smiled apologetically. "But how can you know what there is to see in Great Tipton?"

The road had evened out and the carriage now bowled along smartly behind Rupert's fresh grays.

Benjamin held aloft the program put out by one of the Flower Week committees. It contained names and locations of garden entries in each category from both villages. The paper bore penciled notations made by Benjamin and Sally reminding them to visit "Mrs. James Porter, Larkspur Cottage—Herb Garden

Category" and "The Misses Marshfield, Hedgehog House—Herbaceous Border Category" when they arrived in Great Tipton. Clearly, Miss Hastings had not seen the brochure.

"Here, you are welcome to have a look at ours." He held out the paper.

"Thank you, Mr. Nashe." She examined the program. "So many places to see. It just boggles the mind."

Sally's brows shot up and Benjamin gave her a quelling glance. She sighed with frustration.

"Well, no matter, Miss Hastings. I am certain that Rupert will know just the spots you should see." Sally smiled at her.

"That is right, Sally. Not that I have any firsthand knowledge, this being my first Summer here. But I have been well advised by a number of experts—my gardener, Mr. Dillard; the vicar; Mr. Stevenson, who I am told knows more about herbaceous borders than anyone else in Edenshade; and Charlotte Fayer-weather."

He looked over Georgina's shoulder at the program and scanned the names, pointing out a few recommended for Visiting by his experts. But at his mention of Charlotte's name, Georgina's lips tightened and her chin came up a bit. Even though she had seen little to indicate that Mr. Frost's attention might be fixed on his old friend, she did not intend to allow his thoughts to wander in her direction or, if they did, to remain there for long.

"Mrs. Fayerweather. Such a dear woman. She and my cousin seem to be getting on *quite* well, do they not?" Georgina nodded her head in the direction of the tilbury rolling along just ahead of their carriage.

Rupert barely gave it a glance before his eyes returned to the full lips smiling up at him. "Yes, I suppose they do." He smiled back into her eyes. "How nice for them."

She giggled. "Do tell me, what is your favorite kind of garden, sir? Do you expect that any we shall see today can compare to Sherbourne Place?"

"Without a doubt, Miss Hastings, for even Dillard will tell you that my gardens are not yet what he hopes them to be. I cannot even be certain that Sherbourne Place will be a Survivor until the judges announce their decision late this afternoon. One of the Visits we shall make is to Clayton Park, the largest manor hereabouts. I met the owner at the opening ceremonies—he seems like a right enough fellow, by the way—and I wish to see the competition," Rupert explained, having discovered a real interest in gardens since taking over Sherbourne Place.

It had been evident to the senior Nashes that Georgina Hastings would not let the presence of third parties deter her from pursuing Rupert. But they felt things might develop better for Charlotte and Captain Beddoes if they could enjoy some privacy, so they had suggested the assignment of places in the vehicles that left them alone. The latter couple welcomed this arrangement, though its purpose and advantages were never voiced, and they chatted easily all alone in the tilbury.

There was almost as much bustle in Great Tipton on this second day of the contest as there was in Edenshade. The High Street was fairly filled with conveyances of every description, so the warm Summer air was more redolent than usual of smells of horse, hay, and human. Despite the rivalry of Flower Week—good-natured in all but a few sensational instances—the residents of these two small towns lived peaceably in the valley. Since most did not see one another "from one end of the year to the other," as some put it, there was mingled with the sounds of horses and harness voices raised in cries of reunion and well-wishing.

Some passengers stopped at the local inn for light refreshment before or after turning down the lanes to view the gardens of their choice. Others stood beside their carriages or horses or under shade trees catching up on a Winter's worth of news.

"My Amy—she's the youngest, you'll remember, Margaret—gave birth to her third. Another girl, can you imagine? And just as beautiful as her sisters."

"And I told him, 'Mr. Pollard,' I said, 'I'll not be having low-quality grain like that.' I was that angry, I don't mind telling you. . . ."

"Oh, bless you, Aunt Celia will outlive us all, you know. At least she says so and she's ninety if she's a day and sees the future besides, so who am I to argue?"

"No, no, the hyacinths made a very poor showing this year, *very* poor indeed. Well, I believe the mice or rabbits or some such must have feasted on more than a few of them, so what did come up looked decidedly flimsy. And after last Summer, too. . . ."

Charlotte and Captain Beddoes strolled down the lanes stopping at each house to admire the flowers and exchanging pleasantries with passersby and those cottage owners who were not in Edenshade on their own Visits. Those gardens that had been triumphant in past Summers could be easily identified by the black satin winning ribbon proudly tacked to the garden gate or over the cottage door. Owners stood beaming at their gates, happily answering questions about how best to grow a particular flower or rid a garden of a certain pest or hopefully accepting wishes for "best luck."

Charlotte was amazed to see Lowell Goodspeed standing rather close beside a woman she was certain must be the one who hoped to take the Rose Ribbon from her friend. They were standing in a beautiful rose garden, and as she and Captain Beddoes approached, Charlotte fumbled through her brain trying to find the woman's name.

"Miss Woodland!"

The lady turned to see who called her and found Charlotte, her face aflame and fingertips to her lips—the gesture rather more useful in its intent than use.

"Mrs. Fayerweather!" cried the vicar. "And Captain Beddoes!"

Miss Woodland smiled graciously and Charlotte apologized.

"Not at all, Mrs. Fayerweather. I sometimes do my best thinking out loud!"

"You are too kind, Miss Woodland."

After Miss Woodland and the captain were introduced, Charlotte remarked, "What a charming garden! Oh, the fragrance is heavenly."

"Thank you," replied its keeper modestly. "I am pleased that you like it. Please, I was just about to show Mr. Goodspeed some old favorites of mine. They are just behind this wall if you would like to join us?"

They followed her through a narrow door set in a stone wall and stepped into a small sanctuary, very quiet after the chatter of Visitors and gardeners, except for the fluttering and chirping of birds. The garden walls formed an octagonal shape. Paths of grass led among a variety of rosebushes—some very tall and set along the eight panels of the stone wall, projecting their flowers and branches like sprays from a fountain; others small and shrublike tagging along the pathways. Goodspeed bent to examine a prim miniature shrub with neat pink blooms.

He smiled and inhaled. "Rose de Meaux. I have this, too. Nice little flower, is it not, Miss Woodland?"

" 'Tis. Not as theatrical as some of the others"—she waved an arm at the exhibitionists on the perimeter tempting visitors with their long, elegant arms—"but it never gives me a spot of trouble and has good, dependable blooms." She pointed to her left. "Now, sir, tell me what you think of that!"

Mr. Goodspeed shook his head with appreciation. "My, Miss Woodland, that is an accomplishment." Standing out boldly from its near neighbors of white and soft pink was a slightly shorter plant some four to five tall and bearing startlingly bright flowers of a crimson purple color set off by heavily veined leaves. "Charles de Mills!" the vicar exclaimed, expertly recognizing the flower's name. "Now, you don't see this very often, do you?"

His hostess nodded eagerly and grinned. "He is very flamboyant, is he not?" she anthropomorphized the rose. "Generally, I insist that my roses have a lovely perfume and this has almost none. Still, its petals have a texture like velvet and I like their spiral arrangement. It is so unusual."

Their heads close together, they moved slowly from rose to rose, discussing the merits of gallicas versus centifolias, more commonly known as cabbage roses, and methods and timing of pruning. Had Charlotte not seen it with her own eyes, she might not have believed that the vicar and his archrival would be taking so amiably—no, amiably was not exactly the right word, for she was certain she detected something more in the glances they shared. Could Lowell Good-speed be in love? Charlotte and Captain Beddoes strolled along the path enjoying the intoxicating perfumes and the various shapes, colors, and sizes of the roses set off perfectly against the backdrop of the stone wall.

"I cannot believe how well they are getting on," she whispered to her companion. "Just look at them."

"Why does it surprise you so, Mrs. Fayerweather?"

"Oh, that is right. You would not know." Charlotte explained the facts of life in the two villages, at least so far as they concerned the Flower Week competitors.

Captain Beddoes chuckled warmly. "Well, I do not find it wonderful at all, ma'am, that they should entertain other feelings for one another. Perhaps," he said carefully, "they have actually had a mutual affection for some time, but never found themselves in a circumstance where they might acknowledge it. Don't you agree that this might be so?" He looked at her pointedly, awaiting her response.

"Captain, I do believe you have the right of it," Charlotte replied softly. Then she glanced away to inhale the almost overwhelming perfume of a white Damask rose. Unless she missed her guess, Captain Beddoes was about to declare himself, and she had no idea what her response would be if he did. After all her soul-searching over the past days, after seeing Rupert looking after Miss Hastings time and again, she should have known her answer—that much *was* clear to her. Alexander Beddoes was a good man who did seem to care for her. She did not delude herself that he was in any way head over ears in love with her, any more than she was smitten with him, but she did believe they would rub on well enough together, if they did wed. And she knew it would be foolish in the extreme for her to turn down his proposal, supposing one was forthcoming, even stupider if to do so resulted from expectations or hopes from Rupert's quarter, for he had made his feelings—or lack of them—painfully clear. Still.

"Hallo! Is anyone there? Hallo?"

"Mrs. Pike!" Charlotte called with relief.

"Ah, Mrs. Fayerweather! And Captain Beddoes. How nice to see you again."

"Mrs. Pike, the pleasure is all mine," that gentleman replied warmly.

"Hello, vicar." Mrs. Pike looked at Miss Woodland, then at Mr. Goodspeed.

"Good day, Henrietta. You have met Miss Serena Woodland, have you not?"

Henrietta Pike, never in her life a slow top, beamed. "Indeed I have, my dear vicar." Her voice was hearty. The two women exchanged little bows. "How nice to see you again, Miss Woodland. So this is your garden." She waved her program at it. "I have just been looking at what is outside the walls, but this is your own little paradise, is it not? My dear, what magnificent roses!"

"You are all kindness, ma'am," Miss Woodland replied. "I only hope that the judges are equally impressed."

Mrs. Pike looked to the clergyman. "Well, Lowell, what say you? Will she win this time? I'll warrant she gives you a run for your money! What will you do then?" She watched carefully for his reaction.

Goodspeed smiled benevolently at the tiny woman by his side. "I believe that is very likely, Henrietta. Very likely, indeed."

"Oh, my," Mrs. Pike whispered to Charlotte.

"Just so," she replied.

"Well, I am actually come looking for my friend, Cynthia Ferrars. That creature wanders off without telling a soul where she is going. Thought she might have come in here. In any event, I am very happy that *I* did."

"Mrs. Pike, Mrs. Fayerweather and I were intending to stop for refreshment before returning to Edenshade. Do say you will join us. I am certain that your friend will find you." Captain Beddoes extended an arm to each lady and they all strolled off in the direction of the High Street, leaving behind two contented people who hardly noticed their absence.

Cynthia Ferrars never did find Mrs. Pike, and that lady quickly accepted Beddoes's offer to carry her back to Edenshade in Rupert's carriage. The rest of the party from Sherbourne Place appeared, as scheduled, so that they might all stop and partake of a picnic lunch on the return to Edenshade. Just as they were about to depart, Jeremy Pike trotted up on Jupiter and was pleased to accept an invitation to join the picnic party. While Captain Beddoes drove the short distance to the meadow where they all would meet, he and Mrs. Pike chatted gaily as if they had known one another for years. Since her participation in this effort was not required; Charlotte gazed at the passing scenery thankful that Mrs. Pike's presence meant that Captain Beddoes could not declare himself.

The picnic proved to be of particular importance, even if hardly anyone realized it at the time. It might have started when Jeremy Pike passed the cold roasted fowl to Georgina Hastings, or when Charlotte and Rupert watched Sally lovingly fill her husband's plate, or when Henrietta Pike's eyes sparkled as she sipped at her wine and laughed at something Captain Beddoes said, or when Charlotte heard Sally suggest that Miss Hastings sample a bit of the tart on Rupert's plate. It might have been any of things or none of them, but after the picnic was over, decisions had been made and things in Edenshade were about to change.

Eleven

The parties had returned home in time to hear that Sherbourne Place was not a Survivor. Rupert was simultaneously more disappointed than he had expected to be and relieved to have the burden of the competition lifted from his shoulders. Some Edenshaders, however, were indignant at the results, declaring the judges to be biased in favor of the other surviving entrants, both from Great Tipton. Rupert at last managed to restore their equanimity, chuckling to himself that the whole business was a continually unwinding coil of feelings and relationships that frequently had little to do with flowers and from which he had little hope of ever escaping.

Charlotte had arrived back at Hawthorn Cottage to find Mrs. Ruffle and Mr. Dillard waiting for her. She expressed to him her condolences that Sherbourne Place had not survived the first round and was surprised to find him not the least bit put out.

"As you know, Mrs. Fayerweather, I had not expected to do that well this year. *Next* year"—he grinned—"will be a different story, I promise you. However, ahem, Irene—Mrs. Ruffle—and I do have much happier news." He gazed lovingly at the housekeeper's face. "Shall you tell her, my dear?"

She nodded her head vigorously. If she had been wearing a cap, its streamers would have been dancing a jig. "Mr. Dillard has asked me to marry him, Mrs. Fayerweather, and I have accepted." She could not have grinned more broadly.

Charlotte managed to look a bit surprised, since that seemed to be what the situation called for. "Oh! How wonderful!" She bussed Mr. Dillard's cheek and put her arms around Mrs. Ruffle and hugged her tightly. "I am *so very* happy for you, my dear," she whispered.

The wedding would take place in six weeks' time, and after her fiancé had departed, Mrs. Ruffle talked for hours about her bride clothes. The couple would honeymoon in London—where Mrs. Ruffle, or Mrs. Dillard as she would be then, could spend hours in the warehouses and shops—then in Somerset, where there were gardens her new husband had a desire to see. They would not leave until well into the Fall when he could best be spared from his duties. After the wedding, the housekeeper would leave Hawthorn Cottage for Sherbourne Place, where Mrs. Ruffle would be mistress of her own small house on the manor grounds.

Charlotte sat by her window, looking out at the enormous yellow moon, and sniffed. She had known this was coming, had wanted it to come, but now she found it hard to envision life at Hawthorn Cottage without Mrs. Ruffle. It was not just the woman's excellent housekeeping skills she would lose, though those would be difficult enough to replace. Most of all, she would miss Mrs. Ruffle's cheery disposition, her outspokenness, and her full-blown love of life. Hawthorn Cottage would be a quiet place without the whistle that rang out clear and true as a bird's and drove Charlotte to distraction, without her latest narration of the village gossip or her teasing her mistress to do away with her caps or go ice-skating. Charlotte sniffed again and heard footsteps coming down the hall. She blew her nose quickly and cleared her throat, in case Mrs. Ruffle came in. It would never do to let her see that she was upset. But Mrs. Ruffle's footsteps continued on down the hall and Charlotte crawled into her bed and slept deeply.

The judges had begun to award the ribbons on the third day of the contest. The Norwell brothers, who resided in the handsome old cottage by the river's edge, won the prize for Best Water Garden, having lost it two years running to their own Harland cousins in Great Tipton. The rivalry between the sets of cousins had been characterized by good-natured teasing, but the Norwells were barely able to contain their joy at winning back the ribbon. Numerous other awards were made throughout the day, but the next and final day would bring the prize that held the most interest for so many Edenshaders—Best Rose Garden—for in addition to his particular friends, Mr. Goodspeed's parishioners waited, as they did each Summer, to see if their clergyman would win again.

On the third evening, the Pikes held an impromptu supper on the spacious back lawn of Jeremy's house. Japanese lanterns had been hung in the branches of the trees, more for effect than practical purpose, since it remained so late into the night, and a large table was set up on rugs spread out on the grass. Mrs. Pike, acting as her son's hostess, declared the occasion to be an informal one and insisted that everyone sit wherever they might choose. There were several Eden-

shade residents in attendance in addition to her own
family, Charlotte, and Rupert and his houseguests.

The company drank to the success of the Norwell
brothers, tut-tutted once again over Rupert's loss, and
drank to the luck of their absent vicar, whose fate
would be decided the next day. After friendly wagers
were made on the outcomes of various categories,
Phineas Norwell, who had imbibed much more
spruce beer than he ought, suggested that, for a lark,
they should hide the award ribbons and hold them
for ransom. Silas Trent seconded the notion, but remarked that it would not be a lark for him, for *he'd*
had his fill of gardening and anything to do with it.

"And I should demand a very high price," he
joked, "since any number of otherwise sane folk
would gladly ransom the ribbons, and *next* Summer
I could take a holiday in Paris while the rest of you
endure this whole silly exercise all over again!"

His idea was met with a medley of laughing taunts
and cheers. But he then laughed the whole thing off,
confessing, "No, no, I could not do it, for I am as
mad as the rest of you on the subject of this damnable
contest!"

"I say we should do it," Phineas sang out. "Have
to li-liven up the rest of Flower Week, now that the
important award has been given."

"I hope that you will forgive my brother," Arnold
Norwell laughed. "We can all of us take consolation
in the fact that our cousins in Great Tipton have,
doubtless, drunk even more than Phineas to drown
their shame. If they lived *here* instead of *there,*" he de-
claimed in stentorian tones, "you would truly know
what offensive behavior is!" The guests roared with
laughter. "And now"—Arnold hauled his brother to
his feet and slung the only barely conscious winner

over his shoulder—"I shall take this paragon of recti-
tude home to his bed!" Phineas, hanging upside
down, looked up for a moment, gave the company a
bleary-eyed salute, and collapsed against his brother's
back.

Later, when the party removed to the parlor for
whist, Charlotte could not help but notice how well
her hostess was getting on with Captain Beddoes.
Partners for the game, they had engaged in spates of
lively conversation, and afterward, although he remained attentive to Charlotte, the two continued to
talk and laugh as if they had known one another for
years. It seemed almost as if they were drawn together
like magnets. Mrs. Pike—who could be of an over-
bearing disposition and who, since the death of Mr.
Pike, lived her life vicariously—was clearly having fun
and glowed under the captain's gaze.

Meanwhile, Jeremy spent the greater part of his
evening endeavoring to engage Miss Hastings in conversation and watching her with adoring eyes when
he could not. Rupert appeared not to notice the efforts of the younger man, but Georgina enjoyed their
exchanges and gave him a rather enigmatic look now
and again that left the poor man more bewildered
than encouraged. The senior Nashes were accumu-
lating fodder for pillow talk sufficient to keep them
awake for days.

It rained hard late in the night, but stopped soon
enough to let the ground dry sufficiently for the festivities to resume without discomfort to the participants. As it did every year, the green saw its biggest
crowds on the final day, when the numbers were
swelled by those previously engaged taking their last
opportunity to get in on the fun.

The names of the last few winners were to be announced at eleven o'clock. The ribbons would be formerly presented in a small ceremony at each winner's garden, provided they lived in Edenshade, with Great Tiptoners accepting the prize from the judges at their official table. This was tradition owing to the impracticality of traveling yet again to the other town; Great Tipton winners received their ribbons at their gardens when the contest was held in that town.

Lowell Goodspeed and Serena Woodland moved through the crowd, laughing and talking as if unaware they were not alone. Charlotte encountered them before she met up with Captain Beddoes and the vicar bought them rolls and coffee at one of the booths. The three sat in the shade of an elm to eat and talked of the evening festivities that would bring this Summer's Flower Week to a close.

"The Foxton brothers, not to mention Tommy and Paul, will be retired in favor of a brass band that Rupert has got so that everyone can dance," Charlotte explained.

"Oh, lovely!" Miss Woodland clapped her hands. "Someone told me that there are to be fireworks as well. Is that true?"

The vicar nodded. "A very small display, of course, but it is true. Being a former judge myself, I have some friends on the committee who let me in on the secret—I suppose I may tell it now. The men are arriving this afternoon to set it up. The judges will announce it this morning, after the winners have been named. The committee are very pleased with themselves, as you might imagine. They wanted to keep it a secret for as long as possible and they believe that Great Tipton will have the devil of a time topping this next year!"

"I should say so!" Charlotte laughed and Miss Woodland agreed.

As the hour of eleven drew near, the crowd grew even larger. By a few minutes before the hour, the competitors had all lined up before the judges' booth, their supporters and all the other interested parties behind them. Charlotte was standing near the vicar and Miss Woodland, waiting for the judges to appear, and she soon saw Captain Beddoes and Mrs. Pike coming her way.

"Mrs. Fayerweather!" he called and Mrs. Pike waved at her cheerfully.

"Dear Mrs. Fayerweather, just see who I have met as I came down the lane." Charlotte could not remember ever seeing Mrs. Pike smile so broadly. "Captain Beddoes very kindly offered to accompany me. And now I deliver him to you!" She did not immediately release her arm, which was wound through his in the conventional fashion, rather looking up at him and smiling in a quite different way. "Oh!" she said after a second or two and dropped her arm. "And so, here he is!"

"Well, I . . ." Charlotte did not quite know what to say and the captain looked rather uncomfortable.

Alexander Beddoes was very confused. He had come to Edenshade thinking that his cousin might find herself a husband—and it appeared that this was well on its way to happening, if Rupert's behavior were anything to go by. He had not expected that *his* heart might be touched in any way, and now he found himself attracted to two very different women. He had no idea what he was supposed to do in such a circumstance and even less a notion of what he *wished* to do, except to have the whole problem disappear. He had been paying most particular attentions to

Mrs. Fayerweather and that lady surely must be in daily expectation of a declaration from him. Indeed, he had been prepared—just as she had suspected—to make his feelings know in Great Tipton just before Mrs. Pike happened upon the scene. A most prescient arrival, as it turned out, for he subsequently found himself very drawn to Henrietta Pike in a way that he would be hard put to describe, but which he knew was considerably deeper than his very real feeling for Charlotte. But what could he do? He could hardly cast Mrs. Fayerweather aside at this stage of their relationship. Yet he believed that his feelings for Henrietta Pike would grow and he felt that she returned his sentiments.

His thoughts were interrupted by a prolonged drumroll and a fanfare from Tommy's horn, calling attention to the arriving judges. There was scattered applause quickly hushed by the seven people standing behind the table.

"Good morning to all and welcome to the final day of Flower Week. We sincerely hope that you all have been enjoying the—" Norton Frobisher began to greet the throng.

"Get on with it!"

Mr. Frobisher's eyes widened and his lips pursed at the behavior of this tasteless provincial, who, he was convinced, would be entirely out of place in London. "Ahem!" he said pointedly. "If I may continue? We sincerely hope that you all have been enjoying the festivities of the past few days." A number of people dutifully applauded and called out their appreciation. "As many of you know, Mr. Rupert Frost has been kind enough to engage a band for this evening's concluding festivities and there will be dancing on the green!"

Even Mr. Frobisher seemed to be impressed with this. The crowd expressed its appreciation to Rupert, who was standing in their midst awaiting, along with them, the final contest results. He smiled and waved in acknowledgment.

"In addition to this wonderful treat, I am very pleased to tell you of our little surprise." Mr. Frobisher preened a bit, enjoying the moment. "There will be a fireworks display over the river at ten o'clock this evening and we hope that all of you will be able to join us for the event!"

The people were every bit as thrilled as Mr. Frobisher and the rest of the judges had hoped, but it was not long before they began to call again for the announcement of the winners.

"All right, all right," he chuckled. "We shall now make the announcements of the last winners."

The other judges rose to stand beside him in their official capacity.

"For Best Cottage Tubs, the winners are Mr. and Mrs. Edward Loring of Loring Cottage, Edenshade."

Sustained cheers, for the Loring family was much liked in the village and there was even yet leftover goodwill for the fine wedding breakfast they had provided weeks before for their son, Lawrence.

"Thank you, thank you," said Mr. Frobisher. "Now, for Best Herb Garden, Mrs. James Porter of Larkspur Cottage, Great Tipton."

The Great Tipton judges smiled proudly, as if they had a hand in growing Janet Porter's pennyroyal and chamomile, while she accepted the congratulations of her friends and family.

"And now for the Herbaceous category. The award for Best Herbaceous Border goes to Mr. and Mrs.

Alvin Carbury of Delphinium Cottage, Great Tipton."

There was a collective gasp and a strangled groan from Mrs. Dunstable, from whom the ribbon had been won after eleven long years. The Great Tiptoners erupted into cheers of delight and Mrs. and Mrs. Carbury, shocked and delighted, were carried off by their friends for a celebratory lunch. Goodspeed looked at Archie Stevenson, standing second from the left in the judges' line and looking awfully satisfied with himself. Was it possible that he had cast the deciding vote for the Carburys just to ensure that Mrs. Dunstable would lose even if he could not be the one to take the prize from her? The vicar shook his head as if to rid it of such an uncharitable notion. He decided it would be better for his conscience not to catch Archie's eye.

"And at last, we come to the final category, which so many of you have been waiting for. I do not mind telling you that this was an unusually difficult decision this Sum—"

"Just tell us who won!"

"Who is it?"

Mr. Frobisher, who had prepared a fine speech for this part of the ceremony, reddened and attempted to press on. "All of the entrants this year—"

"Off with his head!" someone shouted in a rollicking voice.

"Hear, Hear!"

Thornton Ellis from Great Tipton and Pansy Shore both leaned close to Mr. Frobisher and said something that made him flush an even deeper pink.

"Oh, very well," he snapped at them. "Quiet please! We are pleased to announce," he glared at all assembled as if daring them to deny him this at least—"the winner of the Best Rose Garden category. The ribbon will go to Miss Serena Woodland of Damask Cottage, Great Tipton."

The silence that fell was even longer than that which had greeted Mrs. Dunstable's loss. While Lowell Goodspeed did not have such a long string of victories behind him as she did, it was commonly understood that his garden was such a work of art that it might never be unseated. Once again, cheers broke out from the Great Tiptoners in the crowd, many of them calling Miss Woodland's name with joy.

"Miss Woodland, may I be the first to congratulate you." Charlotte smiled. "Mr. Goodspeed, I am sorry."

Lowell Goodspeed stood as if turned to stone. Miss Woodland lifted her smiling face up to him in expectation of his good wishes.

"Congratulations, Miss Woodland!" said James Petersham.

"Yes, indeed, Miss Woodland," added Mrs. Pike. "How pleased you must be."

"Well done, ma'am," said Captain Beddoes.

"Thank you," she murmured, still watching her companion, who uttered not a word.

At length, he turned and looked down at her. "Miss Woodland, my heartfelt congratulations."

After speaking this evident falsehood, Mr. Goodspeed turned, calling for Fortune, and strode off.

Miss Woodland called after him, but was ignored. She looked at Charlotte, tears in her eyes, the triumph she had worked so hard for and wanted so badly turned to dust.

"Oh, dear," was the only response Charlotte could think of on the spot.

"But I thought he would accept it, if I did win, which, honestly, I did not think I would this Summer.

He . . . we . . . oh, Mrs. Fayerweather, shall I lose him all for some stupid roses?"

Charlotte could only blink at the blasphemy the woman had uttered. And what did she mean by "lose him?" Did the two have an understanding? "Oh dear," she said again. "Come, Miss Woodland. Let's get out of this crowd."

She cast a glance over her shoulder at Captain Beddoes, asking him to excuse her. That gentleman waved her on with an understanding smile and Mrs. Pike fluttered her handkerchief, pointing out that "a bit of a walk would be just the thing for Miss Woodland."

The two women had not gone far, and Miss Woodland had spoken little, when she said that they must get back to the judges' table for the awarding of the ribbons.

"It is strange—is it not, Mrs. Fayerweather—that not so very long ago, all I dared to hope would happen to me this week was winning the Rose Ribbon. I never thought that Mr. Goodspeed might actually, *finally*, notice *me* and not just my roses. And now this." Miss Woodland blew her nose. "But I shall not let this deprive me of the thrill of receiving my ribbon. I have worked too hard for it!"

"Good for you," Charlotte agreed.

The crowd assembled for the bestowing of the ribbons was considerably smaller than that seen earlier in the day. Now that the suspense was ended, fewer folk cared to view the formality of the ribbon ceremony. Once again, as they had on the first day, the judges opened the velvet hangings, rather the worse for the rain that had fallen on them during the night, to display the box of ribbons. Lined up on each side of the booth and facing the crowd, they were initially bewildered by the gasps and cries of consternation.

"Where are the ribbons?"

"Someone's stolen the ribbons!"

The judges turned to where the large wooden box should rest and saw nothing but an empty shelf!

"Oh, good God, Phineas has done it!"

"Whatever do you mean, Mrs. Fayerweather?" Miss Woodland asked.

"What is the meaning of this?" Mr. Frobisher demanded and was seconded by each of the outraged judges.

Ann Blaine, who was not any more pleased with this Summer's results than she was with those of any other year, screamed at the crowd. "Whoever has perpetrated this infantile joke had better confess now, before we call in the magistrate."

"Yes," agreed Tabitha Hatchton, who much to her consternation had to agree with her fellow judge. "Does anyone know anything about this?"

There were rumblings, giggles and grumblings, some folks finding humor in the situation, others infuriated by it. Captain Beddoes and Mrs. Pike walked over to Charlotte and were soon joined by Rupert, Miss Hastings, and the senior Nashes.

"Good heavens," Sally asked, "do you think Mr. Norwell actually *did* it?"

"Oh, certainly Phineas could not have been so foolish?" Henrietta Pike insisted.

Rupert shook his head. "I don't know. Could he have recovered sufficiently last night, but still been so foxed that he sneaked out and stole them?"

Others nearby overhead these remarks, and soon, half the crowd believed that Phineas Norwell had made off with the ribbons. That gentleman had only now arrived at the green, having had to coax an aching head into settling still on his shoulders before he felt fit to leave the cottage. He looked at his brother, Arnold, who glared back as if he would throttle him.

"Never tell me you actually did it, Phineas."

"Did what?"

"You know what."

"I don't. I've only just got here and . . ." While he was speaking, Phineas had looked up for the first time at the bare table, where the ribbon box ought to lay. He slapped his forehead. "Good God, did Trent . . . ?"

"No, it was never me, Mr. Norwell. And glad I am to say it, now I see how testy this crowd can be. That leaves you as the most likely suspect. At least that's what these good people think." He gestured with a grin at the people whispering and nodding at them. Some of them were beginning to move in their direction.

"Me?" squeaked Phineas. "I never did! Honest!" He gave a rather panicked look at the people coming closer. "I was asleep in my bed all night. Just ask my brother! Go ahead, Arnold. Tell them!"

"And how should I know whether you left your bed or not, you clunch? I was asleep myself in my own room."

"Arnold!"

"Come on, Norwell, out with it," one man shouted. "Where did you stash the ribbons?"

"Yes, tell us!"

"I don't have them, I keep telling you! I swear, Arnold, I shall never touch another drop of mead, not if my very life depends upon it!"

"What is all the fuss about? Does no one here have an ounce of patience?"

As one, the crowd turned to see Mrs. Derwent and

her husband, holding between them the lost box of ribbons.

"Thank heaven," Pansy Shore sighed.

"What are you doing with those ribbons?" demanded Mr. Frobisher, and he was echoed by half the people present.

"Well, it rained last night, didn't it?" Mrs. Derwent explained loftily. "If the ribbons had remained here, the rain would have come right through the velvet curtain and ruined them. So Horace and I came down here—*in the pouring rain, I might add*—to bring them home for the night. And lucky that we did," she added caustically, "because, apparently, no one else gave the matter a bit of thought!"

There being no argument against this, people began to express their gratitude for the Derwents' selfless actions. It was left to Mr. Frobisher to point out that, had they returned the box more promptly, all of the commotion could have been avoided. Mr. Derwent became a bit discomfited at this.

"Well, I do concede that things got just a bit ahead of the missus and me this morning. . . ."

"Don't you dare to apologize for *me*, Ralph. And as for *you*, Norton Frobisher"—she turned on the judge—"your nose is just out of joint because you relinquished your responsibility as senior judge!"

"Well, I never . . ."

"Now, now"—Thornton Ellis tried to turn folks' attention to the intended matter at hand—"the important thing is we have the ribbons back. And now we can get back to the business of giving them out, which is why we are all here after all!"

"That's right! Let's get on with it!"

The awarding of the ribbons was almost dull in comparison to what had preceded it. Serena Wood-

land looked around hopefully for a sign of Mr. Goodspeed, but she was disappointed. She held up well,
nevertheless, and was applauded heartily by her old
friends in Great Tipton and her new ones in Edenshade, who, although they were sorry to see their
vicar lose, found they quite liked Miss Woodland and
her direct ways.

Many of the Visitors from Great Tipton were very
full of themselves after winning so many of the so-
called important categories in this Summer's contest
and eager to extend their success. Since, simultaneously, some Edenshaders were feeling less than
pleased with their results, it was not surprising that
more than one scuffle broke out in the village that
afternoon. None of it amounted to much, however,
until two of the men of the harp-dropping incident
from the previous Summer drank too much ale and
decided that Edenshaders were enjoying the day a
great deal more than they should, considering all their
losses.

The Foxton brothers and Tommy and Paul were
wending their way around the green and along the
riverbank, and Ambrose was maneuvering along behind on his stilts and delighting children old and
young. One grudging Tiptoner nudged his companion and nodded his head in Ambrose's direction.

"Bloody fool, isn't he, Gus? Buzzing around like
some tall, scrawny bumblebee."

"He is. *I* don't know what all the fuss is about anyway. There's probably some trick to making those
things work. He just makes it look difficult, that's all."
He grinned. "Let's send the bee back to his hive,
shall we, Ned?"

They ambled through the happy crowd of people,
who were nibbling fruit and sausage rolls and candy.

Once behind their unsuspecting prey, Gus pretended to stumble, falling against one of the stilts and cata-pulting poor Ambrose off the make-believe legs, through the air, and into the river, where he landed with a loud splash. Ned and Gus doubled over with laughter as Ambrose surfaced. His striped bee cos-tume had filled with water, making the man look, for the first time, like the plump bumblebee he pre-tended to be. His beautiful *papier-mâché* antennae hung, ruined, around his ears, making him look all the more ridiculous.

A couple of Edenshaders saw what had happened and remembered the men from the previous Sum-mer's musical debacle.

"Whoa, look out there," one shouted. "This one was in the middle of the fuss last year, I'd swear it."

"I believe you're right," Ronald Foxton said an-grily. Then he put down his fiddle and thrust his fist into Gus's jaw.

Silas Trent and Mr. Dillard waded into the water to help Ambrose, whose costume was weighing him down. Ronald's brother, Dexter, stood by to lend a hand, if needed, and intercepted Ned, who was run-ning to his friend's aid.

"All right now, that'll do. Isn't it enough that you two have spoiled the little ones' fun? I saw what you did, you know, and—"

Dexter suddenly found himself being pushed to-ward the shore, where Ned, much the larger of the two, picked him up and threw him into the river, concertina and all. Unfortunately, Ambrose and his would-be rescuers, who were, at the same moment, approaching the shore, were in Dexter's path, and all of them, poor Ambrose included, ended up mo-mentarily submerged. The air in the concertina kept it from sinking, but it was ruined nonetheless. Dexter staggered to his feet and managed to snatch the instrument before it floated away, but it wheezed and screeched painfully in his hands. He glared at his opponent, who laughed at him from the shore. Then he waded out to retaliate.

Lowell Goodspeed had returned to the green a short while before, intending to find Miss Woodland and throw himself on her mercy. The raised voices brought him and Fortune to the riverbank, where he was shocked at the spectacle that greeted him. Gus and Ronald Foxton were engaged in an ungainly tussle on the grass, and Ned rushed forward to challenge Dexter as he emerged from the water. A growing crowd cheered—some for the Tiptoners, others for the Edenshaders. The vicar was amazed at the fray and, putting himself between Dexter and Ned, called out to all of the men to stop their foolishness and behave like adults.

All of the participants in the dustup were actually decent, God-fearing men who, normally, would not knowingly harm any living creature. It happened, however, that on his way to the river's edge, Ned had built up a good amount of momentum with an added kick from the downward slope of the bank. Thus, Lowell Goodspeed's well-meant intervention could not have been more badly timed, for Ned was unable to stop and he ran into Goodspeed so hard that the vicar found himself sitting down in the shallow water and feeling very foolish indeed.

Miss Woodland, who had watched for some minutes from a few yards down the green, now flew to Goodspeed and knelt at his side, heedless of the water soaking her skirt and ruining her shoes.

"Lowell! Are you hurt?"

Fortune advanced slowly toward Ned, his teeth bared, and the man trembled.

"It's all right, Fortune. Come here, boy," the vicar called. The dog obeyed his master, who evidently was not in need of his protection after all. A silly smile lit Goodspeed's face. "No, my dearest Serena, I am not hurt, but I deserve to be for the selfish, childish way that I behaved this morning. Can you ever forgive me?"

She smiled sweetly back at him. "Come, Lowell. Let's get you to the vicarage so that you can change your clothes and rest a bit. I expect you to dance every dance with me tonight and then we can see the fireworks and *then* I shall tell you if I forgive you."

"I think that you must already know that I hold you in the very highest regard . . . Charlotte. Please say that you will entertain my suit, for if you will consent to be my wife, I will be the happiest of men."

The sun had begun to slip toward the horizon, and for the moment and in this space, there was relative quiet and privacy. But the thick tree limb that curved and stretched just two feet from the ground proved to be an uncomfortable chair for the few minutes Charlotte had spent on it while Captain Beddoes spoke the words that would commit him to a very different kind of life for the rest of his days. She had tried to stop him when he first began his speech, but she quickly realized that to do so would be rude in the extreme. And so, she had sat quietly, if uncomfortably, both physically and emotionally, while he spoke of her beauty, sweet nature, kindness, and wit, wishing only that he would finish so that she could say what she felt she must.

At length, he finished and she gave a little smile. Not since Edmund Kean, she imagined, had a man so out of love with a woman given such a credible impression of one infatuated. When she was a slip of a girl, Charlotte had sometimes daydreamed of being such an Incomparable that she would turn down suitor after suitor, and she always supposed that it must be done with the greatest care and tact so as to inflict as little pain and embarrassment as possible on the gentleman in question. But now, faced with the situation, she could barely keep from smiling as she delivered what she knew must be the most welcome reply.

"Captain Beddoes, you do me a very great honor," she began in the conventional way. "I must say that any lady who is the recipient of your offer must consider herself to be the happiest and most fortunate of women." Captain Beddoes was looking puzzled, the duration of this preamble being rather longer than he had been led to expect was the norm. "But I am very much afraid that I have, unknowingly I promise you, led you to believe that I felt more, indeed, expected more, from you than was the case." Charlotte could not help it. She shifted in the seat and tried, as unobtrusively as possible, to restore the circulation to her right foot, since this did not appear to be an appropriate time to suggest that they move. "I am certain that, should I wish to remarry, you are the gentleman whose affections I should wish to engage. As it is . . . I can only ask that you try to forgive any pain that I cause when, with all humility, I decline your kind offer."

That was a mouthful, she knew, and only hoped that she had not overdone it, but she felt she had to preserve face for both of them. Captain Beddoes was of a like mind. His previous performance of a man in love he now outdid as he enacted the part of the disappointed suitor. "Mrs. Fayerweather—Charlotte—may I not hope that you will change your mind?"

"Ah, Captain Beddoes. Alexander. How I wish that I had sense enough to do so! But, no. You see, I am quite happy in my single state, set in my ways, as it were. But I shall look forward to hearing that you have found a woman worthy of your affections and who will leap at the opportunity to be your wife." She smiled, suspecting that this would come to pass much sooner than he would wish her to think.

"You are all that is good, Charlotte." He looked at her closely and, she thought, with a great deal more perception than she had expected. "*All* that is good. Although . . . I think you may soon wish to exchange your single state for a wedded one, albeit to a man much more fortunate than I." He kissed her hand and she flushed. "You will save me a dance, at least, will you not?"

She laughed. "Alexander, something tells me that your dances will all be spoken for!"

After long days—and for some, weeks—of suspense and hard work, people welcomed the closing festivities of Flower Week. The brass band was just the right sort of entertainment, its loud and joyous music inviting, almost compelling, everyone to get up and dance. Shortly after the dancing had commenced, the lanterns were lit in the tree branches and flambeaux were staked in the soft earth and set afire. Flickering shapes grew more defined but no less strange as the sky darkened.

Lowell Goodspeed, refreshed from his trip to the vicarage, led Miss Woodland through the lively pace of reel after reel, never seeming to tire. Georgina Hastings sailed gracefully by beside Benjamin Nashe.

"It is wonderful to see Lowell so happy, isn't it, Charlotte?" Rupert asked.

Charlotte smiled in agreement. "Yes. You know, he was devastated when Randolph was killed. Such a loss."

He looked at her, a bit startled. "Of course, you would have known him. I hadn't thought."

She nodded. "I did and liked him immensely. He was so full of life. For a while, I feared that the vicar would be done in by his nephew's death." She looked at him and smiled a little. "I suspect his correspondence with you helped a great deal to keep the poor man sane."

He shrugged. "It helped to keep both of us sane, my dear. I cannot, would not, tell you of the horrors I have witnessed on the Continent." His face darkened. "But always, no matter the comradeship, no matter your rank, there is the overwhelming loneliness and a constant awareness of your own vulnerability. Men and beasts lie dead and dying all around you, screaming in pain, and you come to . . . somehow . . . accept it; otherwise, I suppose, we *would* all go mad. And then you see a friend half blown apart by an artillery shell—sorry, my dear, but there it is— and at first, you can think of nothing but saving your own damned skin."

"But that is quite understandable, surely?"

He went on almost as if he had not heard. "That is only one of the unspeakable obscenities of the whole filthy business. Panic bred from fear for your own life. It is amazing how, on one hand, you guard it, or try to, with a fierceness you would not have believed possible and, on the other, wager it again

and again and again for a cause you are not even
certain you believe in. You cannot imagine the terror
unless you've . . . My God, Charlotte, forgive me.
How could I tell you of such things?"

"My dear Rupert, have you ever told anyone else?"
she asked softly.

"No."

"Well then."

He reached out to touch her cheek tenderly.

"Ah, Mrs. Fayerweather, I see you have been keeping Rupert company while I have been engaged. How
kind."

So, it was "Rupert" now, was it? "As you see, Miss
Hastings. But I leave him to you, now that you are
back. Ah, Benjamin, did you come to ask me to
dance?" The man had just restored Georgina to Rupert and looked winded, but it could not be helped.
She had to make a graceful escape.

"It would be my pleasure, Charlotte."

Later, she lay on a blanket beside Sally and Benjamin, who were keeping one eye each on the fireworks booming overhead and the other on Winston,
who shared a nearby blanket with Violet. Violet's
mother did not seem especially interested in watching
the young people. There was a loud pop and a spray
of brilliant light followed by cries of appreciation.

"Sally, don't you think we should go over there?
Look! I am telling you he is sitting closer to her now
than he was five minutes ago. Before we know it,
they'll be—"

His wife patted his hand and laughed. "Oh, Ben,
do calm yourself! I think I am the one who is expected to be the mother hen!" He tugged playfully
at one of her corkscrew curls. "Honestly, dear, what
harm can they get into in this crowd?"

In fact, both sides of the riverbank were packed with Edenshaders and Tiptoners alike, all gathered to see the pyrotechnic display that was so rare here in the country. Charlotte lay back on her elbows and looked lazily about her as her two friends quibbled genially about their son and his behavior. The vicar, Miss Woodland, and Fortune were several yards away, all three of them oblivious to the beautiful explosions overhead. Fortune's head rested on Mr. Goodspeed's lap, while that gentleman held his lady's hand and laughed at something she said.

Her gaze wandered, past Mrs. Dunstable, being soothed by her devoted husband, the Trents and the Foxton brothers, none the worse for their earlier brawling, and stopped at Mrs. Ruffle and Mr. Dillard. The two were holding hands and whispering in one another's ears—as if anyone could have heard a word they uttered—just like any young engaged couple. Charlotte sighed. Tomorrow she must begin thinking about what to wear to their wedding and what to give them as a gift. All of this was beginning to make her feel decidedly out of place.

There were two loud pops in quick succession and then enough resulting light to momentarily illuminate the crowd scattered beside the river. The loud giggling of some young girls drew her attention to the left, where she saw Captain Beddoes lean over and place a tender kiss on Mrs. Pike's waiting lips. *Well,* she thought wryly, *he wasted even less time than I thought he would!* A soft laugh, heard during a brief lull in the display, made her turn in time to see Benjamin kissing the back of his wife's neck. *Oh, for pity's sake!* She waited until the moment had passed and told them that she was going home to tend to a terrible headache.

It was difficult to negotiate through the crowd in the dark and she stumbled more than once. The last couple she saw just before reaching the lane was Rupert and Miss Hastings holding hands and looking at the sky, their heads together.

"Mrs. Fayerweather, may I see you home? You should not be out here alone at this hour, you know."

It was Jeremy Pike. She did not mention to him that she had felt just as alone by the river.

"How very thoughtful of you. But do you not care to stay for the rest of the fireworks, Jeremy?"

He shook his head. "To say the truth, I am not much interested in them, Mrs. Fayerweather."

She found this rather surprising, considering that pyrotechnic displays were, to say the least, unusual in their little valley.

"I suppose they are not to everyone's taste," was all Charlotte said in reply.

Jeremy apparently did not care to dispute the point, and for a while, they walked on in silence except for the distant, dulled percussion of the remaining fireworks.

"And you do not stay either, Mrs. Fayerweather. Am I to infer that you are as unimpressed as I?" His lips twisted in self-mockery. He seemed to be in a quite peculiar mood.

"No, Jeremy," she corrected, "you may infer that I have the headache."

"Ah." He nodded. "I shall not tax you with idle conversation then."

"I would not generally describe your conversation as idle, and anyway the diversion must only do my poor head some good. So please do not hesitate on my account. Talk, if you like."

He chuckled, then was silent for a few moments. At length, he said, "You knew my Beth, did you not?"

"Happily I did."

Jeremy smiled and stooped to pick up a program someone had carelessly dropped on the path the day before. "I loved her very much."

Charlotte kept silent and watched him. Everyone knew how Jeremy had cared for his wife. For a man who had gone to the altar with virtual indifference, Jeremy Pike had quickly fallen deeply in love with his wife. He had doted on her and taken her sudden demise badly. That was when Henrietta had taken Jaspar and gone to live with her oldest son—for he refused to leave "Beth's house"—and say what you would about his mother, she had done much to get him through his long period of grieving. *What will happen now,* Charlotte wondered, *if Mrs. Pike marries Alex, as I believe she will? Jeremy will be on his own—and glad of it, I make no doubt—but a bit lonely nonetheless.*

"It has been more than two years since she left us. . . ." He stopped.

"Two years is a very long time to mourn, Jeremy. Do you still grieve for her?" she asked gently.

"Not to say grieve, exactly, Mrs. Fayerweather. . . ."

"Please, Charlotte."

He smiled and nodded his acknowledgment. "No, I cannot say that I still feel that constant, profound loss. I miss her still, but now when I think of her, as I often do, I can smile."

"Mmm."

"I do not want to forget her, Charlotte. And I do not wish to replace her," he said forcefully, as if he were arguing a case.

"Surely not. Whyever should you, Jeremy?"

He paused once more. "Is it possible—is it *right*—to

love two people, Charlotte? How can I wish to marry another woman when I still miss my Beth, while I still treasure her memory?"

"Jeremy . . . Jeremy, if you love another, do you honestly believe that Beth would want you to spend the rest of your life alone? I knew her and I cannot believe she would be so unkind to you."

They had reached her cottage and sat on the bench around the old hawthorn tree. He leaned back against the trunk and, sighing, shut his eyes.

"How can I be sure?"

"I am afraid that I cannot answer that. But I do believe that if you love someone . . ." Charlotte could not continue. She could not be a hypocrite and tell him that he must reach out and take the love he wanted while he had the chance to do so. "I just believe that you are entitled to be happy, Jeremy. This woman, whoever she is, if you love her, be glad and for heaven's sake, tell her!"

"But I do not think that she . . . She feels nothing for me—well very little. I can say nothing to her."

It was unlike Jeremy to be so unsure and it made Charlotte smile.

"Um, what do you think of Georgina Hastings, Charlotte?"

So it was that way, was it? "Well, Jeremy, she is, I think, a pretty young woman, bright—oh! and talented—she plays the pianoforte like an angel." She did not say anything about Miss Hastings's voice, for judging by the smitten look on his face, Jeremy would think she sang like a seraph as well.

"She appears to be very taken with Mr. Frost. And he with her." Charlotte did not reply. "You are his friend, Charlotte. Dare I ask you if there is already an understanding between them? Do you know?"

"To my knowledge, there is not. But I must tell you, and I think this can come as no surprise, that I live in daily expectation of an announcement in that regard." Oh, why could he not have chosen someone like Violet Beardsley or Joan Allerdyce, both lovely, biddable girls who would make him a perfect wife? Well, perhaps not Violet, she remembered, for Mr. Goodspeed was sure to be reading *those* banns at any moment.

He had risen from the bench and was pacing around the tree. "Charlotte, I have to have her."

She looked at him and blinked. "Jeremy? Oh, dear, I am afraid it is a little late in the day. I do not want to see you disappointed." He did not sound at all like the Jeremy Pike she knew.

He stopped in his tracks and looked at her with something like surprise written on his handsome face. Then he smiled. "Charlotte, I do not plan to be disappointed."

"I see. Well, how—if one may ask—do you intend to win her?" She knew full well that, in his eyes at least, she had no business to ask him such a question. But then Jeremy was quite unaware of her personal interest in his success.

"I haven't the vaguest idea."

The fact that he was still smiling when he departed a few minutes later did nothing to encourage her. The words "grinning like an idiot" seemed to her appropriate in the circumstance and she let the cottage door slam to emphasize her disgust at having allowed her hopes to rise even for a moment.

Twelve

Charlotte rose late the next couple of mornings, there not being anything particular to get up for. As it was, she found herself exhausted despite the extra sleep and in no mood to receive callers. And so she had advised Mrs. Ruffle. Therefore, when she heard a rap at the cottage door, as she sat in her parlor sketching two days after her conversation with Jeremy Pike, she did not even put up a hand to see that her hair was in place or straighten the tucker at her bosom. And when Mrs. Ruffle scratched at the door to announce herself, she looked up not expecting her to say, "You have a visitor, Mrs. Fayerweather."

Exasperated, she put down her pencil and glowered at the housekeeper. "Mrs. Ruffle, I did say that I am not at home this afternoon."

Mrs. Ruffle raised her brows to a height never seen before in Charlotte's parlor. "And don't I know that? Only *some* people," she spoke in an undertone, "can't take a polite hint like that. Anyway, I thought you might want to see her."

Before she quite finished these words, poor Mrs. Ruffle was virtually pushed aside as Georgina Hastings came through the doorway, content to wait no longer in the hall.

"Good day, Mrs. Fayerweather. I would like a word, if I may."

Mrs. Ruffle looked from one to the other.

"Well, I have never . . ."

"That is quite all right, Mrs. Ruffle."

"Yes, well, I'll be in the kitchen, ma'am." She made this sound as if her employer might feel free to call on her for assistance in removing the recently arrived baggage from the premises.

"Thank you. Do sit down, Miss Hastings." And then, since clearly her guest had no intention of mixing her purpose with politeness, she asked "What is it you wish to speak with me about?"

Miss Hastings placed her parasol on the floor beside her chair and arranged her skirt as if girding herself for battle. She looked more charming than ever in mint green muslin with a lush grass green satin sash tied beneath her bosom. Charlotte looked her in the eye and straightened in her chair, more than ready to do battle, for her dismal mood this morning had prompted her to dress in one of her favorite frocks, a deep rose mull banded at the hem and sleeves with pale pink lace.

"I wish to discuss Rupert, Mr. Frost." A little ridiculous this convention was since both women addressed him by his given name.

"Oh?"

"Yes. I—I want you to leave him alone."

"Pardon me?"

"Oh, Mrs. Fayerweather, do not play the goose cap with me. I see your game."

"Have you gone mad? What on earth are you talking about? I have not been near Mr. Fr—*Rupert.*"

Miss Hastings went bright pink. "Now *that* won't fadge, Mrs. Fayerweather. Not at all!" Miss Hastings evidently had taken more than one lesson in London cant from Hortense Cavendish, and Charlotte had to resist an urge to smile, despite the circumstances. "I *saw* you with him. Just last night," she explained as if to a stubborn child. "You must remember."

"You cannot be serious!" But it was clear that her guest was very serious indeed. Georgina's chin went up and her lips pursed with indignation. "This is because Rupert and I talked last night? Good heavens, Miss Hastings, he and I have known one another forever, as you are aware. Can he not simply *talk* to someone, an old friend, without its arousing your temper?"

But even as she spoke the words, Charlotte recalled the closeness of that conversation—one she somehow felt he would never have with Georgina Hastings—and the way he had touched her cheek. She suspected that the silly woman had not seen that; the good Lord only knew what sort of Cheltenham tragedy she would enact if she had! Ever since she realized that Rupert probably would offer for Miss Hastings, Charlotte had been trying to like the other woman—if Rupert married her, she could hardly spend the rest of her days hating the creature—but just at the moment, she found her task almost impossible.

"Mrs. Fayerweather, you may have a *tendre* for Rupert, and he may speak *constantly* about 'Charlotte this' and 'Charlotte that,' but *I* love him! You cannot have him!"

Charlotte could not put her finger on it, but there was something other than love in Georgina's voice— something much more like panic than passion.

"And what makes you think that I want him, my

dear?" Charlotte's brows were raised in haughty question.

"Well, apart from the fact that he is handsome and good and *very, very* rich, you must want him now that you and cousin Alexander are not to make a match of it." Even the outspoken Georgina Hastings clapped her hand to her mouth and blushed. "Oh, my, I did not mean to . . ."

Charlotte lifted a hand. "Do not apologize, Miss Hastings."

Nettled at being on the defensive, even if she had put herself there, Georgina allowed herself a little smirk. "Anyway, he is going to propose to me and there is nothing that you can do about it."

"Are you so certain?"

"I am."

"Then why in the world are you here?"

"Because . . . because . . ."

"Because you are not so sure, are you, Miss Hastings?"

The look Charlotte received was full of fear. Georgina twisted the reticule in her hands and jumped up from her chair. What was all of this about?

"Are you so certain of yourself? So certain that *you* love *him?*" Charlotte asked.

Her guest had stepped to the open window to breathe in the fresh air, but now she turned around quickly and glared at Charlotte as if she were speaking the greatest blasphemy. "Am I certain that I love him? How can you ask such a question? How could I feel otherwise? Haven't I already told you of his wonderful qualities—his wealth, his looks. Of course I love him! And I *will* have him!"

Miss Hastings stormed out of the room, quite forgetting the parasol on the carpet, and a moment later, Charlotte could see her stomping down the path in a rage. She sat back on the settee. *Whew,* she thought, *I have never seen such a tempest in a teapot! Poor Rupert! And lucky Jeremy, for clearly he is bound to be unsuccessful in his suit; but if he only knew how fortunate he is to lose the silly creature!*

She went to the kitchen for something to drink and found Mrs. Ruffle standing at the window, her hands on her hips, watching Miss Hastings's abrupt departure. She turned to her employer and shook her head.

"And isn't *that* one no better than she should be?"

Charlotte laughed. "Mrs. Ruffle, something tells me that you know exactly what we said to one another. You were listening, weren't you?"

"Mrs. Fayerweather! As if I would! I *happened* to be dusting that old cabinet by the stairs and who could *help* but hear?"

"And since when do you do the dusting, please tell me?" Charlotte teased. "Mrs. Ruffle, you are incorrigible!"

The housekeeper sniffed with disdain. "Well, I had to be sure what she was about. You cannot be too careful these days, you know, not even way out here in the country. For all I knew, she might have tried to strangle you over Mr. Frost and that's a fact."

Charlotte sat down at the scrubbed kitchen table and laughed until tears fell from her eyes. "You have been reading too many of those silly novels. Did you suppose she had a dagger hidden in her skirt? Or a hatchet stuffed in her reticule? Come to that, what would you have done if she had?" But she saw that she was hurting the other woman's feelings. She rose and put an arm around her housekeeper's shoulders. "But I do thank you for the thought, Mrs. Ruffle.

Together we should have overpowered her—I am
convinced of it."

The older woman chuckled. "All right, that'll do,
won't it? But, um, tell me, ma'am. Do you think Mr.
Frost is going to offer for her?"

"Well I should think so, Mrs. Ruffle. Certainly he
has been courting her as if he would these past
weeks." She took her glass and began to walk from
the room. The housekeeper followed.

"And so that is that then?"

"What do you mean?" Charlotte resumed her seat
in the parlor.

"I mean, what will you do then?"

"Pardon?" Her tone was lofty.

Mrs. Ruffle sat down opposite her employer.
"Never mind that. Listen to me, lovey. I've done for
you for how many years is it now?" She did not bother
to wait for an answer. "And in all that time, I've never
put my nose where it didn't belong. . . ."

Charlotte choked on her lemonade.

"Well, hardly ever. But never mind that. *This* is
much more important than caps and hair and
gowns."

"Mrs. Ruffle . . ."

"Tut! Let me finish, ma'am, please. I thought you
were going to tie up with Captain Beddoes. He was
not what I would have wished for you, but the Lord
knows he's a good man and would have treated you
right. There's many that don't, you know. But now,
I hear, *from Louise Barclay*, don't you know, that he's
going to marry Henrietta Pike—and isn't *that* enough
to keep the tabbies talking all next Winter?—not you.
Perhaps you will pardon me for feeling a bit miffed
that the vicar's housekeeper knows more about my
own household than *I* do!" She waved a hand dismis-

sively. "But that is not important. Mrs. Pike is a fine woman and I am sure that I wish her well, but what about you, I ask myself?"

"Me? I shall be quite fine, I promise you."

"Will you then?" Charlotte nodded emphatically. "I am leaving soon, you will remember." The good-hearted woman could not help but weaken her argument by rushing to add, "Of course we shall only be at—well, very nearby. And you know, don't you, that you'll be welcome anytime. Mr. Dillard says the same." Charlotte thanked her solemnly. "Still, it bothers me to leave you on your own now that the captain and Mrs. Pike are to wed. And the vicar and Miss Woodland will announce their engagement any day now. And it looks very like that Nashe boy will make a match of it with Violet Beardsley. Well, the sooner the better. Young blood is hot blood, as they say. . . ."

"Mrs. Ruffle, I am aware of the matrimonial goings-on in our little village."

"Yes, dear, that is the point. The whole village is smelling of April and May and you are sitting here with your sketching block drawing that stupid vase of lilies!"

"Oh, very well, Mrs. Ruffle, if it will make you happy, I shall go out for a walk. At least outside I shall have some peace." She got up and nearly tripped over Georgina's parasol. "I'll return this to the charming Miss Hastings while I am gone."

Mrs. Ruffle would not argue with anything that brought Charlotte into contact with Rupert, so she held her tongue.

No one was at home to receive her at Sherbourne Place, so she left the parasol with the message to return it to Miss Hastings. She stopped outside, hoping to see Mr. Dillard, and spent a pleasant and altogether *un*trying half hour chatting with him about the gardens and his coming nuptials.

Strolling by the river, she heard someone call her name and looked up to see Lowell Goodspeed and Fortune coming toward her in the vicar's carriage.

"Ho, Mrs. Fayerweather. We are going to call on Serena, Miss Woodland. Would you care to join us?" Fortune gave a *woof* to second the invitation, which she happily accepted.

Miss Woodland was happy to extend her hospitality to an unexpected guest. As they enjoyed a fine tea, the vicar took Miss Woodland's hand and they both smiled at Charlotte.

"My dear Mrs. Fayerweather, I am most pleased to inform you that Miss Woodland and I are to be married." His face was flushed with happiness and she leapt from her chair to put her arms about his neck and kiss his cheek.

"Oh, how splendid!" She turned to her hostess. "Miss Woodland!"

That lady extended her arms and hugged her guest. "I am so happy! Will you stand up with me at my wedding? I shall be a nervous wreck, I am convinced."

"I would be honored."

A sleek, very dark brown cat suddenly jumped into Serena's lap and reached up to touch her chin with a dainty velvet paw.

"Lucky, where did you come from? Mrs. Fayerweather, please meet Lucky, who shares this cottage with me."

The cat, clearly a creature impressed with his good looks and winning charm, slid to the floor and rubbed back and forth against Charlotte's legs. She picked him up and sat down again.

"And what of the cottage?" she asked, looking about her. "It is as lovely inside as it is out."

"Yes, I shall miss it a great deal. I shall sell it—it should not be difficult to find a good buyer who likes roses." She grimaced at her intended. "Anyway, I shall be quite busy in the vicarage rose garden improving things there!"

Mr. Goodspeed roared with laughter and her grin broadened. "Well, perhaps, we can somehow contrive to work there together," he teased her.

"When will the wedding take place?"

"We are not quite sure yet. As I was saying to Rupert this morning—I told him our wonderful news when I was out with Fortune and he was out for a constitutional—I do not know who will marry us. After all, I am the vicar! Very likely I shall ask my old friend from Trimble-Over-Water, but I don't know how soon he will be able to perform the ceremony. But we can be patient, can't we, my dear?"

By the time that Miss Hastings returned to Sherbourne Place, Rupert had left with Benjamin for a hike in the valley; Sally was trying on hats at Mrs. Robards's shop, which boasted that it could outfit a lady from head to toe; Alexander was lunching with Mrs. Pike; and Winston was, doubtless, off heaven knew where with Violet Beardsley.

She decided to feed the ducks on the river, but the near side soon became too warm. The stepping-stones looked safe enough, and she lifted her skirt above her ankles and began to cross. But the water level rose toward the middle, and the smooth leather of her soles gave her no purchase on the stones, which, in this spot, were wet and slippery. She felt herself begin to topple and tried to regain her balance, her napkin of bread scraps flying into the air and landing on the grass and in the water, where the ducks feasted, quacking loudly and ignoring her plight.

"Oh! Oh no!" *Splash!* Georgina landed facedown in the river, drenching her entire front but not much else, owing to the relative shallowness of the water. Unfortunately, in trying to get up, her slippers betrayed her once again, and halfway up, she fell again, this time on her bottom, thus managing to soak herself completely. She sat down disconsolately in the river and began to weep for half a dozen reasons, only one of which she could have explained even to herself. As she tried to rise yet again, her wet, heavy skirt hobbled her and she was in danger of falling yet again.

Suddenly, she was seized by a pair of strong arms and carried to the riverbank and deposited on the dry grass in the shade of a tree. Her rescuer smiled and sat down beside her, rather wet himself from the knees down. She removed her ruined bonnet and flung it on the grass and pushed her wet, muddy hair from her face.

"Mr. Pike!"

"Yes, Miss Hastings. I am pleased that you remember me."

"Thank you for helping me, sir. I should have been there the better part of the afternoon, but for you. You are very gallant."

"And you are too kind, ma'am. You are not hurt in any way, are you?" She assured him that she was not. "Did you slip on the stepping-stones? They can be treacherous for all they look so safe."

She nodded. "I was feeding the ducks. I like ducks."

"So do I."

"Only I had not thought to become one of them," she laughed. "Er, I suppose I ought to get home." Georgina could not remember a time when she had not been conscious of her appearance, especially in the company of a man, but he had made her forget.

"Oh, my, yes, you should before you catch cold. You are able to walk?" he asked, helping her to her feet.

"Yes, thank you."

"I should accompany you, however—just in case you feel a bit faint as you go on."

"You are most considerate, sir. Thank you."

Jeremy removed his jacket and placed it around Georgina's shoulders. She looked up gratefully, for even the fitful Summer breeze was chilling in her sopping wet state.

"I hope that you do not take ill from your, um, adventure, Miss Hastings." He smiled. "Summer colds can be an awful nuisance and linger on long after the season for them has passed."

"Oh, I shall survive, sir. You needn't concern yourself, for I am disgustingly healthy!"

"I am glad to know it, ma'am."

The truth was that Jeremy still did not have any notion of how to follow through his rash statement to Charlotte. Now, faced with this serendipitous opportunity, he tried to think how best to take advantage of it; otherwise he knew he would berate himself later for losing such a chance. He glanced at her from the corner of his eye. She was terribly pretty—there was no doubt about that—even with her hair stuck in dripping strands on her neck and mud smudged on her face, hands, and clothes. Her lips looked even more kissable than Ellen Waring's, but kissing was all that Miss Waring ever inspired him to do. It was no more than natural, he realized, for a man to want to kiss a pretty woman, but he was caught by more than Miss Hastings's beauty.

He had seen her flirt with and cling to Mr. Frost and noticed her shoot daggers at any other woman who ventured near him. It was impossible to tell if she were genuinely attracted to the man or if she simply wanted to marry a fortune and was willing to suffer the man who came attached to it. Of course, few women would consider a lifetime with Rupert to be a penance, he knew. And if she did want his fortune, what did that say about Miss Hastings? He supposed that, in all candor, it said no more nor less than it did about half the population of England, who needed to marry money. And that did not mean that such people could not love at the same time, did it? Since Jeremy was quite well off himself, the young lady could do no worse in that respect if she married him instead of Rupert. And beneath her confident, bright demeanor, he sensed something like vulnerability. Jeremy wanted only to cherish her, to give her his love and protection.

"And you like ducks, you say, Miss Hastings?"

"Oh, yes, I do," she said eagerly, glad to help fill the gap of quiet.

"And other birds? Do you perhaps like other birds as well?"

"Yes, but I must confess that I know little about them, sir."

"But that is splendid!"

She blinked her confusion. "It is?" she asked doubtfully.

"Why, yes. Spring, of course, is the best season to look at birds, but even now there is much to see." He smiled at her puzzled expression. "We could ride out of town just a ways and walk through the fields and woods to watch the birds. I could tell you all I know about them—I've made a kind of informal study of birds all my life. You would enjoy it a great deal, I promise!" He nearly stumbled over his words with his eagerness and the now encouraging look on her face. "We could even take a picnic lunch!"

Georgina stopped and turned to face him, beaming. She clapped her hands with delight. "Oh, I should like that above all things, Mr. Pike. When do you think that we might go?"

He could hardly believe his good fortune. "Why not tomorrow? We . . ."

But her face had fallen with her recollection that she could hardly go bird-watching with another gentleman, no matter how kind and handsome he was, while she was supposed to be devoting herself to securing a proposal of marriage from Rupert. Furthermore, she was convinced that such a declaration was imminent.

"Oh, I am afraid I cannot, Mr. Pike."

He refused to acknowledge that this was a rejection, not just a postponement.

"Well, the day after then. Or Saturday or any day you choose, Miss Hastings."

She shook her head and resumed her pace on the lane. "No, sir. Do not ask it of me. I cannot. I shall be . . . engaged."

He blanched. "Engaged? What do you mean, Miss Hastings? Have you—that is, I realize it is not my place to inquire. . . . Has Mr. Frost . . ." He could not bring himself to say the words. "Are you to be married, ma'am?"

Georgina looked at him. How could she say that she hoped so? It would be unpardonably rude, and besides, of a sudden, she was no longer certain she wanted to be engaged to Rupert Frost.

"No," she replied.

"Well then . . ."

"No," she said again. "You are so kind, Mr. Pike. I am sorry that I cannot . . . I mean . . ."

"Miss Hastings—Georgina—do not send me away without any hope. I do appreciate that we have known one another for such a short time, but I . . ."

"Please, sir. I must get home."

"Good God, of course! What a selfish clod I am!"

Jeremy felt glummer after his encounter with Miss Hastings than he had before it. Now that he knew she did not have a dislike of him, that she in fact seemed to like him rather well, her steadfast devotion to catching Rupert Frost made him despair of ever winning her.

Most of the household had returned while Miss Hastings was out. Halfway up the stairs to her room, she met Sally, who gasped at her appearance.

"Good heavens, dear, whatever happened to you? What on earth have you been doing?"

"Feeding the ducks," the young woman wailed and dashed up the remaining steps as quickly as her still heavy skirts would permit.

"Feeding the . . . Oh, Margaret, please see to it that hot water is sent up immediately so that Miss Hastings can bathe," she called to a passing maid. Then she turned and went up the stairs. Feeding the ducks indeed.

She tapped on Georgina's door and entered. "Miss

Hastings? Ah, there you are. Here, let me help you, dear. A nice hot bath is what you need and the water will be up in a trice. Oh, dear, I am afraid your dress may be ruined. The Lord only knows what is in the mud besides mud, but whatever it is, it's all over the hem and I don't think it will come out. You, ah, didn't bother to retrieve your bonnet, I see. That bad was it?"

"Yes!" Georgina burst into tears and threw herself into Sally's arms.

"Oh, my! Don't carry on so, Georgina. It was only a hat, after all. You can buy another tomorrow, this afternoon, if you like."

She walked her to the bed and they both sat down. "Well, I am simply too cloth headed to be alive, for clearly you don't care a fig about the bonnet." She shook her head. "No, I did not think so. Well, I suppose it must be Rupert then, isn't it?" Georgina nodded. "I see. Now, now, chick, you mustn't worry. Rupert will make his offer. It just takes some men longer than others. I remember when Benjamin and I were courting, I thought he would never come to the point. . . ."

"But I don't *want* him to come to the point!"

Sally looked at her blankly. "Well now, you see, there you have me confused, because I was quite certain that you did, you know. And so were a good many other people."

"Well, I did not! That is, I *did*, but now I don't, if you understand me."

"Of course I do, Georgina. Ah good. Here is your bath! You are going to feel *so* much better soon." *And wait until Benjamin hears* this, *she thought.*

* * *

"Here, Daisy. Bring this parasol up to Miss Hastings's room. She left it at Hawthorn Cottage earlier and Mrs. Fayerweather returned it here for her."

Rupert paused on his way across the hall. What had Georgina been doing at Charlotte's house? He asked Georgina this question, although he did word it much more circumspectly, when he saw her late that afternoon in the library.

"I understand you called on Mrs. Fayerweather today."

Georgina had almost forgotten the errand that seemed so important just a few hours earlier. "Yes," she replied, giving him no room for further subtle query.

His curiosity got the better of him. "I had not realized that you and she were friends."

"We are most definitely *not.*"

"Then why did you visit her?"

"Good heavens, Rupert, must I explain my every move to you? And if you think that you may dictate to me where I may go and whom I may see and what I may wear and what I may say and what time I should get up and what time I should go to bed and . . . and whether I should feed the ducks—well you may just think again, Rupert Frost."

Rupert sat for some time in his library, trying to imagine what he had said to set her off.

That evening, Winston joined them for dinner or, as his mother put it, "So nice of you to put in an appearance, dear. I was saying only this morning that I rather *thought* we had a son, but your father insisted that, actually, we have just the two girls." His mother's eyes had a twinkle in them. Just.

"I trust your presence here *means* something, Winston. I am assuming that you have either finally offered for that girl or she's sent you packing!" his father half joked.

Winston smiled broadly at them. "I am happy to say it is the former. Violet has consented to marry me!"

"Congratulations, my boy!" His father pounded him on the shoulders.

"Oh, Winston," Sally sniffed. "What happy news! I do like Violet."

Rupert asked that a bottle of his best wine be brought up from the cellar.

"Ahem, Rupert," Captain Beddoes said. "Think you might want to hold off on that toast. It might be more economical to drink to *two* newly engaged couples instead of one!" Mrs. Pike, sitting across from him at the table, gazed at him fondly.

There were cries of joy and congratulations from around the table and the wine, when it arrived a moment later, was put to good use.

"Henrietta won't marry me until the Fall, because she says there is a great deal to plan." Captain Beddoes rolled his eyes to tease his intended. "So I hope that I may impose on your hospitality until then, Rupert."

"Of course, Alex. Very happy to oblige."

Rupert wondered what had happened between Alexander and Charlotte. He had thought they might marry, but apparently she had meant it when she said she preferred to remain single. As the company filed out to the drawing room to speak at length of weddings, Rupert gently drew Georgina aside.

Drawing her into an alcove for privacy, he tipped her chin up with his forefinger. "Georgina," he kissed her fingertips, "shall we join in their happiness? Will you marry me, my dear?"

The beautiful face that he had pictured would smile up at him at this moment instead crumpled into a frown of indignation.

"No!"

"No?"

"I do not wish to marry you, Rupert."

"Come, Georgina. Are you being coy? You are not still miffed about that silly business this afternoon are you?"

"Silly business, was it?" Then she laughed at herself a little. "Yes, it was, wasn't it? But the truth is, Rupert dear, that I cannot marry you because I do not love you. Oh, I am sorry—that is very harsh. Please know that I am honored by your proposal. And I do appreciate that I must have led you to think that I wanted to marry you, only . . . Well, I am afraid that I have hurt your feelings and I promise you that I do not mean to do so. Oh dear, can you forgive me, Rupert? Can we be friends still?"

He listened in silence, and when she finished, he began to laugh, and he did not stop for several minutes.

Thirteen

Fall

During the days leading up to Flower Week and for a short time thereafter, there had been a brief lull in Edenshade weddings. And then, things got back to normal.

Lowell Goodspeed's friend had been able to travel to Edenshade sooner than the vicar had expected, so he and his bride were settled in the vicarage before the Summer was out. Winston Nashe and Violet Beardsley married three Sundays later, when Goodspeed and Serena had returned from a honeymoon in London, where the Horticultural Society was high on their list of things to do. The Nashe twins had arrived in Edenshade and were resident at Sherbourne Place for more than two weeks before their brother's nuptials, by which time Rupert had begun to reassess his desire for children. Fortune had come to stay while the Goodspeeds were in London and his host was thinking how nice it would be to have several dogs about the place.

Eventually, Mrs. Pike managed to attend to all the little details of planning her marriage and actually *get* married, much to her fiancé's relief. By the time that Jeremy married Georgina Hastings, people in Edenshade were becoming positively jaded with the sacrament of marriage and anything to do with it. Even Mrs. Robards, the milliner, looked forward to the Winter when, she dearly hoped, no one would be shopping for a wedding dress.

Charlotte had looked high and low for a new housekeeper, but so far, had been unsuccessful. She had just left Mrs. Robards's establishment, having been told by a neighbor that the milliner's cousin twice removed and currently living in Great Tipton might be interested in the position. To her dismay, the woman's services had just been spoken for by Violet and Winston, who had bought Serena Woodland's cottage in Great Tipton and were in the process of moving in. The location was ideal for the newly wedded couple, offering both proximity to Violet's family and a ready-made beautiful garden.

Charlotte thought to herself that Violet and Winston probably needed an experienced housekeeper more than she did. In any event, the trip to Mrs. Robards's was not a complete loss, since she had to have the last fitting for the dress she would wear to Mrs. Ruffle's wedding next week. She turned in front of the glass in the shop admiring her reflection. The silk was an elegant violet, trimmed in deep rows of moss green ruching at the hem. The corsage was low, lower than she ever remembered wearing, but she wanted something just a bit daring, although she could not have said why, and this would do the trick.

"No, do not deliver it, Mrs. Robards. I'll just stop by for it on Wednesday. Thank you. Yes, it is lovely, and just as I pictured it. You have done a marvelous job, as you always do."

She kicked a pebble in the lane as she turned back

for Hawthorn Cottage. There was a lot of traffic at this time of day and she nodded and waved to several acquaintances along her way. Rupert was among them. They smiled and exchanged a few civilized pleasantries whenever they met and, she felt, were on their way to regaining their old friendship. And she was heartily glad of it because, even though she could count more friends today than ever before in her life, she often felt a loneliness she had not experienced since . . . well, not for many years. In any event, she was happy that they would be friends again.

Charlotte did not know what had prevented him from marrying Miss Hastings. He had not offered the information and she could hardly ask for it. She supposed that Jeremy, who was still looking happier than she had seen him in years, had worked the magic he had promised and won the young lady's heart away from Rupert. If Charlotte had been compelled to confess the secrets of her heart, she would have said that, when Miss Hastings and Jeremy Pike announced their betrothal, she had harbored for a time the hope that she and Rupert might now—at last—make a match of it. But alas, he had made no overtures toward her and she could not bring herself to make the first move. So their love affair had slipped from their grasp almost before either party knew that their chance had, miraculously, come round one more time.

For Rupert's part, he was settling into his role as Edenshade's nearest thing to lord of the manor and enjoying it thoroughly, no matter that without his guests his house was more silent, more lonely than he could ever have believed possible. He started once to walk to Charlotte's house, but turned back when he was almost there because he could not begin to think how to say to her what a complete fool he had been, and incidentally, would she have him anyway?

And so their relationship had remained at a stalemate all through the rest of the Summer and into the Fall, until today, Mrs. Ruffle's wedding day. The housekeeper was calmness itself. It was Charlotte who was nervous. She hugged Mrs. Ruffle and handed her a box wrapped in gold tissue and tied with ribbon.

"Dear Mrs. Ruffle. I wish I could say all that you have meant to me and how much I shall miss you."

"Oh, Mrs. Fayerweather, pearls! Oh, dear, you shouldn't have! They are the loveliest thing I have ever seen!" She held them out to the sunlight coming in the bedroom window. "Oh, help me put them on."

"You will wear them today? Oh, thank you. That pleases me very much!"

Charlotte sat in her pew, waiting for Mrs. Ruffle to arrive and the wedding ceremony to begin. She smiled to herself. It was just like the woman to be a wee bit late to whet everyone's appetite. She turned discreetly and nodded to Serena Woodland, who had told her just yesterday that she and the vicar were expecting a child in the Spring. Mrs. Robards smiled over at her, obviously on tenterhooks to see how the guests received her creation for one of her best clients. Over to her right, in the Pike family box, were Jeremy and Georgina. The latter, happy and secure now, was in danger of becoming a settled matron. The Pikes, too, would have a child and Charlotte could already predict that next year would be one of births following all those weddings!

Someone slid into the pew on her left and she turned.

"Rupert! Why aren't you in your own pew?" She frowned.

"Because it is lonely in my own pew, Charlotte, and I am very tired of being lonely." She blinked. "Aren't you tired of being lonely?"

"What makes you think I am, Rupert?"

"Charlotte, let's not play any more May games."

"Rupert, please lower your voice. And do stop thinking that you know how I feel."

"Very well," he whispered. "But if you just look around you, you will see that everyone is already looking this way."

She peeked and saw dozens of eyes staring at them. She flushed scarlet. "Oh, Rupert, it is because you are in my box instead of your own. Do go away!"

At that moment, Mrs. Ruffle made her appearance and their conversation had to wait until Mr. Goodspeed had concluded the ceremony and Mr. Dillard had kissed Mrs. Dillard. After they had paid their respects to the newly wedded couple, Rupert steered Charlotte to the church porch.

Taking her two hands in his, he drew her toward him. "Charlotte, my darling, we are two foolish people who keep finding one reason after another not to marry one another. Ah, yes, dearest, I know. I was a beast and you were quite right to throw me over. But I have not been a beast for years now. I am quite a nice fellow actually. Ask anyone in the village—they all like me. Won't you marry me?"

"I would not marry you if . . ."

"Uh, uh, Charlotte. We have played this scene before and look where it got us."

The corners of her lips turned up slightly. "Ah, yes, I know."

"There's my girl."

"Oh, Rupert, do you really think we should?"

He laughed and took her in his arms. "Do you love me half as much as I love you, my darling?"

"I do."

"Ah, there you are. The very words I long to hear. Say that we can spend the rest of our lives together. Please God, tell me yes, Charlotte." He kissed her, as half of Edenshade looked on and very nearly applauded. "We must marry, Charlotte, for it seems no one else wants us!"

"Ha! I will have you know that *I* turned down Captain Beddoes!" Then she touched his lips with her fingertips. "Yes, Rupert, I *will* marry you."

"Hurrah!"

"But I have one condition."

He grinned at her. "And that is?"

"That you agree we shall never name any of our children Rose. Or Astilbe. Or Lavender. Or . . ."

"I swear," he said before covering her lips again with his.